The
Witnesses

Center Point
Large Print

Also by Linda Byler and available from
Center Point Large Print:

Fire in the Night
Davey's Daughter

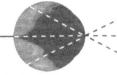

**This Large Print Book carries the
Seal of Approval of N.A.V.H.**

The Witnesses

Lancaster Burning
—Book 3—

DISCARD

Linda Byler

CENTER POINT LARGE PRINT
THORNDIKE, MAINE

This Center Point Large Print edition is published
in the year 2015 by arrangement with Skyhorse Publishing.

The text of this Large Print edition is unabridged.
In other aspects, this book may vary
from the original edition.
Printed in the United States of America
on permanent paper.
Set in 16-point Times New Roman type.

ISBN: 978-1-62899-800-9

Library of Congress Cataloging-in-Publication Data

Byler, Linda.
The witnesses / Linda Byler. — Center Point Large Print edition.
pages cm. — (Lancaster burning ; book 3)
Summary: "Fires have destroyed two more nearby Amish barns, and
many of the farmers are ready to ask for police protection, an unheard
of action. Davey Beiler, the leader of the local Amish community,
counsels against this, but then his beloved daughter, Sarah, is caught in
the flames and severely injured"—Provided by publisher.
ISBN 978-1-62899-800-9 (hardcover : alk. paper)
1. Witnesses—Fiction. 2. Arson—Fiction. 3. Amish—Fiction.
4. Lancaster County (Pa.)—Fiction. 5. Large type books. I. Title.
PS3602.Y53W58 2015
813'.6—dc23
                                                      2015035619

Table of Contents

Chapter 1

He was here.

She could see the sunlight glinting off the roof of his car. The new leaves were pushing out of the buds on the branches of the maple trees in the Stoltzfuses' yard. They threw dancing shadows of sunlight across the vehicle, but she could easily see it from her station at the living room window. She dusted the philodendron plant and clipped a few yellowing leaves from an ivy, attempting to hide the fact that she was unable to keep from longing to see him.

Would it be the same? Would her heart flutter in that same way, her breath quicken when he smiled? It had been so long.

When she could no longer justify her presence at the window, she picked up the yellow can of furniture polish and moved to the sideboard. She lifted the crocheted doilies, the candleholders, and the basket of greeting cards to dust beneath them.

As soon as she had that accomplished, the magnetic pull of Matthew's car began all over again. Quickly, she stole another glance. The same dappled sunlight on the glossy roof of the car. He was still there.

"Sarah."

She jumped at the sound of her mother's voice. "Hmm?"

"When you're finished with the dusting, do you mind washing the floor? When Abram Miller's family was here yesterday, their children got a bit lively, and the grape juice was spilled more than once."

Mam looked up from mixing the Crisco into the mound of soft, white flour, deftly incorporating it for the flaky pie crust she could always turn out. She stopped and blinked, her mouth drawing into a tight line as Sarah turned to glance out the living room window yet again.

Mam knew.

The knowledge rested uneasily on her rounded shoulders and the capable arms that cooked and cleaned for her large family, some of them strapping sons who had married and gone off to Dauphin County, where property prices were more affordable.

Her large, white covering concealed her graying hair, or most of it. Her face was still smooth, though her glasses well worn. She was a comely older woman with years of compassion and hard work molding her features.

Mam sighed and resumed her mixing, absent-mindedly now. She rolled a bit of floured Crisco between her thumb and forefinger.

So he was here.

He came to see her later that evening, when

Sarah least expected him. He bounded up on the porch when she was washing dishes, and she had no time to fix her hair or her covering or have a quick look in the mirror. All she could do was lift her hands from the soapy water and snatch up a corner of her black bib apron, wiping furiously as her heart began its usual wild take-off.

His knock was the same. Rapid, eager.

Sarah flew to the door, her feet skimming the kitchen floor, color rushing to her cheeks as she reached for the doorknob.

Matthew Stoltzfus stood on the porch, his dark hair cut in a stylish manner, polished, in the English way. His eyes were still the same deep brown, but his skin was darker than she had ever seen it. When he smiled, those perfect white teeth dazzled her, and she became quite faint.

"Sarah?"

It was a question, a timid, quiet inquiry.

Her eyes found his, and she was at home. After a long, arduous journey of a million years, she was home. The glad light in his eyes peeled away the thin reserve she had been able to build up, and with a broken cry of welcome, she flung herself into his arms.

"Matthew!"

Her cry was no more than a whisper. She felt his arms gather her trembling form against him, felt the soft fabric of his cotton shirt against her cheek. She closed her eyes to the unbelievable sensation of being in Matthew's arms. Suddenly, the safety of those arms was pulled away as hard fingers closed around her forearms and pushed her away, firmly, cruelly.

"No."

That was all he said. That one small word meant she had been bold, presumptuous.

"I'm sorry."

Her head was bent as she mumbled the words.

"I'm a widower, Sarah."

"Yes, I heard. I was sorry to hear of it."

"Yes."

Matthew cleared his throat and looked around uneasily. He shifted his weight from one well-clad foot to the other.

"Will your mam speak to me? Is your dat around?"

"Yes, come in. Levi will be pleased."

Matthew smiled, and she had to tear her eyes away from his face.

When they entered the kitchen, Mam turned from the pantry door, years of training hiding her emotions. She smiled, greeting Matthew with genuine friendliness.

Matthew grasped her hand, saying, "God bless you," and continued holding Mam's hand until she gently tugged it away, and Matthew asked how she was doing.

She inclined her head and answered, still reserved, but friendly, remembering the Matthew of years past. Hannah's eldest son, the apple of her best friend's eye.

Levi sat at his window, his elbows propped on the arms of the swiveling desk chair, his narrowed, brown eyes alight with interest, his large body leaning forward with anticipation.

"There's Matthew!" he bellowed, breaking into a delighted laugh that bounced from wall to wall.

Instantly, Matthew bounded to Levi's side, one brown hand clapping his shoulder, another pumping Levi's plump hand, leaving him giggling with happiness.

Levi was a special character, the symptoms of Down syndrome endearing him to his family and the community. He often held court from his desk chair or the recliner, spreading humor and goodwill with his sometimes hilarious view of the world around him.

"Levi, old boy! Good to see you!" Matthew said, sincere in his greeting of an old friend.

Sarah stood rooted by the kitchen table, her large green eyes reflecting the worship she felt for Matthew. Tall, athletic, with curly brown hair, she carried herself with a finesse that she was completely unaware of.

"Where were you so long?" Levi inquired.

Matthew laughed easily. Having known Levi as a small boy, he was accustomed to his lack of restraint.

"In Haiti."

Levi nodded sagely, then looked up at Matthew with a cunning glance.

"Snakes didn't get you, huh?"

Matthew laughed again and shook his head.

"No, Levi, they didn't."

"But your wife died."

"Yes."

Matthew's features steadied, folded, the happiness now erased by his sorrow. His brown eyes turned liquid with the pain. Sarah had to grip the back of a kitchen chair to keep from going to him, running her hands over the beloved contours of his handsome face, replacing the pain with her love.

Mam had to turn away from the raw yearning in her daughter's eyes.

They sat together later, on the same swing beneath the grapevines, in the chilly spring evening.

Sarah wrapped her sweater securely around her body and drank in the words he spoke. She savored the sound of his voice, never tiring of hearing about his experiences in Haiti and his marriage to Hephzibah, the black woman he had loved, who had contracted a deadly strain of malaria.

When darkness hid the stark brown vines surrounding them and her teeth began to chatter, Matthew said he should be going as his mother would wonder where he was.

She could not let him go, not without knowing. She could not face the future without the assurance that he would stay.

"Matthew."

He became very still, the desperation in her voice assaulting him.

"You'll be back? You'll return to the Amish? You'll come back to us and pick up where you left off? I mean, quite obviously, God wants you to be here. He took Hephzibah. So now your work in Haiti is done. It was a learning experience, and now you'll be one of us again, right? I just need to know. Matthew, I have to know what you're planning for the future."

She was babbling, becoming hysterical, her voice turning into a thin, reedy whine, and she didn't care. This was her one chance.

Matthew exhaled loudly, then spoke with the patient tone of one far superior.

"Sarah, you just don't get it, do you?"

"What do you mean?"

"I can't come back to the Amish. Your beliefs are all wrong."

"Really?"

"Yes."

"Well, couldn't you believe what you want and still be Amish?"

There was a long silence, stony—hard, gray, and unrelenting.

"Dat says there are many levels of faith. Some

eat meat and others dare eat only herbs. But the way of love is for the lion to lie peacefully with the lamb. He says you don't have to leave us to live as a Christian, the way you think."

Still Matthew stayed silent, which only increased Sarah's desperate desire to win him back—back to her, back to the faith of their childhood.

All her dreams were rolled into the vision of sitting beside him in a buggy, the warm summer air laden with the heady scent of flowers blowing gently through the open window. A good, sleek horse with a spirited head pulled them along, lifting his feet and making solid, ringing sounds against the macadam.

She would be his wife, secure in the knowledge that he loved her, that he wanted her there beside him, and that she was worthy. It was all she wanted.

"And Matthew, your parents would be so happy to have you return to the fold. You should think of them sometimes."

Matthew's words were clipped, harsh.

"My mother gave me her blessing the day I left, and you know it."

There was nothing to say to this.

"I chose to serve God the way I want."

"Yes. Yes, of course."

There was no use angering him further. If she argued, she would lose him, certainly.

"You really don't get it, Sarah. You're always

going to stay Amish and not know any better."

Sarah bristled at the accusation in his voice, but she remained quiet.

"You didn't come to Haiti. You didn't come. It's your own fault that I married Hephzibah."

Sarah sat up very straight, the breath leaving her body in one quick expulsion, a sort of disbelief.

"You didn't want me!"

The tortured words burst from her, lava wreaking havoc as it rained from the still bubbling volcano of her heart.

The swing suddenly came to a stop. Somewhere an owl hooted, probably in the apple tree down by the orchard. Another one gave an answering call. A dog began a deep, anxious barking.

"I did want you, Sarah. I was just afraid that you wouldn't make the break with your parents. Your father is, after all, a man of God, a minister of the Amish church, and—I don't know."

His voice became quiet and trailed off, leaving Sarah hanging on desperately, searching the vertical wall of his voice for one more chance, one more fissure to pull herself up.

"You didn't think I'd leave?"

"No."

A song started in her heart then, the finely-tuned melody of repression and denial. She captured the knowledge that he had loved her, had wanted her, and still did.

"Matthew," she began, then choked and remained still.

"I wanted to go, would have gone."

"Would you now?"

"You know I would."

"I am a widower."

"I'll wait."

"You will?"

"Yes."

Again, he sighed.

"You must be sure."

"I love you, Matthew. I always have."

Victory was hers now, firmly in her grasp, the Olympic gold around her neck and lifted high.

"If you love me, you'll wait six months, and then we'll leave. Your job is to persuade your parents."

"I will."

The old wooden swing creaked. A lamp was lit upstairs, creating a yellow rectangle of light where there had been only darkness. Priscilla and Suzie were getting ready for bed. It must be later than she thought.

There was a woofing sound from the barnyard. The half moon rose above the implement shed, casting soft shadows across the newly tilled garden soil. Sarah thought of the insurmountable task she had promised.

In a very small voice, she asked if he loved

her enough to come home to his Amish roots.

"Well, if that's how you're going to be, then just forget it," he said, without wavering.

"No, no, oh no."

She grasped his arms with nerveless fingers and implored him to have patience with her weakness. Then she gave up and threw herself into his arms, suddenly so aware of her need to feel secure, to grasp the fact that he did love her, without a smidgen of doubt.

He did not resist her, crushing her to him as his mouth sought hers.

Much later, she stumbled into her room and stood alone, her arms hanging by her sides, her senses reeling. A sob rose in her throat, then another. With steely resolve, she tamped down the tsunami of emotion, the quavering doubt and fear that threatened her.

The next morning she was red-eyed but awake, making desperate attempts to act normal. She was kind to Levi, spoke quietly to Mam, answered Dat's questions honestly, but she was glad to escape when the school driver pulled into the driveway.

Entering the schoolhouse, she raised the blinds. The sunshine etched streaks on the glass, highlighting the small dots of residue the sticky tack had left after they removed the valentines, the colorful pink and red decorations the children had made the month before. She would wash windows today, throw herself into her work with renewed energy.

She greeted the children with a pale face, eyes that were brilliantly green, a smile that flashed a little too intensely. Rosanna lifted one shoulder, tossed her head, and said it must be that the teacher has a new boyfriend.

Little David in second grade raised his hand and said Sammy stuck a pin in his arm, whereupon that little person set up an awful howling of guilt and fear. He was duly punished, and quiet was restored.

They decided to begin decorating for Easter that afternoon. Sarah stood with her pupils clustered around her, discussing the artwork they had done for Easter in previous years. She was amazed at their ideas and the willingness to submit them without a trace of the former animosity.

At noon, she sat at her desk, opened her lunchbox, and spread the waxed paper carefully beside it. The thickly-cut baked ham drooped between the sliced whole wheat bread Mam had taken from the hot oven the evening before. The crisp lettuce was piled on top, and small streaks of mayonnaise clung to the golden brown crust. The scent of her sandwich mingled with the delicious smells that always accompanied the opening of twenty lunchboxes, and she could not imagine leaving the only life she knew.

Her classroom was dear and familiar, the only challenge she had faced, the small victories she won here serving as stepping stones to a new and different school environment. Even in the past month, the victories had come one after another as the baby steps of progress she had made developed into toddler steps.

Her reverie was broken by a blonde-haired, round form, eyes alight with pride, bearing a greasy wrapper.

"Here! My mother made these."

"Oh. Oh, my goodness! A doughnut!"

It was a soft cream-filled one, dusted liberally with powdered sugar, wrapped in brown paper.

Surely this was not the same belligerent, impossible child that had entered her classroom that first day?

Sarah's voice shook as she thanked her over and over, an arm hugging the soft, chubby body against her, quick tears filling her eyes.

When Rosanna offered to stay after school to wash windows, Sarah accepted happily. The extra help would allow a thorough job.

They raised the blinds and set to work, efficiently removing every trace of smudges and fingerprints, chatting as if they had always been friends, which Sarah knew had certainly not been the case.

Sarah was caught completely off guard when Rosanna eyed her frankly in that way only eighth grade girls can and blurted, "Hey, what was wrong with you this morning?"

As the heat rose in her face, she rubbed vigorously at one spot on a window, biding her time, desperately trying to hide her face from Rosanna.

"Well, aren't you going to answer?"

Feigning innocence, Sarah muttered, "Why are you asking?"

"Well, you looked different. Sort of shook up."

Should she confide in Rosanna? Should she tell an eighth-grade pupil that her whole world was spinning off its axis, thrusting her into outer space where she wasn't completely positive who Sarah Beiler really was?

No, she couldn't confide in Rosanna.

"Oh, now, why would you say that? I didn't feel different."

"You looked different."

Ah, the social graces of a thirteen-year-old!

Sarah tried to change the subject, but Rosanna maneuvered right back to what was wrong with her teacher.

"I bet you anything that Matthew Stoltzfus came back to visit his parents."

A streak of lightning could not have shocked her more. As it was, she stared openmouthed at the guileless face of her student, studying the blue eyes intently. How could she know?

"Yeah, well, if you're not going to answer,

then I guess I'll know he came to see you. You know he really made a mess of my sister's life—Barbie Ann. She's married now. Thank goodness she had the nerve to step out of his clutches. He said he wanted her, but, well, bottom line, he didn't."

Rosanna sprayed far too much Windex on a window, vigorously pumping the sprayer, the painful memory of her jilted sister lending her strength.

"Whoops! Too much Windex."

Rosanna shrugged her shoulders and set to work, mopping up the excess window cleaner, saying, "You know every girl this side of Harrisburg wanted him."

Sarah nodded agreement, her face averted.

"Did you hear me?"

"I heard you."

"You know you're much too nice to waste your time on Matthew. My mother doesn't let us say certain words, but I could use one to describe him."

Sarah smiled but said nothing. Rosanna was always pushing against her mother's restrictions, which were few and far between as it was.

Sarah decided to conceal any further information she gleaned, cocooning it away to be safely brought out later in the privacy of her room.

She and Rosanna shared a cupcake someone had left in the cloakroom and drank cold water from a cup by the water faucet. They admired the shining clean windows and did not speak of Matthew.

Sarah did learn, however, that Lee Glick and Omar Esh had driven a pair of Belgians to the sales stables in New Holland, and it was the top selling team of the month.

Rosanna giggled and rolled her eyes and said she didn't know how old Lee Glick was, but she wished she wasn't only thirteen.

Sarah listened and smiled and thought of Matthew and wondered why the afternoon took on a dull quality.

When Rosanna left, Sarah sat alone behind the desk as a grayness descended, obscuring the yellow sunshine and puffy white clouds. It stilled the meadowlarks and the chirping sparrows and the warm brown branches of the budding trees, turning them black and gothic and frightening.

Outside the small, one-room schoolhouse, everything went on as before—the sun's brilliance, the moving white clouds, the birdsongs— but in Sarah's heart, a certain sense of despondency took over, a weight of discouragement.

Was it only Rosanna's prattle? What did she know?

Nothing. It was only Rosanna voicing opinions of her own concoction.

But what if Rosanna was right? What if God sent people like this girl to warn her? And what if she held herself in high esteem and pooh-poohed the warnings of one so young?

She would talk to a more mature friend, the Widow Lydia, the most fair person on earth.

Chapter 2

Levi didn't want his chicken and dumplings that evening and became quite ill later, so Sarah knew it was not a good time to visit with her friend Lydia.

Mam was busy making Levi as comfortable as possible, so Sarah washed dishes, straightened the house, and sat down with her schoolwork afterward.

It was a quiet evening, and even Dat seemed preoccupied, hiding behind an opened Lancaster newspaper, the *Intelligencer Journal*. Suzie went to bed early, and Priscilla sprawled on the rug beside the stove with another magazine.

When Sarah heard the rustling of Dat's paper, she looked up, her mind telling her before she actually saw Dat's hooded eyes and his concerned expression.

"Sarah."

"Yes?"

Still she could not meet his eyes.

"I guess Matthew was visiting here last evening."

"He was."

"How is he?"

"Good."

The old clock on the mantle ticked too loudly. Priscilla coughed, cleared her throat, and positioned both elbows so her hands fit over her ears.

"I guess we can trust you, Sarah."

"Yes."

"Did he . . . mention your past?"

"Yes."

At this, Dat sat up, carefully folded the news-paper, and deliberately put it on the sewing machine beside his chair. He rose like an old man, painfully, unfolding his length as if each joint protested its support of him.

When he came to stand at the kitchen table, one large, calloused hand resting on the back of a chair, she could not look up. Blindly, she made a few red check marks, without seeing the fine black numbers on the page of an arithmetic work-book.

"I just want you to know that we are praying you won't be led astray. I know Matthew is a powerful influence in your life, but consider the promise you made to God the day you were baptized."

That was all he said, but his words were seared into her conscience, as red hot and painful as a branding iron.

She saw her father, old, bent, with white hair, years down the road, a silver stream of tears coursing deep ridges of pain in his wrinkled face. Our Sarah, he would say. Our Sarah left us. She stands *im bann* (in the ban, shunned).

Without rebellion, this was going to be impossible.

Sarah left the Widow Lydia a message on her voice mail and then waited to walk past Elam Stoltzfus's till it was fully dark. She did not want Hannah to catch sight of her, furtively scuttling past to dump all her fears and frustrations on the widow who likely had more than enough of her own.

She was cowardly, maybe, but this night she had to talk to Lydia.

It was Wednesday, an ordinary weekday, which was good. She did not want her cousin Melvin to see her either. He never admitted to courting Lydia, although he spent every spare minute within decency at her house, fixing doors or planting shrubs and doing other necessary little duties. He wouldn't be there on a Wednesday.

She tried walking as far off the road as possible, the headlights of oncoming cars an unwelcome intrusion. She did not want to be seen, so she half walked, half ran the whole way, speeding up as she passed Matthew's house.

She was welcomed warmly at Lydia's door and scolded sincerely for staying away so long.

A tray of fruit and dip, cheese and crackers, and a pan of Reese's peanut butter bars stood temptingly on the gingham tablecloth covering the kitchen table, and a pot of tea steamed on the wood stove.

Little Aaron lifted his arms to be held, and Sarah eagerly scooped him into her arms. He was dressed in green camouflage flannel pajamas and informed Sarah immediately that he was an English man and he was going hunting.

Lydia laughed with Sarah, then shook her head. "I shouldn't let him wear them, but Melvin gave them to him."

The girls welcomed Sarah as warmly as their mother had, and she smiled back with sincerity and promised to come more often.

After nine o'clock, the children were put to bed, Lydia poured tea, and they settled comfortably by the kitchen table.

Sarah began to talk, her speech nurtured with the encouraging manner Lydia possessed, unfolding her story, bit by bit, leaving nothing hidden.

Somewhere during the course of the conversation, the exterior door to the *kesslehaus* (wash house) opened, and there was a great clattering, laughter, and talking heard through the closed door.

"Omar," Lydia said quickly.

"Who is with him?"

Averting her eyes, Lydia adjusted the tablecloth. "It's Lee."

"Lee?"

Lydia nodded and sipped her tea.

There was no chance to get away, nowhere to hide, before they burst into the kitchen, their faces alight, flushed with success.

"She did it, Mam!" Omar burst out. "Penny had her colt! It's a filly! A little girl!"

Lydia leaped to her feet, and for a moment, it seemed as though Lee was going to hug her, but he didn't.

What he did do was catch sight of Sarah.

Slowly the elation left his face as he struggled to regain the former feeling of success, but he was clearly caught off guard.

"Sarah."

That was all he said. Not "How are you?" or "Hello" or anything.

She didn't answer, except for a small, frightened smile.

When Omar yelled up the stairs, a great commotion followed—a mad, headlong dash through the kitchen, out the *kesslehaus* door, and down the slope to the new horse barn. Sarah followed along, carrying Aaron a bit clumsily and then stopped to let Lee take him, his hand leaving a trail of awareness where he touched her as he took the small boy from her.

Together, they all huddled by the heavy timbers

forming the box stall, as Omar held the LED battery lamp high, illuminating every corner.

Cries of awe went up as the blonde, spindly little creature wobbled around on new, unsteady legs. The great Belgian mare nuzzled her newborn, batting her eyelashes as if to remind the small group of people that she had accomplished this miracle all by herself, and they had better use the proper discretion—they were dealing with royalty here.

She was truly magnificent, and so was her colt.

"She's so huge!" Sarah said.

"She's a Belgian!" Omar crowed.

Aaron yelled that he was going to ride her as soon as he had breakfast the next morning, and Sarah looked at him, held high in Lee's arms, and smiled, her eyes shining.

Later, Lee would remember every perfect contour of her face, the beautiful green eyes, the generous mouth, and the hair that never quite succumbed to the efforts of a comb, hairspray, or hairpins.

Eventually, the children slowly returned to their beds after glasses of milk and large squares of the chocolatey peanut butter bars. Lee declined an invitation to join them, and Sarah was caught by surprise by the strong feeling of loss when he moved off across the driveway, riding his best horse through the night.

It wasn't safe, Lydia said, but Omar assured her

Lee would ride in fields and along fence rows most of the time.

It was a bit after eleven o'clock when the propane tank ran empty, casting the kitchen into a steadily receding lamplight.

"*Ach*," Lydia said.

"I'll go," Sarah assured her.

"Please don't, Sarah. I still haven't told you everything."

Sarah laughed.

"Just light a kerosene lamp. Here, I'll get the one in the bathroom."

Sarah carried it out and set the small lamp with its cozy orange glow in the middle of the table, as Lydia replenished their tea.

"What I haven't told you is kind of hard now. I feel guilty, being so happy, when you are so obviously tormented with indecision," Lydia said, sighing.

"Just tell me."

"Melvin asked me to be his wife."

She said the words softly, as if they would not hurt Sarah if she spoke as lightly as possible.

Sarah gasped, the words filling her with surprise.

"Oh, Lydia. I am so happy for you. Congratulations!"

Lydia smiled and lowered her eyes, the humility that was so much a part of her so evident now.

They continued their conversation, both of

them aghast when they noticed the clock's hands had moved another two hours.

"I'll walk home with you, Sarah," Lydia offered.

"Of course not. I'll be fine. No one's out at this hour."

They parted with a long hug. There were tears in Lydia's eyes as she promised to pray on Sarah's behalf.

"God does not want us to live in unhappiness or indecision, Sarah. You know, if we are a willing sacrifice, we are able to discern His perfect will."

But when the *kesslehaus* door closed and Sarah slipped out into the frost-tipped spring night, Lydia stood in the middle of her kitchen and clenched her fists. Then she picked up a small, square pillow and threw it against the wall with all her strength. Then she stamped one foot and growled a very unladylike growl and thought she had never wanted to shake some sense into anyone as much as she wanted to shake Sarah until her teeth rattled.

Sarah walked down the sloping sidewalk to the gate, opened it, and let herself out, then walked on down the driveway, the gravel crunching under her feet.

She waited in the shadow of the new barn, allowing a car to pass. She did not want to be caught alone in the middle of the night.

She shivered, stopped to button her sweater securely, and walked on. Lifting her face, she enjoyed the sight of the velvety night sky alive with the stars twinkling, winking down at her the way they always did, a reminder that God was up there in the heavens, the same as He always was, and things would be okay somehow.

Exactly what made her turn her head in the direction of the horse barn, she would never know. She did, however, and caught sight of an orange glow in the small window—the one under the eaves.

Surprisingly, at first, she was very calm. Reasoning, even. The moon was about half, maybe two thirds full. It had to be the glow of an orange moon.

Or perhaps her mind refused to accept what her instincts knew.

Not the Widow Lydia. Please, dear God. If You have to allow another fire, please, not her.

Is a prayer a thought, or a thought a prayer? Can anybody pray when monstrous knowledge slams into them with the force of a sledgehammer?

When the orange glow flickered, Sarah was immobilized. She was frozen to the macadam, as wave after wave of nausea attacked her.

She was only one person, a weak young girl, and who could blame her if she fled to the safety of her father's arms?

As she stood, her gaze riveted to the small second story window, the orange glow became decidedly brighter.

Then she remembered Penny and the newborn filly. She remembered Lydia's humility. This would beat her down so badly, she might never recover. Something had to be done.

Her feet unlocked as anger coursed through her veins. She did not utter a sound. She had no tears. She just clenched her fists and ran. She ran past the house, her only thoughts of Penny and her colt. She had to get them out.

She tore open the main entrance door, groped her way along one wall, trying to remember where Omar had taken the battery lamp. As she entered the row of stalls, there was an alarming roar overhead, gaining momentum by the second.

All her common sense told her to go to the house, but she knew every horse would be lost if she did.

Did she scream, or was it the horses?

She remembered Dat's words. Horses want to stay in their familiar home, no matter how terrified they become.

She whipped off her sweater, called Penny's name, opened the massive gate, called again, cajoled, coaxed, begged. Then, mercifully, her fingers caught the part of Penny's halter below her chin, and she tugged with every ounce of strength.

"Come on, girl. Good. Easy!"

Talking, she coaxed the horse as the crashing

sound of hooves against heavy boards increased. She was so intent on coaxing Penny that the intensity of the flames overhead became lost on her.

Sarah was tall, but Penny was enormous, her head lifting repeatedly as Sarah tried to cover the horse's eyes with her sweater, only to have it slide down around Penny's nose.

Desperate now, Sarah slowly coaxed the great horse to the water trough and clambered up to balance precariously on its rim. With renewed effort, she threw the sweater over the great head, hanging on when Penny lifted her head and shook it.

The hours-old filly bounced awkwardly, its legs splayed out ungracefully like a baby giraffe.

Again, Sarah talked to the great horse, pulled with all her strength on the chain that opened the door facing the house, and with one final heart-stopping leap, they made it through.

Sarah was crying now, her relief was so great. Opening the gate to the pasture, she turned them loose, peeling the black sweater off as the panicked horse shot through the opening to safety, the squealing little filly cavorting along as best it could.

The barn was fully engulfed, although it was contained to the upper level.

Sarah raced up the driveway, through the gate,

and pounded on the house door with all her strength, crying hoarsely now, then resorting to an otherworldly scream of fear.

When Lydia came to the door, it was as Sarah had feared. The defeat in Lydia's eyes was already evident.

She turned and ran back down the slope, leaving the gate swinging drunkenly on its hinges, aware of only one purpose, to save the horses.

Behind her, she heard Omar cry out, warning her, but she ran, crashed through the door, yanked open the door to the stables, her black sweater clutched in one hand, her chest heaving, her breath coming in great, tearful gasps.

The horse stable was strangely quiet, except for a lone whinny at the far end. One horse remained. It must be the great stallion. They had likely turned the rest of them out to pasture.

She was aware of another presence.

"Sarah!" Omar screamed her name, again warning her.

Silently, she handed him the black sweater, then stood back, as he worked swiftly, efficiently, covering the massive head with her sweater, as the crackling roar overhead became a raging inferno.

Should she go? No, she'd stay. She wanted to be certain Omar and the stallion made it out safely.

"Get out!" he screamed, as the stallion plunged past, dragging him along.

Turning, she took one last look around, making sure there was nothing in the box stalls, as the roar overhead shut out all other senses.

Sarah was moving toward the door and could see the cool, clean night beyond, when a fiery beam exploded over her head. She looked through the opened door, wide, beckoning, and she knew she could make it out. When she heard the cracking, tearing sound, she was puzzled by it.

The great, blackened beam slowly tilted to the side, gathering momentum, and crashed to the cement floor below. The only object cushioning its impact was Sarah's bent form. When it hither head and neck and shoulders, the sparks and flames from the burning wood ignited the soft fleece of her headscarf, which instantly caught on fire.

There was a moment of blinding, indescribable pain, and then nothing as Sarah's world turned darker than black.

Omar could not hold back Dominic, the great Belgian stallion, as he hung frantically to the thick leather of the halter. He had no regard for his own safety as the stallion reared, lifting him off the ground. He talked to the animal, he screamed out his fear, but in the end, he had to let go and watch helplessly as the enormous giant tried to return to his stall.

Horrified, Omar could only stand helplessly as the horse tried to crash through the opened door. Omar let out a desperate cry as a woman, skirts billowing, darkly clad arms waving, stepped directly in front of the plunging behemoth, turning him aside at the very last minute.

Snorting, eyes rolling in terror, the stallion wheeled, galloped down the driveway, and up the road in the direction of the Beiler home.

Omar skidded to a stop, panting.

"Mam!"

Lydia stood beside him, watching Dominic race out the drive.

"Where's Sarah?" Lydia asked.

"Where is she?"

"Don't you know?"

"No!"

"Omar! Oh, please!"

"She was in the barn!"

"With you?"

Omar didn't answer, he was already through the door, into the mouth of the roiling, smoking, crackling furnace that had been the proud handiwork of Lee Glick.

"Sarah!"

He screamed and screamed.

Smoke filled his eyes, his nose, and his mouth. He gagged, choked, couldn't breathe. Faraway, as if in a dream, he heard the thin, panicked voice of his mother, but he could not go back.

Somewhere, Sarah might have fallen, been overtaken by smoke inhalation.

He bent low and stumbled, falling headlong to the fiery concrete floor, aware of the dark still form beside a flaming timber.

Lifting an arm, he coughed into the inner elbow, the fabric of his shirt mercifully allowing him one more gasp for breath.

In one swift movement, he turned and found her, inert, the length of her completely engulfed in small flames.

Without knowing how, he rolled her, shoving, gasping, choking, until every devilish, dancing little flame was extinguished.

Disoriented now, the forebay spun around him as he staggered and fell to his knees.

It was the popping, cracking sound of the great timbers overhead that infused his veins with the adrenaline he so desperately needed.

In one swoop, his strong, young arms scooped up the charred, heated body that was Sarah. With flaming lungs bursting, he stumbled through the door and across the cold gravel to the frosty grass on the other side.

Lydia could not control her voice—hoarse sobs and cries emerging in unearthly wails as terror consumed her. Omar lay face down, gagging, as wave after wave of nausea expelled his stomach's contents.

Her cries reduced to moans and sobs, Lydia

bent to Sarah's charred form, tenderly laying her sweater over the burnt body. Then she removed her housecoat and covered her legs as well.

Lydia stood in her homemade, flannel night-gown, her large eyes pools of shock and incomprehension, as Elam Stoltzfus and Matthew came gasping up the driveway, Hannah's large figure behind them, crying, questioning, answering herself.

Immediately, they heard the high, thin wail of the vehicles from Gordonville Fire Company heading their way.

"What happened?" Elam gasped.

Matthew remained silent, surveying the almost fully engulfed barn before turning to look at the covered form on the grass.

"Who?"

Lydia, slowly entering the first state of shock, shivered, crossed her arms, and rocked from side to side, as small beads of sweat formed on her forehead.

Matthew yelled at her, not realizing what was occurring, "Don't act so dense!"

Grasping her arm, he lowered his face and yelled again, but Lydia's head wobbled on her shoulders, a rag doll now, as she slowly sank to the ground.

It was the brilliant, bluish headlights piercing through the orange, smoke filled night that illuminated Sarah's still dark form with Lydia sitting beside her, awake, but not aware. Omar sat up, tears streaming down his cheeks, and told Elam and Hannah that it was Sarah lying there, and, no, he did not know if she was dead or if she still lived.

Chapter 3

The trained individuals, both Amish and English, that answered the call of 911 that night all agreed. They thought she had died and then wondered why she hadn't. It was the worst case they had ever seen.

They found a weak, fluttering pulse and sprang into action. Radios crackled, lights flashed blue and orange, sirens wailed repeatedly through the early spring night. The fire raged, roared, and crackled. The walls collapsed, then the roof.

Neighbors came on foot. Men had thrown on their clothes haphazardly and jammed straw hats backwards on their heads.

Women left at home hovered on porches or at upstairs windows with blinds rolled up, curtains held aside. Children pressed against them, and the mothers stooped to answer childish questions as their hands dried frightened little tears.

Davey Beiler was awakened by his wife, Malinda, with a soft, repeated calling of his name. At first, he was bewildered, but then he knew with the assurance of experience. Some-where, there was another fire.

When Malinda told him it looked like the Widow Lydia's barn, he groaned within himself. Why her? Why a second time?

He fought back a rage so intense it filled his mouth with a metallic taste. He yanked on the strings of his brown, leather work shoes so hard that his ankles hurt.

Who was demented enough to return and do this same evil to Lydia a second time?

Davey pulled his broad brimmed straw hat down on his head, smashing it angrily. The rough straw beside the soft cloth lining inside of the crown scratched his forehead, but he was beyond caring.

"Take care of the girls and Levi," he said roughly, before lunging through the door.

His thoughts were tangled, his steps long, as he hurried up the road past Elam's. Cars were now vying for position to get near the fire, sirens wailing repeatedly through the night.

Men were directing traffic around roadblocks, their fluorescent vests gleaming in the night. Davey was glad. No use having all this traffic around.

As he neared the scene of the fire, he noticed the Gordonville ambulance at Lydia's gate. Had someone been hurt?

As he hurried, his mouth turned dry, and a

premonition pushed its dark head into his mind.

Omar?

The Widow Lydia?

He remembered Sarah then. She had gone to visit her friend. Hadn't she returned?

He was fighting emotions as he walked up to Elam, his neighbor for almost thirty years, and touched his elbow.

"Who?"

That was all he could think to say.

When Elam looked at him and his mouth twitched downward, Davey knew it was Sarah.

When Elam's lips compressed in an attempt to check his emotions, and his great, calloused hand was clapped on Davey's shoulder, he knew it was bad.

"*Iss noch laeva dot* (Is there life yet)?"

"*Ach, ich glaub* (Oh, I believe so), Davey."

Davey nodded.

In the kaleidoscope of lights and sound, he singled out a member of the trained personnel and plucked at his sleeve. He pushed his white face towards the worker's and asked who it was, his capable fingers shaking, useless now, devoid of their usual power.

"I understand it's a neighbor girl."

"Sarah Beiler?"

The man inquired, returned, and nodded his head, affirming the premonition.

"I am her father."

Davey bowed his head then and let the tears roll down his cheeks. He shook like a leaf. He jammed his hands into the pockets of his broadfall denim trousers to still them, acknowledged the arm thrown about his shoulders.

He prayed silently that God would spare her life, but that His will might be done. He knew God ruled omnipotent, His ways so far above his own, and who knew if God would choose to take Sarah as well as Mervin, his beloved, towheaded six-year-old?

He could feel the submission come, the calming arrive, as he prayed on. Slowly, the night, the sounds, the smoke, and flames receded, and he focused on the interior of the red and white ambulance, where four people hovered over the figure on a stretcher.

He saw the tubes, the stethoscopes, the tanks, the lights, and knew there was nothing he could do. She was in good hands.

A driver came. He was ushered into the front seat of the ambulance.

"Remember to tell Malinda. Bring her."

Elam bowed his head, shook it. Matthew stood beside his father, his face waxy, white.

Hannah was illuminated in the lights of the ambulance as she knelt by her neighbor Lydia, a hand on Omar's back, the girls huddled around their brother.

The last thing he saw was the streams of

water directed on the new dairy barn, keeping it safe from the overpowering heat from the burning horse barn. Then the ambulance crunched down the lane and turned onto the road, on its way to the emergency room at Lancaster General.

A sharp sense of reality made the night, the headlights, the two yellow lines on the road, the frosty grasses by the roadside, come into a clear focus.

When the driver turned on the siren and pushed down on the accelerator, Davey pressed back in his seat as they shot forward.

He sat immobile, as they raced through the night, picking up speed as they turned onto 340, the Old Philadelphia Pike, on their way through Bird-In-Hand and towards the city of Lancaster.

His lips moved in prayer, his shoulders slumped in submission, but his hands continued their weak trembling, so he stuck them both between his knees to still them.

As a minister of the Old Order Amish church, Davey was no stranger to the ER or the Lancaster General Hospital. His duties took him there many times. The lights, the automatic doors that slid quietly open, the voices of doctors and nurses as they padded down glistening tiled hallways in professional footwear—it was all familiar.

The night air revived him, helped stabilize the feeling of defeat, but there was nothing he could do about his trembling limbs, so he stood, shaking, in the cold night air as the ambulance doors were flung open.

He cried slow, hot tears when the realization hit him.

A helicopter was standing by.

Men and women clad in pastel colors rushed out, swarmed the stretcher. Without thinking, acting solely on instinct, Davey rushed to the stretcher. He bent over, peering frantically between the doctors and nurses, trying to see until he was pulled gently away.

"I want to see her," he pleaded.

No one answered.

Inside, he sank to a chair in the waiting room and did as he was told. He answered questions, nodded his head, said yes or no, provided an address, a telephone number, her birth date.

No, he didn't know her Social Security number. He produced his own and felt like crying all over again because the small blue card was so old and worn, and he shouldn't carry it in his wallet, he knew.

He showed his ID, his wallet slapping against his knee as he tried to insert it back into the plastic sleeve.

He wished for Malinda intensely. She was quicker, smarter, better spoken at times like this. Small, stout, quick, she was so capable.

They didn't let him see Sarah. That was the hardest part. And he didn't know they'd taken her until she had already gone. He'd signed forms but wasn't aware how swiftly they would convey his daughter away from him.

Mein Gott (My God), he cried inside.

The Amish were forbidden to fly. They were not allowed to enter an airplane, small or large, so they didn't. Except when medical aid was needed.

It was hard to be alone, waiting, without knowing. He felt as though he was the one suspended in mid-air, dangling, fighting fear.

He kept his head bowed, his straw hat beside him, occupying a whole chair by itself. He should hang it on the steel hooks provided for that purpose, but he felt better having his hat close by, a familiarity, an old friend to wait with him.

He looked at the round black and white clock. Three eleven. Or twelve. Not quite quarter after three. He wondered when Malinda would come. Who would do the milking?

Panicked, he turned his head to the left, then to the right. The waiting room was fairly empty. A few weary people slumped in their seats, and a couple was having a quiet conversation in the corner.

Rising slowly, he went to the desk window and waited before asking if there was phone service available.

When he was led to the nurses' station, he followed instructions carefully, relieved to hear

Malinda's greeting on their voice mail. He left a message, saying Priscilla and Suzie would have to milk as best they could, and the vet was coming in the morning for number 84 in the box stall.

He returned to the waiting room, his eyes filled with a new light when he found his wife standing hesitantly inside the automatic doors, wearing her black shawl and bonnet.

Quickly, he was by her side. They did not hug or touch at all, but their eyes spoke volumes. They understood each other's pain, the fiery trial, and the endurance that would be required. They were not strangers to suffering.

Together, they sat quietly, and Davey spoke in hushed tones as Malinda silently wept, her flowered handkerchief lifted repeatedly to wipe away the tears.

Finally she burst out, "But will she live?"

"I can't tell you. I don't know."

They sat, waiting, drawing comfort from one another.

When a doctor came to the door and asked for David Beiler, Dat almost leaped to his feet, but after shaking the physician's hand, he sat back down, weakly.

Mam lifted a white, ravaged face.

His name was Dr. James, and he was the specialist on call.

"Your daughter's injuries are extensive."

Mam caught her breath.

"We have what we call 'the rule of nines,' referring to the percentage of the body that is afflicted. The head and each of the arms make up nine percent, the back, front, and each leg eighteen percent, and so forth. We don't know the exact invasion on the epidermis or the deeper tissue, but most of one whole side of her body was in contact with the flames. For how long, we don't know. The actual depth of her wounds will be determined at the burn center near Philadelphia. That's at the Crozer-Chester Medical Center in Upland. There, she'll be given the best treatment possible."

The doctor paused.

Dat swallowed, his mouth gone dry, remembering horrific tales of children enduring the removal of dead tissue from a burned area. Debridement, they called it, the unusual term now springing unexpectedly to his mind. They'd once said no parent could stand to watch or to hear the cries.

Mam bowed her head, weeping quietly.

"Our first concern is the trauma. She was in shock and will need transfusions. Another big concern, of course, is the smoke inhalation with the risk for infection in her lungs and pneumonia. So far we can offer a fair evaluation. She's young and was seemingly in good health. Are there any questions?"

Dat shook his head.

Mam lifted her gaze to Dr. James and asked what percentage of Sarah's body was burned and how bad it all really was.

The doctor remained forthright, saying the evaluation would be much more accurate at the burn center. His answer seemed to satisfy Mam, and she nodded assent. They shook hands, thanked the doctor quietly, and turned to go.

Dat hadn't thought to ask who the driver was and if he was willing to drive them to the burn center at this time of the night.

It was Wendell, the good, dependable driver who knew every route in and out of Lancaster and the surrounding counties and states. A retired truck driver, he was competent and skilled at *goot zeit macha* (making good time). It was a term often overheard in Amish circles, an analysis of each driver's ability to efficiently get his load of people from point A to point B.

How could a night be so long? The sky was still pitch-black as they travelled along on the interstate highway. The stars twinkled above them, and the half-moon hovered to the west, yet it seemed the time moved twice as slowly at this nightmarishly early morning hour.

Davey hoped that the hovering, man-made wonder called a helicopter had landed safely. Would Sarah's burns be so severe she may be better off perishing because of them?

Just help us through, guide us, let us accept what You have for us.

His prayers kept him calm, centered, in the middle of this giant whirlwind that had whisked him off his feet and thrown him into a nameless land where nothing made sense, except to blame himself.

"You're going to keep this up until someone gets hurt!" Melvin's words rang in his ears now, and Davey laid his head against the van seat, drew a shaking breath, and closed his eyes.

He had not allowed it, in the end. No media or private detectives. God had allowed this, the spate of fires, barns burning at random, hadn't He?

Yes, it was wrong. But as Davey had said a hundred times before, the Amish were a non-resistant people. If a man takes your raiment, give him your cloak also. If he smites one cheek, give unto him the other. If he asks you to go with him one mile, you're supposed to go with him two.

But did it apply? If a man burns your barn, give him your house as well? The principle was insane when it came to personal loss. Or was it?

God's people were peculiar. They did things differently than the world, and it appeared a foolishness to many.

Davey Beiler knew God's people were every-where, in many modes of dress, many cultures, and ways of life. Not only the Amish knew God's ways. Sometimes, in matters he kept to himself, he thought the English were the ones who came through with great, undeserved love and kindness, the spine of Christianity.

And now, his daughter, somewhere alone in a great hospital far from home, was severely injured. Was it because of his inability to "do something"?

Dozens of bishops and ministers agreed with Davey. The old way was best—the principle of forgiveness—even at a time like this.

Self blame edged out his conviction, causing an unrelenting torment in his breast as the van bore to the left, passing yet another tractor trailer.

Levi was awake.

He wasn't completely sure why he had been awakened, but when he heard a rapid pounding on the front door, he rolled over and opened one eye to peer at the alarm clock. He could see alright with only one eye if he wasn't wearing his glasses.

Two o'clock.

Throwing back the covers, he took his time pushing his feet into the corduroy slippers by his nightstand.

Checking the buttons on his flannel pajamas, he buttoned one that had come undone and pulled the fabric down over his ample stomach.

Shuffling to the bedroom door, he called for Dat, then Mam. When there was no answer, he shifted his gaze to the living room couch, then caught sight of the blaze beyond Elam's place and heard the thin wail of the fire sirens.

Ach, du lieva (Oh my goodness), he thought.

Another sharp rapping assaulted his slow senses, and he snorted impatiently. Well, if Mam and Dat were not going to the door, he guessed he'd have to.

"Hang on!" he bellowed, exactly the way he heard his brother Allen say at his house.

He was not afraid, didn't even think of such a thing. He simply yanked the door open, stuck his great tousled head out, and peered into the youth's face. Levi asked, in a voice as English as he could possibly make it, "May I help you with something?"

The tall, thin youth with the shaggy hair moved uncomfortably from one foot to another, his hands stuck in the pockets of his short jacket.

"Your dad here?"

"No. I'd say he's down at the fire."

"Oh, yeah. Guess he would be."

Levi checked his face for a full minute, thoroughly examining every angle, the plane of his nose, the way he held his head, the shaggy hair.

Yep, Levi decided. It's him.

"You can come in. I'll light the kitchen lamp. He should be here."

"Okay."

The youth moved through the door and stood

awkwardly by the counter while Levi slowly lifted the lighter to the mantles of the gas lamp and turned the black knob. The tall youth blinked in the bright, yellowish light.

"Sit down," Levi said.

He sat down.

"Now, I have to go to the bathroom, so are you alright if I leave you awhile?"

"Sure."

"Alright, then."

Levi disappeared through the *kesslehaus* door, closed it behind him, and instantly moved as stealthily and swiftly as his bulk would allow. Through the side door of the *kesslehaus*, across the frosty lawn, and into the phone shanty he sped, closing the door as quietly behind him as possible.

Lifting the small LED penlight, Levi peered at the buttons, then deliberately punched in the nine, then two ones in rapid succession. He told the dispatcher he needed a policeman, or two, if she could, at the Davey Beiler farm on Irishtown Road in back of Gordonville. He thought he had someone they might want.

He replaced the receiver, swished through the cold, wet grass back to the *kesslehaus*, and entered noiselessly. He reached into the small alcove and flushed the commode, then washed his hands, splashing and humming, biding his time, before reappearing.

"Sorry about that."

The youth said nothing, his face working.

"You want coffee? Shoofly? Mam made whoopie pies."

"No, thanks."

"Okay then."

"When's your dad going to be back?"

"Oh, I'd imagine before too long. He'll need something after awhile."

The youth cast a dark look at Levi and was greeted by a look of childlike innocence from the narrowed brown eyes.

When they heard someone on the front porch, Levi knew it wasn't Dat, but he went to the door and said, "Oh, you're here. Come on in. Your company is waiting for you."

When the first policeman entered, the youth leaped to his feet and made a mad dash for the *kesslehaus* door, but Levi had locked it from the other side. He crashed into it, swore, and tried an alternative route, straight into the burly officer's arms.

Levi hopped up and down with excitement, but then sat quietly as the youth was questioned.

When it was his turn, Levi answered the policeman's questions well. He believed this boy was "sticking on" (lighting) the barns. He had believed it ever since the very first night the small white car moved past their barn with no lights. He never told anyone that a teddy bear drove the car, because everyone in his family and the church would laugh at him. But his hair was shaggy, like a stuffed bear. Levi saw this boy at the funeral of that pretty English girl, and he thought his name was Mike.

The youth glared at Levi, then became quite somber. The boy leaned forward and lowered his face in his hands, and Levi knew without a doubt that he was *buze fertich* (repentant).

Too bad the policeman didn't want any shoofly either. It was pretty lonely eating it all by himself at such an early hour in the morning. He hoped Dat and Mam wouldn't return too soon. They'd be needed at the fire, he reasoned, as he cut his second wedge of shoofly pie. And he deserved a treat for his work that night. It had just been a matter of waiting till the time was right and knowing when to go to the bathroom.

Chapter 4

Finally, when David and Malinda Beiler thought they would go mad with impatience, another doctor appeared in the doorway of the waiting room and asked them to accompany him to a room where there would be more privacy. Their despair had become a steadily rising foe, and it was about to grow bigger.

In the private room, they were told the truth,

bluntly. Nothing was held back, but in precise, physician's language, the doctor relayed Sarah's situation in a professional manner laced with empathy and kindness.

They were left examining the burden of information he dropped on them, an unwelcome weight dumped on their shoulders, impossible to carry. They tried to contain their emotions, but that, too, was an impossibility. Tears slid unheeded down their exhausted faces.

For now, she was stable, though her condition was critical. She had lost a lot of blood.

The burns covered roughly fifty percent of her body, the worst of the damage on one side, the right. It was centered on her upper chest, arm, neck, and face.

Mam gasped as the doctor said, "face."

The deepest burns had been caused when her headscarf caught fire.

The biggest concern was the possibility of pneumonia and infection. They would need to take it a day at a time, the extent of skin grafting and surgeries depending on the severity of the tissue damage.

The recovery would be weeks, months. There were facilities provided for family within walking distance from the hospital, where they could stay free of charge.

They asked their only question, "When can we see her?"

He made a few quick phone calls, a nurse appeared, and, after shaking the doctor's hand and thanking him, they were on their way. Into the elevator and up to the third floor, they moved along behind the nurse with their heads bowed, avoiding gazes that were curious, kind, or puzzled.

They were joined by another nurse, a tall, angular woman with graying hair, who introduced herself as Junie Adams, the head nurse. She explained the tubes, machines, and monitors they would see, then asked them to don gowns and masks, remove their shoes, and wear only sterile slippers.

Quickly, they complied, then followed her into a cold, dim room, alive with clicks and whirs, lights, IV bags, poles, and a figure swathed in white bandages.

There was no trace of Sarah anywhere. Even her eyes were covered. That was the hardest part for Mam. If only she could see her eyes, she'd be able to find her Sarah.

As it was, they stood together, their clothes touching, the feeling of being joined at this hour absolutely essential.

"You may talk to her. She's on morphine, heavily drugged, as you can see, but she may respond. Her mouth is lightly covered, the same as her eyes, so go ahead, see what happens."

They could not speak, at first. It wasn't that

they didn't try, but nothing would come except more tears, more pain, as they struggled together.

Finally, Mam said, "Sarah," and was instantly consumed with a flood of weeping so intense she sagged against her husband, and his arm went around her to hold her steady.

Then he spoke. He said her name. He told her not to be afraid; they were here with her now. Mam told her they loved her and were waiting until she could speak to them.

A long, hoarse moan came from the swathed mouth, then another. The nurse assured them it was okay.

They spoke again, but the first few moans were the only ones that came in response, and they had to be satisfied with the knowledge that perhaps she had heard.

It seemed more bearable now, somehow, since they had seen her.

They sat in the large room, after following a bewildering number of people to another floor and through an archway with a cafeteria sign above it. They had followed others, picking up plastic trays and silverware wrapped in white napkins, and chosen the food they would need to sustain them, for the forenoon hours, anyway.

Mam ate dry toast, without realizing it wasn't buttered, and Dat drank his coffee black, unable to find the creamer and not wanting to make his way through the crowd again.

It was alright, they could face each other, read the depths of one another's eyes, and drink greedily from the comfort and assurance they saw there.

When Dat reached across the tabletop and grasped Mam's hand, he told her she was all the support he needed and thanked her for being strong. And she knew her Davey was a man she still admired even after all these years.

Together, they were a mighty fortress.

Back in the waiting room, they leaped to their feet at the appearance of Ruthie and Anna Mae, their husbands in tow. Priscilla and Suzie followed them shyly, their eyes huge in their pinched white faces.

A clamoring ensued with talking, hugging, and crying. The girls needed to find out every single detail they could gather about Sarah.

Then Priscilla told them about Lydia and Omar's situation. The horse barn, of course, had been burned to the ground, but the dairy barn was saved, and not one horse was lost. Dominic, the crazy thing, ran clear out to Ben's Sam's in Gordonville and was being kept in the bull pen for now.

Melvin had stayed with Lydia, and so far, she did not seem to be sliding into despair, her spirits being bolstered by Melvin's unfailing optimism, which was good.

No one was allowed to see Sarah. Suzie sat

close to Mam and would not leave her side. Priscilla stayed on the other. Ruthie talked and fussed on and on about what she knew about burns—the miraculous work of the B and W salve and burdock leaves. Dat nodded assent but said, "Not for now, Ruthie, not for now. This is way above our home remedies. Our Sarah almost died."

"Could she still?" Suzie asked, her terrified eyes large and intense.

"She could, yes. We'll take a day at a time—no, an hour at a time," Dat said.

Eli's Sam had stayed with Levi. They played game after game of checkers, and Levi did not say a word about the shaggy-haired youth or calling the police.

Priscilla and Suzie had slept through the ruckus, and Levi figured he'd not mention it until Sarah was better. Sarah was tough, he reasoned, but she was, after all, a girl, and you had to take care of them. Why, they screamed terrible when he took his dentures out of his mouth.

The Crozer-Chester Medical Center was a great earth-hued building, rectangular, seven stories high. It had an enclosure along the one side, a porch of sorts. Trees surrounded it and some newly planted shrubs and flowering bushes. They were dormant now, waiting for their time to join the greening of spring, the bark mulch around them weathered by the snows of winter.

The parking lot spread across acres of former agricultural land, the parking spaces painted white, like a crossword puzzle mapped out with signs—who could park where, this space reserved. Usually most of the spaces were occupied, the gigantic building a beacon of hope and caring for families whose loved ones were severely burned or burned beyond the realm of home care, in any case.

Hundreds of doctors, nurses, and other trained individuals worked within the tiled walls of the hospital, devoting their lives to the care and healing of unfortunate souls who had to endure one of the most severe forms of nature's suffering.

The Beilers' second night at the burn center was almost spent. The moon had descended far to the west, its bluish white glow turning the indigo blue night sky a bit silver. The parked cars took on the glistening luster of moonlight, and small shadows appeared on the east side of every object.

Inside, on the third floor, the figure in Room 312 moaned, sighed, then fell asleep, her limbs twitching after she attempted to verbalize her thoughts. Images spun through her head, but they made her too tired, so she let them go.

There was no use. The weariness was much too heavy. It lay on her chest like a fifty-pound bag of potatoes, slowly pressing out her will to live.

Those potatoes needed to be taken down to the

root cellar. The garden must not have produced enough this year for Dat to have bought them in a fifty-pound bag.

She groaned, tried to roll out from beneath it. No use. She'd just have to breathe as best she could.

She was picking up potatoes now, the breeze soft and mellow, the earth still warm on her bare toes, although the summer was fast coming to an end, and most of the harvest was in.

There was still the cabbage Mam had planted late, and the celery, banked up with hills of loamy brown soil.

She stooped, felt the satisfying mound beneath her fingers, and brought up a big one this time. The biggest potato of the season. She tossed it into the wooden crate, then bent for another.

Mervin was with her, laughing, throwing small potatoes at her. She was puzzled that he was there, but the weight on her chest made it too tiring to ask.

Mervin sang, he laughed, he smiled, and all the potatoes he threw at her hurt so badly, she wanted to make him stop.

She cried out, "Mervin, *do net* (don't)!"

The more she pleaded, the harder he threw them, still singing and laughing.

The pain was unbearable now.

She begged for mercy, asked him to stop.

Where was Mam? She had to have help.

Someone had to help her get out from under this weight. She called and called, but no one would come to her.

Sarah's parents sat, one on either side of her bed, with their heads resting on the backs of the vinyl-covered chairs. Their eyes were closed, mouths slack as sleep loosened the muscles and tendons.

Rest had come suddenly for both of them. After almost forty hours, there was no alternative. They slept.

While they slept, Sarah called, over and over. Or so she thought.

Mam still slept with the trained senses of a mother of ten, but there was no sound from the still, white form on the bed. It was the swish of the nurse's scrubs that first woke Mam. She sat up immediately, adjusted her covering, smoothed her skirt, and felt guilty for having dozed off, away from Sarah.

The nurse didn't speak, just edged silently past Mam, checked the blips and beeps on the monitors, inspected the IV bag to check its level, then patted Mam's shoulder as she moved past.

She was efficient and kind, even at this hour, Mam thought. It was a miracle the way these people knew exactly what they were doing.

A low sound came from the bed.

Mam turned, grasped the arms of her chair, and got to her feet. The sound was different this time.

"Mm. Mm!"

Quickly, Mam bent over Sarah, placing her hands lightly on her face, her shoulders.

"Sarah. Sarah. *Ich bin do* (I am here)."

Then, decidedly, from the thin confines of the white bandages, came a garbled sound, altered by a swollen throat.

"Ma-am."

"I'm here, Sarah. Can you hear me?"

Hoarse breathing, accelerated now, came rasping from her mouth behind the gauze. It sounded like fabric tearing as Sarah regained consciousness. The only form of expression her body allowed was a long, hoarse whisper of misery. A silent scream.

"Sarah. Sarah."

Mam was completely distraught now, afraid Sarah would choke. Forgetting the button she was supposed to press for help, she moved past the foot of the bed and out the door. Turning her head from left to right, she scuttled in the direction of the nurses' station.

The station wasn't there. Not where she thought it should be.

Oh, there was someone. She stopped the harried looking nurse.

"Can you help us? She's awake!"

The nurse, all six feet of her, looked down at the weary Amish woman plucking at her sleeve and resigned herself. These Amish were all the same. Inevitably, they all came looking for help, forgetting to use the call button.

Mam's feet slid across the tiles, following the long-legged stride in front of her, so befuddled she didn't even notice when the nurse stopped at a long, high enclosure and said, "312."

Instantly, the nurse—the same one who had checked the IV—rose and walked swiftly to Sarah's room, awakening Dat as she went to his side of Sarah's bed.

She pressed the button for help with one thumb, while her other hand reached for the thin gauze around Sarah's mouth. Mam stood by, her hands clasped in front of her, her mouth working, as the agonized sounds continued.

Another nurse, younger, with a tanned complexion and short, brown hair, joined the other one. Together, they began loosening some of the bandages around Sarah's face.

"If you would rather not be here, you can step out of the room," the first one informed them.

Dat's eyes questioned Mam, but she refused to budge. Sarah was "coming to," and there was no way she was leaving this room.

The pain was a white-hot, blinding force that took her breath away before she had a chance to finish it. She let out a small puff of air, drew one back, and then another, before the hoarse screams would stop them entirely.

Slowly, the light above her head came into focus. The doorframe, the track beside her bed, the sour green of the walls, the clashing color of the beige curtain.

Then the waves of pain pounded across her, a tsunami, a devastating wall that set all her nerves shimmering with unaccustomed intensity, like a razor blade drawn horizontally across her wounds.

As the nurses allowed a minimal opening, her eyes or the small, red swollen appendages that had been her eyes, opened far enough to search, desperately, for someone to help her.

A face, hands, voices, but not someone who would help.

"Mm. Mm." She strained to call Mam's name.

Stepping aside, the nurses allowed Mam into Sarah's line of vision. Mam never wavered. There were no tears. Her daughter was awake, she was calling for her, and she had a duty to perform.

Many nights Mam had nursed cranky babies. She had comforted her children after disturbing dreams. She had wiped vomit from their bed-sides, gagging as she did so, bathed little ones smelling so sour she could taste it, poured baking soda on soiled mattresses, and tucked the sweet-smelling children back into beds made up with clean sheets—only to have the exact same scene repeated a few hours later. Those times, she didn't think of herself, her weariness. She just went ahead and did her duty, the same as she would do now.

"Sarah."

"*Helf mich* (Help me)."

"I will help you, Sarah. I will do everything I can."

Dat stood, helpless, his eyes pooled with tears, but calm.

"*Voss* (What)?"

The croak was barely audible, but the question, the plea, was known and recognized, the way it banged on Mam's heart.

"Sarah, the barn at the Widow Lydia's? It burned. Can you remember anything at all?"

"*An drink.*"

Immediately, Mam understood. Of course, she was thirsty.

"She wants a drink," she said to Dat.

Mam asked the nurses for a cup of water, but they provided only ice chips, which made Mam breathe hard, the way she did when she was huffy inside, though she was trained to be quiet, submissive.

So she held a plastic spoon of ice chips to Sarah's swollen lips, lovingly, expertly. She held very still when Sarah gurgled, choked, and began a labored breathing that concerned the nurse. Mam figured that the ice was too cold and a cup of water would have been much better.

She needed comfrey tea and B and W salve and

burdock leaves she had gathered from the fence rows and dried in the hot August sun. She needed the spring tonic she made with garlic and red pepper and aloe vera, but she knew all that would come later.

For now, they needed the care of professionals, the sterile environment, doctors with experience and knowledge far above their own.

"It hurts," Sarah moaned.

"Sarah, you'll need to be brave. You have to gather all your courage, every ounce of strength within you, to be able to heal. A beam fell on your head, and your clothes were on fire."

The only answer was another onslaught of ragged cries, and the nurse tugged gently on Mam's sleeve, drawing her away, then explained very gently about upping the pain medication, so Sarah would sleep for another few hours. The need to keep her quiet was explained in careful detail, and Mam folded her small form back into a vinyl chair and acknowledged their counsel, but the moment the door closed behind them, she turned to her husband and sputtered with indignation and suppressed emotion.

The morning sun made its appearance through the east windows on the third floor, as Sarah lay quietly. She was breathing in and out slowly, but then more shallowly as her breathing accelerated.

Over the course of the sun's ascent, she lay, as her parents spoke quietly, with furtive glances in the direction of their sleeping daughter. They both knew the weeks ahead would tax their strength to the breaking point, but with God's help, they would make it through.

When three doctors entered at once and stood gravely at Sarah's bed, then turned and introduced themselves, still grave, Dat's heart plunged within, and he felt physically ill from the feeling. Would she still not survive?

The oldest, with white hair in a semicircle around his shining bald crown, had square glasses and a goatee. He spoke first.

He addressed Dat as Mr. Beidler, and Dat did not bother correcting him.

"Her burns are severe, especially on the right side, where the beam hit. Her neck, ear, and right side of her face have mostly third degree burns, some second degree perhaps. We are still deciding about complete isolation in a room with laminar air flow, to keep her as free from microorganisms as possible."

The second doctor addressed Dat as Mr. Beidler as well, then stroked his dark moustache thoughtfully, lowering and raising his eyebrows, two perfectly matched black caterpillars.

"She's young, very healthy, and she may be okay here—strong enough to ward off possible infection."

Dat nodded.

Mam thought about vitamin C drops and

capsules, and echinacea, but she didn't say anything. A woman was subject to her husband, and if she needed to know anything, she could ask him at home.

The third doctor was short and round, with a thatch of black, well-groomed hair lying flat along his crown. His Asian features were pleasant, his accent thick, his speech rapid. Dat nodded, his head inclined, but he did not understand a single word he said.

Finally, Dat spoke. He told the physicians that the decisions they made were theirs to exercise, and he would abide by them, and he wished them God's wisdom. He said, at times like this, he could only be thankful that God had imparted this learning to them, and he hoped they could communicate well and understand the process.

Mam nodded and smiled, but said nothing.

They were escorted through the door and walked like an aging couple to the waiting room, their steps slow, their heads bent, weary, defeated suddenly.

Why? Why had God allowed this devastation? Wouldn't it have been easier to let her die?

He didn't have the nerve to ask about the disfigurement. Surely, her face and neck would never be the same. She would carry horrible scars all her life, and folks would not be able to keep from staring at her. Davey and Malinda had been through all that with Levi.

The glances, quickly, then away, only to return—the pitying looks that came along with carrying her imperfect baby wherever she went. Mam knew the feeling well.

Yes, she had taken pride in Sarah's beauty. A nontraditional beauty, perhaps, but still. And now God had chosen to chastise her.

Together, they sat, side by side, three floors above the large parking lot, and stared through the immense glass windows without seeing, losing ground as they flailed themselves with harsh thoughts of self-judgment.

Because of my sin, my daughter lies in torture. Because of my sin, God is chastening me. Oh, I know that He loves me. But I have gone astray. Without knowing, my heart has turned to stone, and now He must bring me back.

Individually, but almost as one, they repented, asked forgiveness, prayed silently, separately, but found no peace.

The windstorm of self-blame had been efficient. It had wrecked their mighty fortress, leaving them both on high, bitter, arid ground, separating them as each sought to withstand the blows of fortune. Or of God.

Chapter 5

Back home in the area between Intercourse and Gordonville, the neighborhood buzzed with activity once again. Black exhaust poured from the smokestacks of great yellow earth movers as they cleared wet, charred beams and twisted metal. They formed a huge pile of useless, wasted material that had been the fine horse barn housing the Belgians. It had been the pride of the Widow Lydia's son, Omar, and his older friend and mentor, Lee Glick, the blond, strapping young man who lived with his sister Anna and her husband, Ben Zook.

Truckloads of yellow lumber made their slow, noisy way past Elam Stoltzfus's house, and Matthew was awakened by the sound, one he considered unnecessary.

His mood already foul, he dressed carefully, as he always did, in a white short-sleeved t-shirt with navy blue pinstripes and a clean pair of jeans. He pulled on a black leather belt and admired the buckle, thinking how much better it was to wear a belt than those elastic suspenders he used to wear.

Naturally, his mother was up at the Widow Lydia's, so he broke a few eggs in a bowl and beat them with a fork, set them aside, and searched the bread drawer.

No bread?

The door opened, and his mother walked in backward, holding the big plastic coffee container with both hands. Her black scarf was settled haphazardly on her head, her sweater closed with safety pins, as usual.

"Oh, Matthew, you're up!"

Her tone took on that high, desperate whine it always did when she wanted him to be in a good mood. Irritation welled up as he watched her slam the coffee container on the countertop.

"Matthew, Sarah is burned! She's burned bad. Oh, I think it can't be! Why did she ever go into the barn?"

"Mam, we went over all this before. She just wasn't thinking."

"No, she wasn't. She wasn't."

Bustling now, talking to herself as much as to Matthew, she chided Sarah for going into the burning barn, scolded Davey for allowing this to go on, scolded Malinda for letting Sarah go to talk to the widow that night. She was simply unable to come to terms with Sarah's suffering.

Matthew remained quiet, listening to his mother with an air of patience and understanding.

"Where's the bread?" he asked.

"Bread? There's no bread in the bread drawer? *Ach my*! I think there's some in the freezer."

Hastily, she ran over to the refrigerator, yanked the freezer door open, and searched frantically.

"Well."

Matthew watched from his perch on a kitchen chair.

"I don't know how I managed that. I'm out of bread."

"You manage that quite often, if I remember right."

"Now, Matthew. Don't be mean."

"Half the time, you're out of bread."

"No, not half the time."

"If you'd bake your own the way Malinda does . . ."

"You have a car. You could run out to Kauffman's."

"Nah. I'll just have scrambled eggs."

"There's sausage."

"Where?"

Hannah yanked open the refrigerator door, pushed containers aside, and produced a Tupperware bowl of ground sausage, her face alight, eager to make up for the missing bread.

Matthew lifted the lid, sniffed, slowly replaced it, and pronounced it spoiled.

"I'm not eating that stuff."

"Matthew. *Ach*, I just bought it."

"Where?"

"At Centerville."

"Hard telling where that junk comes from."

"We have bacon."

"What kind?"

"John Martin's."

"Is it fresh?"

"Oh, I think so. Surely. The package hasn't been opened yet."

Matthew found the bacon to his liking and proceeded to make his own breakfast, without toast. Hannah bustled about the kitchen, making more coffee, collecting sugar, milk, flour, and apple pie filling from the cellar. She was always hopeful that Matthew was pleased and not too put out by her poor management.

"Are you coming to help today?" she asked finally.

"Why would I? I'm not Amish."

"Oh, now, that doesn't matter."

"I don't want anyone staring at me or asking questions, okay?"

"Oh, alright."

"I'm going to have my devotions. My Bible is my strength now as I travel life's pathway alone."

"Oh, so true, Matthew. I'm so glad you have your faith, your Christianity."

Her hands clasped, her eyes lifted to her handsome son, the poor, hurting widower, the love of her life. She was so glad he was able to carry on alone, glad he was so well versed in the Bible. That was all that mattered.

Juggling her bags and boxes, only dimly aware of the fact that Matthew did not offer his assistance, she loaded the wagon, that ever-present and faithful conveyor of all things wagon-able, and was on her way, doing her duty at yet another barn raising.

Well, where there was life, there was hope. Sarah had not died, and Matthew might still be glad to make her his wife.

And they could be Amish, too, she decided, the very thought making her yank on the wagon handle energetically.

Lee Glick sat beside the coal stove in his sister's kitchen, his hands held to the warmth, as Anna stood by the gas stove, flipping pancakes skillfully, landing the golden brown orbs perfectly on her two-burner griddle.

Little Elmer walked over, lifted his arms, and smiled. Lee bent and picked him up, his chin nuzzling the top of the plump little boy's head, but he said nothing.

Anna slid a look in his direction, as tears sprang to her eyes, and her nose burned. She bit her lower lip to keep from crying.

Lee was pale, he would hardly eat, his eyes full of unshed tears every time she dared look at him.

"Is Ben done yet?"

There was no answer, so Anna let it go, as she slid the casserole dish containing the fluffy pancakes into the oven to keep them warm. She plopped a pat of butter onto the skillet and began breaking eggs onto it, sniffing.

She hoped Lee could handle this.

When her husband, Ben, entered the kitchen, she looked up and gave him a smile, which he returned, saying over his shoulder, "Hear anything?"

"Not since last night."

"Is she awake?"

"Not as far as I know."

They sat together at the table, the two school-aged children subdued, hesitant to speak of Sarah, their beloved teacher, who was in a faraway hospital, badly burned.

Ben bowed his head, and the others followed, for the time of silent prayer that was customary before every meal.

When Ben raised his head, the ones seated around the table did the same. They raised their glasses of orange juice and set them back carefully, avoiding the eyes that bore too many questions and no answers.

Lee took a thick slice of homemade whole-wheat toast and reached for the butter, spreading it slowly without looking up, as if the concentration he devoted to this small task was absolutely essential.

He passed the plate of fried eggs without helping himself to one, bent carefully toward six-year-old Marianne, and raised his eyebrows.

"Want one?"

She nodded eagerly, anticipating the wondrous

breakfast, her round little body already taking on her mother's proportions.

Lee sat back after helping Marianne, raked a hand through his short blond hair, and looked at his sister with blue eyes reflecting the misery he had been experiencing since the fire.

"How, I mean, how severe do burns have to be before they kill a person?" he asked, his wide shoulders leaning into the chair, as if to shrink away from the truth.

Ben was intently spreading homemade ketchup on his mound of steaming stewed crackers.

"Oh, I imagine it would have to be pretty bad. Sarah is young. She's what 20 or 21? She's a hard worker, healthy. I can't imagine it would actually take her life."

Lee nodded.

"Didn't anyone hear anything?"

Anna shook her head.

"At the barn raising, they'll know. Someone will have heard something. Aren't you going to eat, Lee? There are three eggs left."

He shook his head.

"Toast is okay for now."

Ben met Anna's eyes, raised his eyebrows. Anna shook her head only slightly, then looked at her brother.

"Lee, she'll be fine. With today's methods, they can work miracles."

He nodded.

"It's just so hard to understand why God would allow someone as kind and caring as she is to get burned like this. The only reason she went into the barn was to save that colt. I could see how she loved it, how completely taken she was after the birth." Lee shook his head. "She's a special girl," he finished, so soft and low that no one heard what he said.

At the barn raising, Lee lifted Omar's spirits by telling him to come with him to watch the new colt. They stood side by side, their feet propped on the aluminum gate, as the long-legged colt galloped around, cutting a ridiculous figure, its legs way out of proportion with its body.

"Now, that is a blessing, Omar. Our first colt, alive and well."

"Sarah . . ."

Omar looked desperately at Lee, then ducked his head. When he looked up, his eyes were dark pools of torture.

"She's not going to die, is she?"

Ashamed of his tears, his lack of "big guy" composure, he blinked miserably.

Lee put a hand on Omar's shoulder. When his back heaved and a sob emerged—a ragged cry of pain and inability to understand—Lee hugged him hard and said, "It's okay, buddy."

They stood. The black debris was rolled away now. The stench still hovered, but the bare earth was visible. Cement blocks and mixing machines and new lumber awaited the men clad in black, their varying shades of yellow straw hats bobbing amid the dark outer wear. The brown pasture showed a hint of green, a mixture of a remembrance of the past winter and of new life awaiting, a promise of spring just around the corner.

Word came via Hannah. Malinda had left a message.

The Widow Lydia waited with bated breath as Hannah relayed her friend's message, word for word.

"Hannah, this is Malinda. We are at the burn center. I think it's called Crozer-Chester or Chester-Crozer Medical Center or Burn Center—something like that. It's near Philadelphia. Sarah woke up, but they have her heavily drugged again, sedated. Her burns are serious, and they're going to put her in a special room with different air, so that she stays germ free. She's in pain, too much to bear, Hannah. Please *halted au in gebet* (pray for her)."

The word spread among the women and from the Widow Lydia to Melvin, her beloved friend, her betrothed. Sarah's garrulous, big-hearted, twenty-eight-year-old cousin—with a personality that was larger than life—immediately carried the long-awaited news to the men.

When it reached Lee's ears, he was bent over a cement block, cutting it with the edge of his block hammer. He stayed in his bent position, hoping no one could see, no one could gauge the intensity of the relief that flooded through him, leaving him light-headed, his face blanched, his eyes dilated with feeling.

Melvin waved his hands and said he'd heard of Crozer-Chester. Wasn't that the place Abner's Joe was taken that time when he cut into an electrical cord and could have died?

Yes, yes, it was.

The sun was warm on their backs that day, the first serious promise of a gentler time ahead, and hearts swelled with gratitude that the winter would finally be over, without fail.

At lunchtime, Matthew Stoltzfus appeared at the doorway. His hunger drew him, and he was eager to fill his plate from the great kettles containing the variety of home-cooked dishes he had missed so much in Haiti. He didn't care if he never saw another piece of broiled fish in his life. He had been raised on good grass-fed beef and homegrown chicken, fried with flour and butter, with thick gravy on mounds of white potatoes. He considered it a privilege to join his mother now, at the lunch hour.

He figured seventy-five percent of the people he met would treat him respectfully, so he responded in a like manner. He met curious stares, smiled back when someone smiled at him, and answered inquiries in a level tone, being careful, wary, not disclosing more than he had to.

Hannah filled his coffee cup repeatedly, hovering close by like an annoying wasp. That was most of the reason for his being tight-lipped. He knew how desperately she wanted to sweep him back into the fold, and she wasn't going to accomplish it.

He watched the women and single girls, missing Sarah. She had always been at barn raisings, her bright expression and wavy hair a familiar sight, like a white fence freshly painted or a red barn beside fields of waving summer cornstalks, pleasant, a piece of home.

He wondered where Rose was, wondered how he'd feel if she was to arrive here, on this day, and find him back in his old neighborhood.

Digging into his second slice of chocolate cake with a mound of peanut butter icing on top, he chewed, then slid over on the bench to make room for Omar Esh.

Eyeing the Widow Lydia's oldest son, Matthew thought he was a looker with those black eyes and impressive height. He had grown at least a foot taller. Matthew remembered him as a pesky little eight-year-old, his father batting him around in church when he refused to behave.

"Hey, Matthew."

"Hey, yourself, Omar."

"Good to see you."

"You too."

"Sorry to hear about your wife."

"The Lord giveth, and the Lord taketh away."

Omar was unsure how to answer this, so he didn't. People like Matthew were *fer-fearish* (deceiving), and his mother had often warned him not to become entangled in a discussion with someone like him. He didn't fully understand what the big deal was, but he figured he'd better listen to the voice of his mother.

"Looks like the Lord chose to take from you as well. This second time around you really must admit you're doing something wrong."

Omar shifted uneasily, lowered his head, and slurped his coffee.

"You know you Amish should not be hiding the fact that you are being punished for your weak faith, which is a sort of disbelief in the Holy Scripture. If you took God at His word, you wouldn't need to justify your life by works, dressing that way and driving a horse and buggy."

Matthew stopped and looked up when there was a tap on his shoulder. Infinitely pleased, he scrambled up from the bench and walked outside with a blushing Rose Zook beside him.

Everyone saw it. The older women narrowed their eyes and compressed their lips. The younger ones whispered behind extended palms, "My, what a couple they still make."

Lee was chewing a toothpick absentmindedly. He heard the familiar high-pitched giggle and watched Rose talking animatedly with her former boyfriend. He showed no outward sign of emotion at all. He simply extracted the toothpick from between his teeth and threw it in the plastic garbage bag hanging from a nail on the porch.

Not much had changed, in his opinion.

When Friday's paper arrived at the David Beiler residence, Eli's Sam, or Sam King as he was known, brought it in with the rest of the mail, laid it on the counter by the sink in the *kesslehaus*, and forgot about it for a minute. Joe Kauffman, coming to do the milking, had distracted him with his speedy entrance into the forebay, his horse rearing and fighting the restraint on his bit.

Levi was by the kitchen window, mixing some powdered Tang with lukewarm tap water, and almost had a fit, the way Joe couldn't hold his horse. Joe was a bit of a character, he thought, but Sam King was a good chap to have around, and Levi enjoyed his company immensely. An extra bonus was the fact that he was allowed to have that second slice of shoofly when Sam was there.

Levi pitied Sarah, felt sorrow for Davey and Malinda, and understood the events that caused their suffering. He was kind and considerate of Priscilla and Suzie, glad to see the arrival of his three brothers, and just as glad to see them go to the burn center. Davey liked those three—Abner,

Allen, and Johnny. They'd make their father happy, for awhile.

So in his own simple realm, his life was upset, but not by too much, with Sam playing checkers with him and Priscilla to do the cooking.

Levi never bothered much about the mail. Unable to read, he sometimes looked at bright flyers and glossy advertisements and enjoyed the magazines, but deciphering the articles printed in the paper was beyond his limited ability.

Joe and Sam entered the house together. Sam scooped up the mail, unfolding the paper as he settled on a kitchen chair.

"Joe, you want a cup of coffee before you start the milking?"

"No, thanks. I'm a bit late as it is."

He turned, his kindly face breaking into a smile at the sight of Levi coming to join them.

"How's it going, Levi?"

"Real good, Joe. Real good. Sam is really good to me, a nice chap to have around. Priscilla made soft pretzels last night."

"She did?"

"Oh yeah. Were they delicious? Yes, they were. Did you know I don't use mustard to dip them in?"

"You don't?"

Levi shook his head, his eyes narrowing.

"I use ketchup!"

Joe opened his mouth to answer Levi when there was a decided yelp from Eli's Sam.

"What in the world?! Joe, check this out!"

Spreading the newspaper on the tabletop, Sam started reading aloud, his gnarled forefinger following the newsprint.

There was a young man in custody—a Michael Lanvin. He was the suspected arsonist in the barn fires and was being held in the Lancaster County jail on $75,000 bail.

"Oh my goodness," Joe said, very soft and low.

Sam read on. He had been taken into custody at the David Beiler residence.

"Which David Beiler? There are dozens of them here in Lancaster County."

"Here!" Levi shouted.

They turned in unison, disbelief stamped on their features, mouths agape.

"What?"

"Here!"

Levi stood by the table, his wide girth lengthening as he pulled himself to his full height, hooked a thumb beneath his suspenders, and snapped them against his great chest.

"It was me."

"Come on, Levi."

Sam shook his head.

"Do you know this guy?"

Levi walked around the table, bent over, and cocked his head to peer closely through his thick bifocals at the paper. He began nodding his head.

"Oh yeah, that's Mike. That's the long-haired

young man that cried at the pretty girl's funeral, and my dat, Davey, gave him a long hug, and he talked to him with nice words. He didn't know that Mike was the same man that drove his car in our drive that night, the time when our barn burned. I didn't either, for sure, but sort of. Then he came to our house, when the widow's barn burned. He wanted to talk to my dat, you know, Davey. And . . ."

Here, Levi paused for a moment, taking in the two men's undivided attention, reveling in his self-appointed position as conveyor of wonderfully astounding news. He leaned forward, his eyes narrowing with conspiracy.

"I told Mike to sit down, and he did. Then I told him I had to go the bathroom, which . . ."

His voice trailed off, making sure the two men were on the edges of their seats, as he played the drama to its fullest extent.

"I didn't really have to."

He almost hissed the words. Sam's and Joe's eyes opened wide in bewilderment.

"I just said so. Then I went quietly out the *kesslehaus* door and to the phone shanty. I ran. I can really run if I have to. I know my numbers. Did you know that? I punched the nine and the one two times, and I told the lady I needed the policemen. They came, but not before I asked Mike if he wanted shoofly or whoopie pies. My mam had just made them."

"What happened when they got here?"

"Mike tried to get away, but he couldn't very easily do that. The *kesslehaus* door was locked."

Incredulous now, Joe Kauffman slowly shook his head.

"Levi, you are something. May God be praised."

"It wasn't God. It was me," Levi said, scowling at the thought of his rightful honor going elsewhere.

Eli's Sam threw back his head and let out a great roar of delight, and he and Joe laughed until they had to wipe their eyes with their navy blue handkerchiefs.

Clearly, that set everything right. Levi grinned widely, happy to be able to produce that sort of reaction.

"You know, they were saying at the barn raising that someone heard somewhere that they had caught the arsonist, but we've heard it dozens of times, and it's never been true—just a rumor," Sam said.

Joe nodded, then glanced at the clock above the sink.

"I have to begin milking right now. Levi, would you send Priscilla out to feed calves?"

"Suzie can help her."

"Alright."

Joe went out, the keeper of his neighbor's cows while they were at the distant hospital with their suffering daughter, and his heart twisted within his chest, keenly aware of their pain. He'd have to set up a trust fund at Susquehanna Bank tomorrow. They had some staggering medical bills coming their way.

But wasn't that Levi a corker?

Ah well, the least of these my brethren, and who would have thought he had it in him?

Chapter 6

The newspaper article set up a great cloud of speculation, suspicion, and disbelief that hovered over the Amish community. It reached for many miles as housewives chatted at quiltings or sisters' days. Men working on construction sites tipped their hats, put down their nail guns, and gave their opinions. Many of them were like-minded, their voices laced with exasperation. They were just plain fed up, weary of the barn fires and their aftermaths.

What if someone was in custody? That didn't hold much clout, in their opinion. He'd lie his way out. No one had caught him actually setting fire to a barn. If the courts tried this Mike in a few months, who would testify? Who would press charges? Very likely the ministers would not allow it, so there was no point in getting excited about this guy's picture in the paper.

And now there was the minister's daughter, completely disfigured, some said, and Davey was the main one who had held back, not allowing the usual investigation.

Some said this would bring him round. Others said maybe this really would put a stop to the fires. And didn't Davey Beiler's Levi have Down syndrome? You just couldn't believe everything you heard.

Sarah was fully awake, her wits about her after that horrible battle to summon enough willpower to withstand the sensation hovering mostly on her right side.

She could not turn her head, and her vision was limited by that as well as the swollen lids of her eyes, but she could see the room and her parents' faces, briefly. She knew she was badly burned and had come to grips with it, sort of.

Each day, in the forenoon, they unwrapped the bandages, and the taking away of the dead tissue would begin—the debridement.

It was beyond anything Sarah had imagined the human body could withstand. She shook with uncontrollable spasms of fear and pain. She clenched her teeth to keep from crying out, but in the end, she gave up trying and begged them to stop. She cried and pleaded, thinking she would surely die.

Always, the nurses and doctors were kind,

explaining over and over how absolutely essential this procedure was for the healing.

When she tried to tell her parents about it, after
that first time, her hoarse voice caught on a sob,
and she couldn't convey the overwhelming pain.
Her father's face became grim, and he said he had
to leave—he was going home to see to things.

His wife's eyes questioned him, and when she
saw the raw agony in her husband's eyes, she
became very afraid. Reaching out, she placed a
hand on his trembling arm.

"Davey, are you alright?"

"No, I'm not alright," he whispered. "Who
would be? Who could stand to think of their own
children being tortured? Who?"

Turning on his heel, he left and stalked down
the hallway, the soles of his high-topped black
Sunday shoes ringing on the glossy blue and
white tiles. His shoulders, clad in the black *mutza*
(Sunday coat), were held stiffly, his face white
and set, like granite.

The driver, Wesley, told old Dan King that he'd
never seen Davey Beiler like that. He was afraid,
so he was.

When Sarah woke up that afternoon after her
father left, she found her mother dozing in the
vinyl chair beside her bed. She called her name
hoarsely, then cleared her throat and tried again.

"Mam."

When there was no answer, she lay back and

closed her eyes as warm tears coursed down her cheeks, soaking the fresh bandages that covered her face. She felt alone, defeated.

How badly was she burned? Why wouldn't they let her have a mirror? Was she hideously disfigured, or could the doctors fix the worst of it? Surely she still had a nose and ears. And she had her eyes.

Sarah tried raising her left arm, but instantly felt a stinging sensation across the muscles in her upper back, so she let it go.

Every twitch, every slight movement sent shivers of pain through her body, like a million stinging needles pricking her skin.

She'd probably have to get used to that, wouldn't she? She'd have to work up some kind of resolve against the pain. She thought of her cousin who had a severe case of juvenile diabetes, plunging a needle into her stomach every day. She'd said that after awhile she hardly felt the *gix* (needle), and Sarah believed her.

She'd try hard to bear the pain the best she could, which wasn't the worst of it at all. The worst was the fear of disfigurement. The realization of it rolled into her consciousness like a fog on a wet spring morning, obscuring any hint of hope or encouragement.

She was accustomed to the stares of curiosity whenever Levi went somewhere with the family, but he was born with his disability. His features from Down syndrome and his tendency to be overweight drew looks, but his mind was immature enough to allow him to live among his beloved friends and family with a childlike innocence. Levi was genuinely happy.

Sarah felt trapped, not knowing her fate. She hung suspended between anxiety and acceptance.

And what about Matthew?

She groaned within herself, sharply aware of his dark good looks, his tendency to seek perfection in others. He'd never look at her again.

His perfect features were etched into her brain. She could conjure up any picture of him she wanted, anytime she wanted. Laughing, scowling, moving away, walking toward her, playing volleyball or baseball, or sitting beside her in the buggy, his profile was as handsome as that of any model she'd ever seen.

Oh, Matthew. You'll never want me now.

Closing her eyes, she prayed, asking God for one more chance, one more time to be with Matthew. Perhaps her injuries would soften his heart.

Alone in the confines of the small shed storing wood and coal, David Beiler fell on his knees, the rough bits of bark and chunks of coal biting into them through his denim trousers.

He reached up, removed his straw hat, and bent his head above his calloused hands, which were clasped in prayer, but nothing, not one word could he utter. He felt infinitely alone.

Puzzled, he remained on his knees, the futility of being there slowly seeping into his mind.

He could not pray. The words, the lifting of his spirit, would not come, so he rose stiffly, brushed the bits of dust and dirt off his knees, and turned to go. Opening the door of the woodshed, he stopped. He leaned against the dusty doorframe and looked out across the night sky. The soft glow of lamplight from the upstairs windows, the neighboring lights, the silhouette of the new barn and outbuildings against the twinkling stars arrested him and he held himself still. Perhaps if he waited, God would come to him and peace would be restored, along with the ability to communicate.

The only emotion he felt, after a long while, was anger. Unresolved, boiling anger, as hot as the falling beam that had hit Sarah. It had scraped and burned her shoulders and back raw, like ground beef. Now, she lay in that hospital, tortured every bit as badly as the Anabaptists had been tortured, as told in *Martyrs Mirror*.

It was his fault. He'd clung to the old ways. How much of it was tradition, how much was pride, and how small was the slice of heartfelt conviction?

Was it really expected of him? This forgiveness? How could he forgive an arsonist who had burned his daughter at the stake?

He had no tears, only a pounding heart and a clenched jaw. He'd go, read his Bible, and try to get back on track.

Instead, he found himself sitting at the kitchen table, staring at the picture of Michael Lanvin, the shaggy-haired youth, looking at him from the photo above the article where he said he'd been the arsonist—was the arsonist.

Had he actually hugged that arrogant youth? Blessed him and wished him well? That had been pious of him, obviously. That was, of course, before Sarah had been burned.

Who knew? Did they really know he lit the barns? What was truth? Why? Why did a loving God allow his daughter Sarah to go through this senseless burning? Anger churned through his veins as his Bible lay unopened on the table, his breath coming in hard, frustrated puffs.

Did he believe in God? Had he ever been fit to be a minister? Outwardly, maybe, but had his heart ever been right?

The clock on the wall loudly banged out the seconds, and the refrigerator hummed quietly. Somewhere a wall creaked, and Levi mumbled in his sleep as the mattress beneath him groaned. David Beiler bowed his head as he wrestled with his demons—the purveyors of doubt and self-loathing, of discouragement and a lack of faith.

Suddenly, he sat up, drew back his fist, and slammed it into the black and white photograph of the man that was supposedly the arsonist He tore the newspaper with the first assault. A coffee cup rattled, tilted, rolled off the kitchen table, and fell to the floor, breaking into dozens of pieces.

Again and again, he slammed the newspaper as great, hoarse sobs tore from his throat and tears rained down his cheeks.

David Beiler's Gethsemane had come.

Much later, he lay prostrate on the floor, his body convulsing as the force of his cries continued to shake him. His supplications rolled from him in whispers, cries, and questions as he railed before the throne of his God.

Slowly, peace and acceptance emerged, driving back the darkness and the void he had experienced in his place of anger and misery. Gradually, a quietness in his spirit led him to real communication with the One who resides in heaven, supreme. The way before him was clear.

There was no substitute for forgiveness, no question of its balance. But it first had to start with him. He could not allow himself to become short with his brethren. There would be a way. All he needed was the strength to face each new day, for now.

He felt deeply ashamed of his anger. It seemed so wrong, and yet hadn't Paul said the things he did not want to do were precisely what he ended up doing? David's human nature hung on his frame like an unbearable cloak, stifling, woolen, and extremely uncomfortable.

Rising, he went to the pantry, found the dustpan and brush, then lowered himself to clean up the broken coffee cup, sweeping up every bit of glass carefully.

Ah, yes, so symbolic was this mug. We need to be broken, again and again, to allow the waters to flow, those life-giving waters of love.

Before David went to bed, he checked on Levi. He adjusted the quilt and patted his son's shoulders as he did so. Sleep well, Levi, sleep well, he thought.

A love for his handicapped son welled up within him, and he turned, stumbling over the rug as tears blinded his eyes.

Yes, God did know, after all, exactly what He was doing. There were just too many knotty problems to understand the big picture.

After the morning milking, David sat at the breakfast table. He ate the eggs that were fried beyond any hope of having soft, yellow yolks. He also had some burnt toast and the saltines swimming in hot milk, devoid of browned butter. And he praised Priscilla's attempts at cooking breakfast.

Suzie smiled up at her father.

"I made the toast!"

Levi was scraping anxiously at a blackened slice.

"You left it in the broiler too long."

"Nah, Levi. It's good that way," Suzie answered.

Levi chose to ignore her and asked instead when Mam was coming home.

"Soon, Levi. As soon as Sarah is moved into a regular room. Then you can go see her, and Priscilla can stay for awhile and let Mam come home."

"Nobody makes me anything to eat," Levi said so pitifully that Dat smiled widely behind his napkin.

As if someone had planned their lines, there was a knock on the door.

"Come in," Dat called, without getting up. He simply motioned with his hand, the way country folks living in rural Amish settlements often do.

Matthew was smiling, his handsome face alight with good humor. He was genuinely glad to see his old friends, especially Levi, who returned his sunny greetings effusively.

Matthew was laden with food. The cardboard boxes contained a casserole of lasagna and one of baked corn, loaves of homemade bread, pies, macaroni salad, sausages, and a quivering Jell-O pudding, all leftovers from the ongoing barn raising at Widow Lydia's.

Matthew inquired about Sarah's well-being, his face serious, benevolent, and said anxiously that he needed to see her. When Dat told him about the isolation and the upcoming surgeries she would need, the skin grafting, he reconsidered but begged Dat to let him know the minute he could go and would be allowed in her room.

Dat remained kind and assured Matthew he would do everything he could, but he thought that the sooner he saw her, the better. He knew.

Matthew surveyed the now empty breakfast table, looked at Priscilla, and asked if she was the cook. Blushing, she nodded, her large green eyes lowered, the lids heavy with thick, dark lashes serving to enhance her prettiness. Eyeing her a little longer than necessary, Matthew's face took on a smile of appreciation and something else that Dat labeled silently.

The surgery went well. The skin they harvested from Sarah's left side served as patches that they transferred onto the worst of her wounds on her right side.

A few days later, she was allowed to have a mirror, although the doctor counseled her wisely, preparing her for the shock of seeing the damage the fire had done.

Sarah insisted she was prepared. She had braced for the worst scene possible, she really had.

She searched the nurses' faces for signs of pity or horror, but they remained impassive, professionally trained.

She felt the bandages being unwrapped, the

cool air frigid on the newly exposed skin, then took a deep shaking breath and held out her left hand for the mirror.

The skin on her arms and back still pulled painfully, but she moved everything she could, repeatedly, to acquaint herself with the sensation.

When the mirror was before her face, she squeezed her eyes completely shut and lowered it, courage eluding her.

The doctor encouraged her again, and this time she took the mirror and held it up unsteadily, but she did not lower it.

Slowly, a grotesque being came into focus.

Sarah's first impulse was to open her ruined mouth and scream and to go on screaming and protesting, raging against every force that had brought this bizarre accident into her life.

She was, by all accounts, truly hideous.

Determined, she kept holding the mirror at slightly different angles, examining, peering closely in the garish light from the overhead fixtures.

No hair, anywhere, although there was a slight fuzz on the left side, perhaps. No eyelashes or eyebrows. Red, peeling eyelids. A swollen fore-head that was purple, red, and pink on one side. The only way to describe the other side was as some kind of meat, like ground turkey or pork. She guessed that would be sausage.

Well, she had a nose—a good sturdy one at that.

The skin was just falling off of it in great peels, like a tomato skin in hot water.

Her lips looked as if she had at least fifty cold sores piled all over each other.

Her neck was barely burned on one side, especially on the underside of her jaw. The right side was where they had done the grafting, which looked much the same as she imaged it would. Skin from her back was adhered to her neck, and, incongruous as it seemed, it did look hopeful.

She smiled to herself. There was one good thing—if her back became itchy, she could scratch her neck.

When she lowered the mirror to her shoulders, she could not keep from crying, helplessly allowing tears to slide down the damaged skin on her cheeks. It was awful.

But she was alive. She was here. The doctors told her that the current methods at the burn center were just short of miraculous, and she was young and strong, something they had assured her repeatedly.

She clung to the words now.

She was taken out of isolation, and her family surrounded her. Allen, Abner, and Johnny must have made a no tears pact—joking and smiling, bringing her silly cards and balloons.

Their wives were less audacious, more reserved, so much so, in fact, that Sarah asked if she looked better or worse than they'd thought.

No one provided a forthright answer, so Sarah knew they were shocked at her appearance. Well, so be it. They certainly weren't the last ones who would experience disbelief.

Maybe she should spend the rest of her life with a paper bag over her head, she told her brothers.

"Make sure it's one from a chain store that would pay you for the advertising, like Walmart or Target," Allen said, laughing.

"They use plastic," Abner said loftily.

Sarah's back hurt, trying to keep from laughing.

Anna Mae and Ruthie held nothing back, crying until their faces were blotchy and red. Their eyes were swollen, and Ruthie's glasses were messy with smudges. They said things that weren't helpful and lots of things that made no sense at all, but they were her sisters. And sisters are like good apples, even the cores and the little black seeds can be eaten and tolerated.

Anna Mae said her eyelashes would grow back. Ruthie said if they didn't, they'd take Sarah to a face place and have artificial ones sewn on.

Sarah couldn't smile, but she asked, why bother, a face that looked like meatloaf was not improved by eyelashes. Johnny said if he had a choice, he'd definitely take the meatloaf with artificial eyelashes.

Then Priscilla came, along with Omar and Lydia, who had hoped they could gain entry to her bedside, but it was not to be. Not yet.

Priscilla walked over to Sarah's bed. Her face turned a sickly shade of green, and she folded up like a graceful ballerina as she drifted slowly to the floor. Allen caught her on the way down.

What a flurry then! Anna Mae and Ruthie had conniption fits, fanning her, sending Allen for Pepsi, saying her blood sugar was way down, she worked too hard, she was always dieting, and somebody needed to go ask a nurse for smelling salts.

No one did their bidding, and Priscilla woke up, blinked a few times, and was fine. She was accosted by her sisters for the next five minutes about protein and energy greens that come in powder form to be mixed with milk or water or juice. They insisted that if she took that, she would never pass out, no matter what.

After they all left, Priscilla and Suzie walked over to Sarah and told her she looked awful. Sarah said she knew that, but it wouldn't always look this bad.

Suzie, in all seriousness, said she looked like a catfish.

That time, Sarah cracked the skin on her lips. She couldn't help it, the laughter on the inside wanting to escape so badly.

After they all went home, Sarah slept the first deep sleep since the accident, relaxed in the knowledge that her family loved her, and for now, that was enough.

When she awoke, she was ravenously hungry, pressed the bell, and asked if she'd be allowed a snack.

Almost immediately, her favorite nurse, Alison, brought her apple juice, graham crackers, and peanut butter. She pulled up the blinds, letting the afternoon sun into the room. She told Sarah it was wonderful to hear she was hungry.

She made her spread the peanut butter on the crackers herself, even if it was painful to hold the graham cracker with one hand and spread the peanut butter with the other.

They got her out of bed again, for the third time, and there was nothing to do but grip the walker until her knuckles turned white, bend over as far as they'd allow, and shuffle along as best she could. She clenched her teeth, sucked in her breath, and kept going, refusing to admit defeat. If the hospital staff thought she was capable, then she was.

Tomorrow, the physical therapy would start. For now, Sarah was blissfully unaware of that additional form of torture.

The flowers began arriving then—vases of fresh-cut daisies and carnations and gerbera daisies and little white baskets of potted ferns and peace lilies and vines. They all came with attached cards of well wishes from neighbors and friends.

The largest, most flamboyant bouquet of

flowers was from Melvin, and Sarah smiled. The card with a flowery verse written in small letters reminded her of him. He had no doubt driven the florist crazy, reciting these eloquent words for her. They had to be perfect.

So many greeting cards. Eagerly, she read each one, but none were from Matthew. And the phone did not ring, ever. Even if it did, she would not be able to answer it. She found herself gazing at it, thinking how it would be to have only one short conversation with him.

He probably wouldn't call.

She opened an especially large envelope containing homemade greeting cards from all her pupils at school. That was the highlight of her week. Over and over, she read the words, the innocent get well wishes, and traced the hand-drawn pictures with the tip of her finger, as if to permanently impress every outline in her memory.

Rosanna wrote that she cried for her every day, and Samuel said school was like an empty silo that had no silage in it if she wasn't there.

Well, now she was like silage. An improvement from a catfish. She grinned to herself.

When Alison poked her blonde head in the door, asking if she needed anything, Sarah said, yes, more graham crackers and peanut butter, but she wanted them with marshmallow cream and coated with chocolate.

Alison laughed and said, "No way, ma'am."

Before long, another skin graft was done, and Sarah become feverish and short of breath as she came down with a classic case of pneumonia, just when things were going so well.

It was a serious time, a setback for a condition that had been improving far ahead of schedule, the healing multiplying in leaps and bounds.

Rumors abounded, until some well-meaning folks actually asked their friends in church which arm of Davey Beiler's Sarah had to be amputated —the right or the left?

Oh no, they said, nothing was taken off that they knew about. She just had pneumonia. Burn victims often do.

"*Vell, my oh* (Well, oh my)."

"Who starts this stuff?"

Chapter 7

Matthew Stoltzfus was the first one to come see her, after visitors were allowed.

She lay on her pillows, her bed raised to a comfortable position, with her eyes closed, half awake, still weak from the powerful antibiotics used to fight the infection in her lungs.

She wasn't aware of the fact that visiting hours had started and was shocked to see Matthew, alone, knocking softly on the door frame.

She wanted to pull the sheet up over her head

and roll herself into a cocoon, a shroud, and never let him see her.

She could see him recoil, saw the nameless distaste, the horror, and his inability to conceal any of it.

Slowly, he walked closer, his hands clutching his belt, his shoulders hunched beneath his blue shirt.

But, oh, the beauty of him! The sheer wonder that he was here. He had come!

"Sarah. Sarah." The first word was stammered, as he tried desperately to right himself.

"Hello, Matthew."

Again, he drew back, and a hissing sound escaped his lips. She was now accustomed to the croak that served as her voice, immune to the shock value of the sound that emerged from her swollen larynx and the tender walls surrounding it.

"How are you?"

She could only nod her head, the lump in her throat now causing an obstruction too painful to allow even one word.

"Are you in pain?"

Again, she only shook her head, realizing the effect of her croaking attempts at speech.

"Can't you talk?"

"Yes. But my throat is damaged."

"Always?"

She shook her head.

The visit fell so far short of her expectations

106

that the pain of it was almost as bad as the physical pain of her wounds.

He volleyed questions at her, hard and rapid. Was she prepared to meet God? Was she born again, truly? Was she willing to confront her parents?

The wearying, mind-numbing questions sent her tumbling down a precipice, where she lay, battered, bruised, reeling mentally from the awful disappointment of his lack of empathy, his selfishness. She finally admitted to herself that that was his problem.

How long would she torment herself with Matthew?

One thing grew relentlessly in her under-standing. It was a flowering seed and had lain dormant, but it was growing steadily in the sunshine of her family's love. She knew she could never leave them.

And the conviction that she wouldn't have to do that in order to be a Christian grew alongside it, like a sweet-smelling rose.

If God was love, then He was with her family. He was in the imperfect fuss of Anna Mae and Ruthie; He was in their tears and stupid advice. He was in the mood-lifting banter of her married brothers and their faithful wives. He was in the whole circle of them—Mam clucking and stewing and wanting only what was best for her family, and Dat's agony, his self blame, and

Suzie's comparison of Sarah with a catfish.

As Matthew spoke, quoting endless Bible verses to justify his own desires, she heard only a small part of what he said. She silently nurtured the newfound wisdom that had been imparted to her since the fire as she had endured the agony of debridement, the surgeries, and skin grafting and pneumonia.

Wearily, she nodded or shook her head in response to Matthew's ramblings, but her heart was faint with fatigue, burned out with the whole deal.

"So, Sarah, what percentage of your hair do they think will grown back? I mean, seriously, you don't have any."

"I'll always be bald."

Why did she find such complete satisfaction in saying that if it wasn't really true?

Matthew snapped to attention.

"Ew. Really?"

"I'll wear a wig."

That clearly gave him the creeps.

Still, if he stayed quiet long enough, she could admire his good looks and hang onto the past, but she really just wanted him to leave.

Just go, Matthew. Go. You know you don't want me. She was surprised she hadn't said it out loud, surprised he still sat in that vinyl chair. For what?

"You think you'll ever look like yourself again?"

That was her undoing. That one unnecessary question that was brought on by his fear of having a less than perfect wife.

With all the strength she could muster, her voice a rough squawk, she asked him why he cared.

"You don't want me, Matthew. I won't leave my family. I don't have to. Just go, and stop tormenting me. Maybe God allowed me to suffer because I would not have given you up any other way."

Her voice turned to a whisper.

"You know there is nothing colder than ashes, after the fire is gone, just like that old love song Mam used to sing."

"You scare me, Sarah. You're losing your mind."

She looked directly at him.

"No, Matthew. You have it all wrong. I am finding my mind."

She began crying then and did not care that Matthew cast her a wild-eyed look and began backing out of the room. He would always remember a caricature of the former Sarah, misshapen, peeling, bandaged, hideous, but inside her a marvelous thing was slowly taking shape.

It was like a new barn rising after an arsonist's foolery, a beautiful thing, a symbol of caring, people working side by side, a whole community of love, including English, Mennonite, Hutterite,

German Baptist, all following their Christ, all different, and all the same.

Strong and sure, grasping the truth handed down through the ages, Sarah's faith was alive and well.

Three weeks after the burning beam hit her, Sarah had made remarkable progress. Steadily, the healing process brought changes. Her hair was now a light copper-colored sheen over her scalp. Her eyelashes were short but coming in thick and fast, and the perfectly shaped wings of her eyebrows showed promise as well.

She walked the hallways, unassisted sometimes, enjoying an easy friendship with the staff, other patients, and the scores of visitors that entered the hospital daily.

She watched the red buds of the trees by the parking lot turn a beautiful lime green color. Then tiny leaves as big as quarters grew into small leaves of a darker hue. Lawn mowers appeared, landscaping companies mulched around shrubs and flowers, and she could only watch, her hands aching for the soil in Mam's garden back home.

Matthew never visited her again. It didn't surprise her. It left only a dull ache for a time remembered when he had been her utmost goal in life. The fact that he was the one who had brought all that yearning, the sweetness of young love to her life, always made her sad, but it was a fading melancholy feeling now.

When the doctor took the bandages off one day, he was pleased. In fact, he was so pleased that he forgot his professional manner, if only for a minute or so.

"Marvelous!"

Sarah smiled as best she could, a warm glow beginning to spread through her senses.

Would the time be close now? She eagerly anticipated the long-awaited moment when she would be dressed in her usual garb, the Amish colors and fabric she missed so much, and walk out the glass doors and never look back.

Her physical therapy sessions on the first floor went well after the first few times, when she had thought her skin would split open with the force of simple movements. She worked with the therapists, gritted her teeth, and kept going, pulling ropes attached to pulleys with weights on the other end, or simply lifting light weights, or raising and lowering her arms and legs.

She had started looking forward to physical therapy as she became acquainted with the therapists and those around her, other burn victims who shared their stories and formed a bond of closeness based on their shared experiences.

It was ironic, the way there were not Amish or English or Mennonite in a burn center. Each patient wore the exact same shapeless, colorless garments that tied in the back. Her bandages served as a covering, and no one could tell she was Amish.

For the first time in her life, she knew the feeling of blending in with other people with no distinctive dress or mannerism to set her apart. It proved to be very interesting.

The usual questions were always about school. Had she graduated? Was she in college?

In Sarah's culture, any young girl in her twenties would have been asked about her marital status, her situation as a dating or non-dating young girl. School was out of the question, except for being a teacher in a one-room parochial school.

There were no goals as far as a career was concerned. Marriage, managing a home, and motherhood was the only route, chosen for her by her parents' wishes. A rarity was the young girl who preferred to stay alone, becoming self-sufficient as a teacher or storekeeper.

Sarah walked the hallways wearing the light robe her sister Anna Mae bought for her. It was green, the color of her eyes, with a belt that tied around her waist, the hem reaching almost to the floor. She felt good when she wore it, sweeping along, her gait improving as each day went by.

She talked on the phone to well-wishers, looked forward to her family's visits, spent hours with a small handheld mirror searching for all the small improvements she could find.

She grimaced as she checked the growth of the new hair sprouting from her head.

She'd even prayed it would be straight, wryly remembering Dat's words about asking God for selfish favors. Just let it be straighter. It doesn't have to be perfect, just not as curly as it used to be, she had pleaded.

Sadly, the new growth on top of her head looked a bit like steel wool, only a dark, copper color. She could not bear to look at it or touch it. What would she do if her hair was curlier still?

Sitting on the side of her bed, she pushed her feet into the slippers Mam had supplied for her, a pair of green and beige plaid Dearfoams that matched her robe.

The bandages were mostly gone, except for on her right shoulder and that side of her neck where the skin grafting had taken place. Her face was still discolored, scarred, but her eyes were open. The lids were a dark shade of red and still peeling, but so much better.

She walked down the hallway to the lounge area by the vast windows, to gaze out over the lawn as the sun sank below the horizon.

A sort of melancholy settled over her shoulders, and she sighed, crossed her arms at her waist, and stared unseeing, as distant lights came on, winking along the streets as folks warded off the night, turning homes into cozy, light-filled havens.

At home, Mam would be holding the lighter to the mantle of the gas lamp, turning the knob, and infusing the kitchen in the homey hiss of the standard Amish source of light. Levi would lift the glass chimney of the kerosene lamp in the bathroom as he prepared for his nightly ritual of showering, teeth brushing, and gargling with his green mouthwash—not blue or purple or yellow. It had to be green.

A wave of homesickness washed over Sarah. She wanted to eat shoofly pie with Levi and tease him about the amount of milk and sugar he put in his coffee. She wanted to sprawl across her bed and play Yahtzee with Priscilla. The low IQ game, they called it, but they loved to roll the dice and say silly things and laugh with quiet heaves and great guffaws, the way only sisters can.

She stood in the dim light of the lounge, watching the twilight settle over the unfamiliar land, oblivious to those around her as tears welled up in her eyes.

No one had come to visit today, which was unusual, but she'd talked to her mother and understood. Allen and Rachel had become parents to a little boy named Samuel Lee, and Mam was going to Dauphin County while she had the chance.

Sarah tried to form a smile as she glanced at an

older couple sitting on a sofa. She reached for a Kleenex and blew her nose, hating her own weakness, her moment of self-pity.

The elevator doors opened, disgorging its occupants. Sarah paused, watching the people step out.

A head taller than anyone else, his blond hair shining in the yellow lights of the elevator, Lee Glick stepped out, looked to the left, then right, before his gaze traveled the lounge area.

He found her.

His gaze rested on her with a fleeting moment of recognition. He stood completely still, his hands at his sides. He was dressed in a navy blue polo shirt, his neat black Sunday pants, and a pair of black and navy blue sneakers.

His eyes found hers, and he moved toward her, as if in a dream, his gaze never leaving her face.

When he reached her, he stopped only a short distance away, but she could see the expression in his eyes.

What was she supposed to do when tears welled up and flowed unchecked down her discolored cheeks?

"Sarah," he whispered.

Then he put his hands on her shoulders, his touch so light she barely felt it. He leaned forward and placed his lips on her forehead, on the side that was scarred most. He kissed her cheek, the scarred one. He stepped back, his eyes searched hers, and he breathed out, quietly, and then pulled her close, so gently, she could barely call it an embrace.

But she felt the fabric of the navy blue shirt, the line of his suspenders, the muscle of his shoulder, and she closed her eyes. He held her, as the hand on the clock ticked away the seconds.

The old couple on the sofa bent their heads and whispered knowingly, then looked up, watching eagerly, remembering the time when their love was young.

Finally, he let her go, but he kept her hands in his. The blue eyes were intent on her face, examining, savoring.

"How are you?" he whispered.

"I'm doing well, as you can see," she said quietly.

"You're beautiful," he breathed.

She was surprised when he dropped her hands. He drew in his breath, then exhaled, almost a groan, before he gathered her back into his arms and held her there.

She had been crying before Lee arrived, the homesickness unbearable, and now she wanted to stay here in this room and never leave the circle of his arms. She had come home, to a place where she belonged. Of this, there was no doubt.

Once more, he released her, stepped back, and searched her eyes.

"Sarah, you're alive. You're here. You did a

very brave thing. You are an amazing person. No one but you would have risked her life to save a colt."

"The colt was not the main thing," Sarah said, very soft and low, embarrassment welling up, ashamed of the croak that was now her voice.

Bending his head, Lee questioned her.

"The colt . . ." Sarah began.

She placed a hand on her throat, grimaced, her eyes begging him, and whispered, "My voice sounds terrible."

"Your voice?"

Sarah nodded miserably.

"Let's sit down, shall we?"

Taking her hand, he led her to an alcove, away from prying eyes. They sat, side by side, and he did not relinquish his hold on her scarred fingers.

"What's wrong with your voice?" he asked as gently as possible.

"My throat was burned, damaged from the heat and smoke."

"It's okay, Sarah. It's okay. Just talk to me. Tell me everything."

And so she did, beginning with her first memory, which was waking up in the room at the burn center. He listened, rapt, as she described the pain, the hopelessness of the first look in the mirror, the surgeries, the visitors.

Lee became very quiet.

"Was Matthew in?"

Sarah nodded.

A silence followed, as Lee separated the space between them. Suddenly, he got to his feet and walked away, over to the windows, his hands gripped behind his back as he watched the twilight.

The elderly lady sitting beside her husband raised her eyebrows and pursed her lips, while her husband lowered his head and whispered, "What do you think is going on?"

"Let's find out," she whispered back.

In complete agreement, they rose stiffly to their feet. He extended his arm, she placed her hand comfortably on it, and they shuffled their way back to the alcove. They gleefully found a sofa within earshot, where they settled. He produced a magazine to look at, and they both became cunningly absorbed in it.

When Lee stayed at the window a long time, Sarah slowly got to her feet. She felt unsure, but the need to be close to him overrode her hesitancy.

Placing a hand on his arm, she said, "Lee."

He turned, and she was alarmed at the bitterness in his eyes.

"It's . . ."

"Sarah, listen. I can't take one more minute of this, knowing you are going to throw your life away with Matthew. I should have never come."

Turning on his heel, he stalked away.

The old couple was left in the alcove, unable to

see or hear the conversation. Like dominoes they leaned to the right, peered around the corner, their eyes wide, straining through the thick lenses of their trifocals.

"What do you think is going on?" she hissed.

"Mom, now hush," he hissed back.

Sarah followed Lee. Her pace was steady, her footsteps quiet, her heart swelling as the strains of love rose and fell in her heart, a rapturous symphony that swelled to a crescendo. She had never been more certain of anything in her life.

Her steps quickened.

"Lee?" she called, a question, a bewilderment.

He turned, his face a mask of pain.

"Sarah, if Matthew was already here, I'm just wasting my time, okay? I'll go now, and I'll talk to you later. Be careful."

"Lee, don't go," she said.

"I think it's for the best."

The elevator door opened, he stepped inside, gave a small wave, and was swallowed up as the doors closed. She stood, her entire being straining toward him, but it was too late.

Slowly, her hands fell to her sides. Sighing, she retraced her steps, without noticing the elderly folks examining the pages of their magazine, and returned to her room. She let the green robe slide from her shoulders, kicked off her slippers, and crawled into the high, narrow bed.

Well, he had come to see her. He was the

polar opposite of Matthew. Even their hair color couldn't be more different. Where Matthew recoiled, worried over the future of her appearance, Lee had told her she was beautiful, which she obviously was not. And he had told her she was an amazing person, which she obviously wasn't either.

She blushed and put her cold hands to her warm face. Well, one thing was settled. The thought of it made her bounce a bit, shifting her weight from side to side the way a child does before opening a candy bar, so delighted with his gift.

Yes, it was a gift, this knowing, this undeserved reality check, this discovery.

She did not love Matthew. She was consumed by her wanting of him. For what? His good looks? The pride of having him? The winning of the race, beating every other girl that had ever wanted to be his girlfriend?

Sickened by her own human nature, she recoiled from the virtual mirror held to her heart. How long she had strained against the reins of her Creator! How long-suffering was her God?

She bowed her head, clasped her hands, and thanked Him for allowing her this one chance at true love. The future was still suspended, the question hanging in midair, but her heart was at rest.

When the telephone rang, she reached for it, answered quietly.

"How are you, Sarah?"

Matthew.

"Good. Tired. Ready for bed."

"Have any visitors today?"

"One."

"Who?"

She had a notion to tell him it was the man on the moon, but she didn't. When her answer was not forthcoming, he repeated the blunt question.

"Who was it?"

"A friend."

"Can I come see you tomorrow?"

For only a moment, the old anticipation crowded out her common sense, but it was instantly replaced by an anger that shook her to the core.

"Why would you want to, Matthew? You have nothing to say to me, and you know it. No, you may not come to see me."

"Wow!" Matthew answered.

Sarah didn't bother replying. She was plain down too mad.

"You still there?" he asked, his voice mellow.

"Yes."

"So this is it. Really it?"

"Yes. It is."

Firm and hard, her words were spaced, set in concrete. They were sure, sturdy, and full of conviction.

"Matthew, just go live your life. Forget about the gangly little eighth grader who thought the sun rose and set on you and you alone. You have wrung my heart for the last time. Let's just say the fiery trial I've been through has worked very well in producing a solid vessel, shining like crazy."

"Are you really losing your mind?"

"No, sir. I told you before, Matthew. I just found it."

"I'll be up to see you once you get home."

"Don't bother."

"You're serious, aren't you?"

"Yes."

"Goodbye, Sarah."

Gently, she replaced the receiver, then pressed down on it, firmly.

Chapter 8

On the day Sarah came home, the sun shone warmly through a haze that promised rain. The grass on the front lawn had been freshly mowed and trimmed. The tulips had already bloomed, surrounded by a thick layer of mushroom mulch, and newly-planted petunias lifted cheery faces as they turned their purple stripes to the warmth of the sunlight.

Everything appeared dreamlike, with an air of the unfamiliar. Sarah was surprised at the lump in her throat, the heavy feeling of sadness in her chest.

The pink banner strung between the two porch posts that said, "Welcome Home, Sarah," dissolved the sadness and replaced it with anticipation. Then the front door burst open, and a horde of her family members appeared on the porch, all with varying expressions on their faces. They tried to produce wide smiles of happiness at her homecoming, but most of them didn't accomplish it, their faces contorting into all sorts of grimaces as they did their best to control the flow of tears.

Dat held her suitcase, and Mam stood by offering assistance, but Sarah unfolded her stiff joints from the backseat of the car and stood erect on her own. She breathed in deeply, savored the smell of the fresh-cut grass, the mulched flower beds, the cows, and yes, even the manure that had just been spread on the fields.

She was hugged, touched, fussed over, and leaning on her brothers' arms, taken inside where a huge brunch awaited them.

Her appetite was alarming, and Sarah swallowed as she asked Anna Mae to load up her plate with some of everything, please.

Her blue dress hung on her thin frame, and her black belt apron was pinned too loosely, but Mam said it wouldn't fit otherwise.

Sarah did not wear a covering. She didn't have enough hair to pin it to or hardly enough to consider it, her sisters said. Mam told her a *dichly* (headscarf) would suffice for now, until she had more hair again.

She sat on the recliner in the living room. Ruthie put warm woolen socks on her feet, Priscilla spread a soft blanket over her lap, and Levi brought a table leaf to put across the arms of her chair.

He stopped, looked at her gravely, and said, *"My oh, do gooksht different mit kenn hua* (Oh my, you look different with no hair)."

His brothers smiled, but they did not laugh, knowing Levi tried his best to say and do the right thing, earnest in his speech.

Sarah smiled up at Levi.

"Yes, Levi, I know. It's pretty easy to take care of."

Levi nodded seriously.

"Do gooksht ova shay (You look pretty, though)."

"Thank you, Levi."

Levi swelled with pride. His sister approved of him, and that meant a great deal. He had done well on the day Sarah came home.

The brunch began. Plates were loaded with egg casseroles, sausages, bacon, waffles and pancakes, home fries, and applesauce. Homemade ketchup glugged from the narrow openings of re-used Heinz ketchup bottles, butter was spread thickly across the pancakes, and syrup was poured liberally over everything. The grandchildren sat at the small plastic picnic table brought in from Levi's room where it was usually folded and stored.

All except for a few bites of bacon or pancake remained on the children's paper plates. The eggs had green stuff in them, or tomatoes, so they remained untouched. Scolding mothers scooped up the plates, but they allowed the children their freedom for this one day, this celebration of Sarah's healing.

The children ran squealing outside to play on the swing at *Doddy's* (Grandfather's). Grown-ups slowly savored the shoofly pie and homemade cinnamon rolls frosted with caramel icing. They finished their coffee and began asking Sarah questions about her experience.

They showed her the newspaper article about Michael Lanvin and were surprised to find tears of sympathy in her eyes. She read the article and shook her head from side to side.

"I can hardly believe he actually is the real arsonist," she said finally.

Dat looked at Sarah, his gaze piercing.

"Why do you say that?"

"It just seems as if he is a weak, sniveling sort of person. He did not treat Ashley right, I know, but he often seemed scared of his own shadow. He just never struck me as someone who would intentionally kill harmless animals. I think his bullying of his girlfriend was his portrayal of the weak person he is, same as his substance abuse."

Dat nodded soberly.

"You think they have the wrong person?"

"I don't know. If I said yes or no, I would only be surmising."

Levi drained his coffee cup, sat up straight, and said he was the one driving the little, white car though. And he had all that shaggy hair.

Allen said he believed Levi, but Dat said just because he drove the white car did not mean he actually lit the barn, which caused Levi to leap to his feet, one finger held aloft, and shout about another person hiding in the backseat.

This topic was a large, succulent bone for Levi. He'd chew on this subject for days, letting go of his captured suspect and honing in on another. He'd get it figured out eventually, sustained by his own ego, his sense of self-worth.

A serious conversation followed about the process in the court system for a case like this. Would Michael Lanvin be tried in court, and if he was, would any Amish person press charges? Would they testify against him?

David Beiler shook his head, his face grim.

"We are not supposed to go to court. We are not to take any part in testifying against another person. We are non-resistant people. That means exactly that. We don't resist. We don't believe in war. If someone takes your coat, give him your cloak."

Johnny, the youngest of the three married

126

brothers, pulled at his short beard, his face turning redder by the second. Sarah could see the rebellion rising against their father and hoped the onslaught would remain reasonable.

"Dat, I disagree. What about Abraham Lincoln and the Civil War? He agonized over that, but he knew lives had to be lost for the greater good. Do you believe in slavery?"

"I'm not talking about slavery. I'm talking about someone doing evil against you. We are taught to return good for evil."

Johnny's face turned redder still.

"So when that overseer on his horse cracked the whip over the stumbling slaves, exhausted in the 100-degree heat, they were expected to turn the other cheek?"

Dat did not answer. Mam opened her mouth and closed it again.

"So when Michael lit your barn, the Bible instructs you to go out and tell him to light the implement shed as well? I mean, come on, Dat. Get with the program."

There was a long, tense silence as a gray cloud of discord settled over the happy family celebration. Dat blinked and took his time considering Johnny's words.

Outside near the swing set, a child was heard, crying in pain. Suzie took one look out the window, then ran outside to assist the victim who had fallen down the slide.

Finally, Dat spoke.

"I am with the program, Johnny. I understand your point of view. No, that would not have been feasible, the way you put it. But think. If a fellow was intent on burning my barn, and I would have gone out and offered the implement shed, he'd thought I was out of my mind. Would he have done it?"

"Of course! Without a doubt!" Johnny exclaimed.

Allen agreed.

Abner waited, leaning back in his chair, picking his teeth with a toothpick, one ankle propped on the other knee, his brown sneakers matching his brown shirt.

"A shot of lead in his britches would get him out of here faster. He'd never return. He'd be GONE!" Johnny continued, bolstered by Allen's approval.

"Wait a minute, Johnny. He'd be gone, alright, but how would he reciprocate?"

"Talk Dutch," Johnny growled.

"Respond. Give or take."

"That would be up to him. At least my barn's safe."

Abner added his thoughts to the conversation.

"I can see Dat's point of view. In the long run, which would serve to make the guy lighting the barn feel as if he was in the wrong? He already knows that it's wrong, okay? And he doesn't care.

He's out to hurt someone or something, full o rage and rebellion, just evil inside.

"So what if you shot his hind end full of lead'. That's evil for evil. An eye for an eye, if you will I think what Dat means is which response wil. help this person to accept forgiveness, which is in the long run, the whole point. The person lighting the barn is perhaps a lost soul or some-one gone astray, filled with hatred toward someone else."

"Oh, come on," Johnny growled.

"Hey, either you're Amish or you're not. Many in our generation do not fully understand the old ways. We think nothing of going after what is rightfully ours, in this dog-eat-dog world. But that's not really what it's all about."

"Some English people are kinder than we are," Johnny said, the wind fast dying out of his sails.

"I agree. Of course, Johnny. Good people are everywhere, in every walk of life. Dat is just trying to remind us why we as a community shouldn't be determined to have our own way— to put the arsonist behind bars, the way we members of the younger generation would like."

"You boys have to understand what I went through when Sarah was burned at Lydia Esh's fire," Dat said quietly. "I wanted to literally beat up the person who did this. I am ashamed to tell you what I wanted to do. But there is only one way through this, and it's forgiveness.

"We don't need to *bekimma* (bother) ourselves about this Michael. We'll leave him in God's hands. He'll unwrap everything, and when it comes to the light, it will be done properly."

Johnny shook his head in disbelief, incredulous now.

"You're just going against common sense, Dat."

"We'll see."

The days turned warmer as the season progressed into summer. Sarah rested, ate, and slept. The hours of deep, restful slumber restored her spirits as nothing else had.

Mam had begun her home remedies the first day Sarah had returned, and she continued faithfully with her homemade salves and steeped burdock leaves. She used vitamin C in liquid form, an assortment of herbal capsules, and "body builders," as she called them, which conjured up visions of men lifting heavy weights, their oiled skin bulging unnaturally with muscles of iron. Sarah just shook her head and laughed and said they were not called body builders.

"What then?" Mam asked simply, slapping on yet another limp green burdock leaf as Priscilla stood by with the bandages.

Sarah did not visit her school, afraid her appearance would shock the pupils. If the healing progressed throughout the summer as well as

Mam predicted, she'd be almost completely restored by September and could go back to teaching again then.

It was another lazy day in late June, and Sarah sat in the shade on the porch, shelling the last of the late peas. A bushel basket containing the oblong pods sat on one side of her, an empty box on the other. Her thoughts were dreamlike, resting on nothing in particular as she watched Dat cutting hay in the alfalfa field, the mules' heads bobbing in rhythm.

Why mules? she wondered.

They were the lowliest of God's creatures. They had to be. In fact, He hadn't even thought them up, they said in Dutch. She smiled, heaped another pile of pea pods on her lap, and wondered why Dat didn't buy a nice pair of Belgians from Omar Esh.

She wondered if Lee Glick had anything to do with the raising of the new colt. Or if he still existed.

She sighed.

Alles gutes nemmt tzeit (Every good thing takes time). It was an old saying, but tried and true.

Over and over, she'd relived Lee's visit to the burn center. Over and over again, she'd wondered at his mistrust of her. She had no one to blame but herself, obsessed with Matthew for too long.

A rich smell wafted through the kitchen window and circled beneath the porch roof.

131

Sarah lifted her nose, sniffing. Mam was frying chicken. Fried chicken, mashed potatoes, new peas, and creamed lettuce with slivers of radish and onion and hardboiled egg. Mmm.

She had never appreciated her home the way she did now. It was so secure, so free from harm and pain and bright lights that hurt the eyes and attacked the senses.

And yet, she was grateful for the burn center. She still remembered to pray for the good doctors and nurses at Crozer-Chester. They had become her friends, mentors, a much-appreciated network of support when she needed it most.

She was surprised to see Hannah hurrying across the yard, her apron pinned with silver safety pins, unnamed bits of food clinging to her dress front, her covering strings flapping with each step.

"Sarah!" she called, throwing up a hand.

"Hannah. It's good to see you."

She stumbled up on the porch, fell heavily in a chair, and looked long and hard at Sarah's right side.

"You look amazing."

"I do?"

"You really do."

"Thank you. Mam has steeped tons of burdock and slathered gallons of homemade salve all over me."

"That's stretched," Hannah observed dryly.

Sarah laughed. "Yeah, it is."

"*Ach*, Sarah, you're a girl dear to my heart. I still wish that Matthew was different." Her voice trailed off, a wistful note suspended and hovering above them, echoing the sad repercussions Sarah knew came from her heart.

"What happened when he visited you in the hospital?"

Sarah told her, sparing nothing, and watched as Hannah bowed her head, then lifted it bravely to face her.

"You know, Sarah, I admire you. You see Matthew in the right way. Perhaps in the way I should. But he's my son, and a mother's love is unconditional. We love our boys, no matter what they do or who they become. But you know, I worry. He doesn't always have a nice way with me, and I'm afraid he'll treat his wife in much the same way. You know he's talking to Rose again?"

A familiar pang of jealousy tore through her mind, but she was able to quench it quickly, her new realization of the love she felt for Lee the only form of weaponry she needed to defeat it.

Rose had visited her many times, and she had never mentioned Matthew. Sarah wondered about it now.

"Is he?"

Hannah nodded.

"I'd be happy for him with Rose, but if he's not Amish, then he'd drag Rose along with him, creating bad feelings between her parents and us. Well, Elam says they're pretty liberal, so maybe they wouldn't care as much as we think."

"Hannah, I didn't know you were here." Mam came out on the porch, wiping her clean, wet hands on her black apron.

"It's just me, Malinda. Just me. I was chatting with Sarah."

"Doesn't she look good?"

"Oh my goodness! Yes!"

"Except for my hair," Sarah laughed.

Hannah laughed with her.

"You know what it looks like? I cleaned a house for an English lady once, and the hair on her poodle looked exactly like yours!"

Hannah shrieked with laughter after that remark, and Mam chuckled quietly, her rounded stomach shaking with mirth.

"Yes, Hannah. Just call me 'Poodle.'"

"Give me a handful of peas."

"Shell your own."

Hannah laughed again.

"They spoiled you at Crozer-Chester, didn't they? Your meals brought on trays, your bed changed every day."

"Her skin scraped off," Mam added wryly.

They joked, exchanged pleasantries, and laughed plenty. Sarah soaked up the camaraderie, keenly aware of the fact that all the ill feelings between them had gone away, proving their true friendship. The hurt was swallowed by the past, time healed the rift, forgiveness worked its magic, and life resumed its safe, comfortable routine of days past.

Here she was, exchanging barbs with Hannah. She could even joke about her horrific experience at the burn center, and she was glad. She was happy to be alive, grateful for her health.

Only God would have to know about her future.

That Sunday, Dat pronounced Sarah fit to go to church. She no longer needed visible bandaging, although parts of her right shoulder were bandaged, covered by a white t-shirt beneath her dress.

Mam said she could wear a colored *halsduch* (cape), as the stiff white organdy was too irritating against the tender new skin on her neck.

Sarah demurred at first, but Mam assured her everyone would understand. Sometimes the rules had to be bent to allow what was merely common sense in a case such as this.

Her hair was every bit as hopeless as she knew it would be. She plastered it down with gel as her hair spray was much too harsh for the delicate skin on her scalp.

She wore a new white covering and was pleased with the results, grateful her hair was now long enough to wear a covering. A navy blue dress and *halsduch*, and a black apron, shoes, and stockings, and she was ready to attend church services once again.

Sarah sat in the back seat of the carriage with Priscilla, who was making all sorts of snorting sounds, trying to keep her white organdy apron from getting wrinkled.

"Things never change much, do they?" she observed, picking at her mouth to rid it of loose horse hair.

"Didn't you brush Fred?" Suzie shrieked, sticking out her tongue as she raked her handkerchief across it.

"Yes."

Dat never said much on the way to church, especially when he was prepared to preach the sermon. He remained stoic, spoke only when he was spoken to, and Mam sat devoutly by his side, as traditional as the special open-front carriage the preachers drove.

Sometimes the carriage seemed holy, or something close to it, and Sarah felt guilty for complaining or talking nonsense on Sunday morning.

"It will be warm today," Mam said, worrying about Sarah's bandage and the t-shirt beneath her dress.

"I wouldn't be surprised if we have a thunderstorm later in the day," Dat remarked.

Sarah took stock of their surroundings. Why were they going to Ben Zook's? She swallowed nervously but could not collect enough nerve to mention it. She was relieved when Priscilla spoke up.

"Why are we going to Ben's? I thought church was at Joe Fisher's."

"We were asked to come here. One of their ministers went to Indiana."

Sarah's heart beat harder, and she felt the color leave her face. Would Lee be at Ben's, at his sister Anna's house? Did he attend church services at all?

Well, she was being conveyed there at an alarming pace, with no alternative, and her face was as multi-colored and pieced together as a jigsaw puzzle, but so be it.

"What's wrong with you?" Suzie asked loudly.

"Me?"

Priscilla turned to check out her sister's face, grinned cheekily at Suzie, and whispered, "It's called Lee Glick Syndrome."

Suzie giggled, put her hand across her mouth, and hid her smile. They rode solemnly up to the shop on the Ben Zook farm, neat and prim and proper.

Sarah walked bravely to the side of the shop where the single girls were assembled, greeting others and smiling. She knew some of them, but was not acquainted with the younger ones.

She was completely aware of the curious stares, the pitying glances, but she feigned indifference, making it much easier for herself and those around her. Nothing was said, conversation resumed its normal tone, and Sarah relaxed and enjoyed the beautiful morning. She noticed Anna's yard and garden, tended to perfection.

"Sarah."

She looked around and saw her oldest pupil, Rosanna, dressed in a garish shade of green, her hair combed in the latest style, her covering sliding around on the back of her head.

"Rosanna. Why, of course, you'd be in this church district. It's so good to see you."

Rosanna shrugged her shoulders and tried to regain an air of indifference, but she looked again at Sarah's scarred and discolored face, stammered, and threw herself into Sarah's arms, bursting into little girl sobs. Sarah held her shaking form, patted her back, and looked at her through misty eyes.

"It's okay, Rosanna, really. It'll get better."

Rosanna was sniffling, wiping a finger viciously across her nose, her eyes lowered, so miserably ashamed of herself.

Sarah looked around at the cluster of girls and found only sympathy and tears of pity for Rosanna. She assured her again, handed her a Kleenex, and slid an arm around her waist.

"I can barely wait till we have time to talk, okay? I have missed you so much this summer. I can hardly stand the thought of returning to school and you not being there. You're done with school!"

Rosanna nodded.

"You look awful," she said sadly.

"I know. But I won't always look like this."

"You think you'll need a helper this year?"

"I might."

Rosanna looked straight at Sarah, and they exchanged a look of confidence and trust.

"We'd have so much fun," Sarah said.

Anna came to lead the girls to their designated benches, and Rosanna left Sarah's side to follow the girls her own age.

Her eyes averted, knowing all eyes were on her injured face, Sarah walked slowly into the large building that would house the church service, gratefully sliding onto the bench, out of sight and away from prying eyes.

When the single young men filed in, there was a short, dark-haired youth leading them. So. He was not here. As Anna's brother, Lee would have gone first.

Bitter disappointment took her breath away, but only for a minute. She had the rest of her life, and this was the first day of it. Life was much easier when she thought along those lines, she mused and opened the black hymnbook after the song was announced.

Chapter 9

It was good to be back at the Sunday services, the traditional gathering of friends and family. In each district, a group of about twenty-five to thirty families took turns hosting church services at their homes.

The districts were areas agreed upon by the ministers and laymen, usually bounded by roads or other landmarks. When the district grew to more than forty families, causing challenges for hosting so many people, the murmuring would begin. The women grumbled to their husbands about baking forty pies and the necessity of having to make eight batches of homemade bread. It just took too much food, they said.

The women were to be keepers of the home, quiet, prohibited from speaking in church, but they carried considerable clout when the time came to divide a church district into two. They were the ones who fretted and stewed about hosting the ever-growing congregation in their houses or shops or basements, always concerned about the allotted spaces.

On Sarah's first Sunday back at church, Davey Beiler's family had gone to church at Ben Zook's farm, meaning they had gone to the district beside their own home church. They went because the lead minister had gone to attend services in Indiana and had asked Davey to preach instead.

Despite her earlier confidence, Sarah was suddenly not sure she should be there at all. She felt lonely, self-conscious, and now, noticing Lee's absence, a bit put out. But maybe he'd think she was running after him, coming to Ben's church service with her scarred face. Well, she wasn't. Most of her pupils went to church in this district, so what was wrong with that? Besides, her dat had been asked to come.

As the rising volume of the plainsong swelled around her, she opened her mouth and joined in. Few things could lift her spirits like the singing in church. The slow, undulating cadence sent chills down her spine. It was the sound of home, safety, and belonging.

Suddenly, she stopped singing, lowered her head, and kept it hidden behind the woman sitting directly in front of her.

Lee!

He'd just walked in.

Oh, my. Oh, my.

All thoughts of singing were completely erased from her mind. In fact, everything was. She hadn't seen him in church clothes since Susan and Marvin's wedding when he had selected Rose to take to the wedding table. His blond hair was cut short. She'd think he was an embarrassment to his parents, or to Ben and Anna, with hair like that, but it did look handsome. His shirt was so white, his eyes so blue, his vest and *mutza* (coat) fit so superbly, it actually took her breath away.

He was not yet a member of the church. He had never been baptized and taken Christ as his personal Savior. He was already 23, maybe 24. Suddenly, he seemed far away, unattainable. What had she done?

Why, if he was still so worldly, did his values and his attitude seem the opposite of Matthew's, who was born again, saved, without one doubt in anyone's mind? Matthew read his Bible endlessly and had a heartfelt testimony to back his knowledge of the Bible, but in so many ways, he still behaved like the same mama's boy he'd always been.

It was not her job to decipher the difference. It was God's. Dat had been very firm about that.

Over and over, she relived that last encounter with Lee at the burn center. Now the blinding fog of Matthew was completely gone, the warm sun of her understanding obliterating it, leaving her weak with gratification and the wonder of her love.

The difference was astounding. Where she'd felt desperation, heart-pounding greediness, really, with her desire to be Matthew's wife, this was slow, easy, secure. It was bliss borne of knowledge, knowing the wait was all a part of God's plan.

After the singing ended, there was a soft tap on

her shoulder, and Sarah turned, meeting Anna's lowered face, her eyes bright with concern.

"*Komm* (Come)."

Sarah shook her head.

"Yes, Sarah, you can't sit on that hard bench. You're still weak. Come, sit with us. I have a chair for you with cushions."

Sarah waited until Anna left, then summoned all her courage and rose in one swift movement, flustered and painfully aware of the discoloration of her skin, the deep and angry scars.

Gratefully, she sank into the soft cushions placed on a patio chair, keeping her head lowered, her eyes on the bench directly in front of her.

How ugly she must appear!

A little girl turned around on the bench, gave Sarah a frank appraisal, and asked Anna innocently, "What is wrong with her?"

She was shushed instantly by her harried mother, who was holding a grunting infant over her shoulder.

When Sarah looked up, Lee's eyes were directly on her face. They both looked away, unanimous in their decision to avoid eye contact. Immediately, they both looked back, and just as swiftly, lowered their eyes again.

When the singing stopped, Dat got up, cleared his throat, looked around the congregation, and began to speak. His voice was deep and low, well modulated, a tone that carried well.

Sarah had never heard her father speak the way he did that day. He was kind and loving, but he firmly shared his new-found insights on non-resistance. He spoke of the test of his faith, when his daughter was burned, and said that on some days, he still wanted to testify against the man in prison. In fact, he'd imagined the hangings of old, the gallows, and any form of punishment man had ever devised, because he was human.

Human nature, he said, wants to slap back immediately. It's a natural response. Someone smites your cheek, and you want to hit back, but that is not what the Bible teaches us.

Christ's way is to turn the other cheek. If we return good for evil, it's like piling coals of fire on our enemies' heads. It becomes a misery, and it works.

He spoke with conviction, yet he remained gentle.

When Sarah began to feel faint, she put her head on the back of the cushioned chair and closed her eyes, but the room tilted and spun crazily. She gripped the arms of her chair and prayed the weakness would pass.

Recognizing the nausea that welled up in her throat, she got up, immediately grabbing the chair back for support as the room spun around her. She made it to the doorway, gulping as she headed to the house.

The fresh air and brilliant sunshine revived her

for a moment. When she got to the kitchen, she sank gratefully on a chair, lowered her head in her hands, and closed her eyes.

She felt a presence, then a light touch on her shoulder.

"*Bisht alright* (Are you alright)?"

Startled, Sarah lifted her head. Two bright blue eyes peered at her from behind round spectacles, a kindly smile accompanying them.

The older woman was as round as Anna, shaped like a little human barrel, except much softer. Her face crinkled with lines that were likely formed by all the smiling she did.

Sarah nodded, weakly.

"You're that Sarah Beiler, *gel* (right)? I am Anna's mother, Rachel."

So. She was Lee's mother. That was interesting. She could see where he got the color of his eyes.

Clucking to herself, Rachel placed a soft hand on Sarah's face, turning the scars to the light, adjusting her own face to peer through the bifocals on her glasses.

"*My, my. My oh.* You really did go through something, didn't you? *Siss yusht hesslich* (It's too bad)."

Stepping back, she tilted her face, turned Sarah's cheek to the light again, and kept examining the burned area.

"You are using the salve?"

Sarah nodded.

"I still have one surgery to go through. The spot on my shoulder that was burnt worse than anything else."

"I guess you're thankful to be alive."

Sarah nodded.

"It could have been Lee, you know. It worries me the way he gets so involved with the people who have fires. I mean, that's why he's here at Ben's. He feels bad for Ben's loss and does whatever he can so Ben doesn't have to hire someone. And now he's so involved with that widow's boy Omar and his horses. I guess it's okay, as long as he doesn't do something foolish yet."

There was nothing to say to that, so Sarah merely nodded.

Likely, the busy little woman had no idea about Lee's relationship with Sarah. Or the lack of it now.

Rachel suddenly changed the subject.

"I'm hungry. You look like a bit of food would do you good. Let's sneak some cheese and *blooney* (bologna)."

Giggling like a schoolgirl, she searched the refrigerator, coming up with a plastic bag containing at least ten pounds of sliced sweet bologna. She proceeded to open the wrapper on a loaf of homemade bread and spread it with the cheese spread that was so much a part of the noon meal following Sunday services.

"I just didn't have time to eat breakfast."

Rachel handed a small plate of the bread and bologna to Sarah with one hand, stuffing a large portion of her own slice into her mouth with the other.

She turned her back, guilty now, as a young mother rushed into the kitchen with a screaming baby, a crying toddler hanging onto her apron.

Rachel polished off the slice of bread, then scuttled after the toddler and picked him up, saying, "Hush, hush, my goodness. Here, here. You want a slice of *blooney*?"

When the angry little boy's screams increased, she fished under her ample apron and produced a string of bright colored toys on key chains.

"Here. Look! Here. Now, now. Don't cry."

She pressed the button on a small flashlight, which did the trick. The cries dissipated as she clicked it on and off.

Sarah observed Rachel's motherly skills, the way she saw the helpless expression on the young mother's face and instantly bustled after the crying toddler. She thought of Lee being here, on this farm, for his brother-in-law, as well as helping Omar Esh.

She nibbled on the smoked sweet bologna, broke off a corner of the homemade bread, and appreciated the mellow taste of the cheese spread. Looking up, she saw Rachel with the toddler encircled in one arm, holding out a glass of orange juice to her.

"Orange juice. It's the best thing for low blood sugar. You're not hypoglycemic, are you?"

Sarah shook her head and accepted the juice. Then she moved to a rocking chair, where she leaned her head back against the cushion and closed her eyes.

No doubt about it, she was still not as strong as she would like to be, so she'd better stay in the kitchen and rest awhile.

The young mother fed the infant, turned her head to observe Sarah's face discreetly, then bit her lip and looked away.

Rachel fussed to the now happy toddler, showing him each trinket on the chain. She observed Sarah as well and pursed her lips.

The door was pushed open, allowing Anna's buxom form to enter. She was puffing slightly, the color on her cheeks high, her blue eyes alight with excitement.

Church was at her house, and everything had to be perfect.

"Forgot paper cups," she whispered to her mother, yanking on the pantry door with enthusiasm.

"Did you remember sugar this time?"

"Uh. No. I forgot."

Rachel's round form shook as she heaved with silent laughter.

"Best stop cleaning and remember you have church, Anna."

In answer, Anna swung the plastic packet of paper cups in her mother's direction, batting her eyelashes as she did so. Rachel ducked her head. The woman on the chair looked over and smiled. They all knew Anna.

Comfortable now, relaxed, Sarah smiled to herself. She savored the easy relationships passed down through the generations. There was a congenial acceptance of one another, at church services, quiltings, school programs, wherever there was a social gathering.

It didn't seem so long ago that she was a little girl dressed in a pinafore-style white apron, in a kitchen such as this. Her hand firmly grasped in Mam's, she was led to the bathroom or for a drink of water, as the singsong voice of the preacher rose and fell in the shop or the living room or the basement below.

Mam would meet a good friend, and they'd talk in hushed tones, only a bit, not too long. But they leaned in, touched a forearm as they quickly exchanged a community tidbit, swapped knowing looks, and passed on quickly.

It was rude to stay away from the service for an extended period of time, especially for a minister's wife. A baby that had to be put to sleep was an exception, however, so the kitchen or living room of the house was often a place where mothers put the little ones down for a nap, relieved to have a few free moments to absorb the sermon without squirming infants on their laps.

Motherhood was an eagerly awaited event for Sarah. She looked forward to cozily sitting together with other young mothers, comparing experiences about births and babies, raising children, the various ways of canning and freezing, cooking and baking. It was an objective for every young girl, and Sarah was no different.

She opened her eyes as the grateful young mother rose slowly from her chair, carefully carrying the sleeping infant into Ben and Anna's bedroom, where she laid a pre-folded diaper in the middle of the high king-sized bed, gently placed the sweet baby on it, covered her with a light blanket, and tiptoed out, closing the door lightly behind her. Going to Rachel, she bent over and held out her arms for the little boy, smiling as she did so.

"*Denke* (Thank you)."

"*Siss gaen schoene* (You're welcome)."

They exchanged smiles, and the young woman whisked her son back to the shop, where services were continuing.

Other young mothers milled about, changing diapers, getting their children cold drinks, sitting down with crying little ones—all a part of the usual church Sunday.

Sarah leaned her head back, closed her eyes wearily as the sounds ebbed and flowed, waves of laughter and talk coming and going.

"Did you hear about Anna's brother Lee?"

Instantly, Sarah's eyes flew open, before she caught herself and closed them, afraid someone had noticed.

A young mother folded a snowy white diaper across one shoulder, lifted her daughter, and draped her deftly across the cloth. She lifted her eyebrows and shook her head.

"They say he's going to Alaska."

"Whatever for? Is he going hunting or what?"

"I have no idea. He probably won't be Amish if he goes up there. He's pretty old and hasn't joined the church."

Sarah's mouth went dry. She took a quick breath to steady herself, then sat up to look for Rachel, his mother, but she had gone back to the service with her daughter.

Alaska. He may as well go to the moon.

"What happened between him and Rose Zook?"

"Who knows? The youth are always going through some sort of drama. Worse than we ever were."

Nodding righteously, the listening young mother inserted a pink pacifier into her sleeping baby's mouth, turning to address her friend.

"You know he won't be back. I pity his parents."

Sarah could not sit on the chair another second, so she rose, walked stiffly across the kitchen, looking straight ahead without acknowledging either woman, as if obliterating them from her vision would also dissipate the fact that Lee was going to Alaska.

She didn't believe it. He would not leave Ben and Anna, or the Widow Lydia and Omar. He was the most unselfish person she knew, as kind as her father, by all means. Why would he do something so completely out of character?

She entered the shop, her eyes downcast, and found her chair. She listened to the voice of the aging minister whose turn it was to speak as he expounded the Scripture in a meaningful way.

He spoke of faith, the essence of believing that which we cannot see, but Sarah's mind was churning with unanswered questions now, her attention diverted by the bit of gossip from the kitchen.

That was all it was. Two young mothers bored with their own lives who circulated rumors like that among themselves to make things more interesting. It simply was not true, Sarah told herself.

After the last hymn had been sung, services were over. The single boys and girls filed out in solemn rows until they reached the open door. The small boys pushed out between the young men, eager to grab their black felt hats from the back of the bench wagon.

The bench wagon was a large trailer built to carry the wooden benches from one service location to the next, usually pulled by a team of strong draft horses. As time went on and more Amish left farming for other occupations, the need to hire a pickup truck to pull the bench wagon became more and more apparent. It was frowned upon at first, but common sense eclipsed tradition, and the practice was accepted. A tolerant hired driver patiently traveled at a slow pace, the tongue of the bench wagon secured firmly to the pickup truck's hitch, rattling along from one Amish home to the next.

After everyone had left their appointed seats following the service, the murmurs swelled into a near roar as friends met and greeted one another. The men folded the legs of some of the benches and set them on trestles to create long tables with the remaining benches set along side.

Women scurried out with white tablecloths draped across their arms and snapped them across the tabletops that had been benches only five minutes before. Plastic totes containing plates, tumblers, saucers, knives, and forks appeared like magic as many willing helpers scurried from the house bearing trays of sliced homemade bread, plates of butter, and dishes of jelly. There was also a delicious concoction that Sarah always anticipated. It was made with boiled brown sugar and water that was cooled and poured over great gobs of peanut butter and marshmallow cream. It was a part of her life, a tasty tradition at church dinners.

Cheese spread, the smoked sweet bologna, dishes of pungent little slices of bread and butter pickles, savory red beets, seasoned pretzels, and *snitz* (dried apple) pie completed the meal.

In years past, apples had always been dried and stored in a cool place to be used later for *snitz* pies. Water was added, and the dried apples were cooked, mashed, and flavored with sugar and spices.

Somewhere along the way, a wily housewife had discovered an easier version for *snitz* pie. She mixed applesauce, apple butter, sugar, and spices with an almost identical result. It took only a few minutes, with no cooking or mashing necessary.

Snitz pies were delicious, in Sarah's opinion, although each housewife's version varied slightly. Sometimes a wedge of pie proved to be almost inedible, leaving a sour aftertaste when a well-meaning baker had spared the sugar and cinnamon.

Crusts varied as well. In some pies, the crust was thick and hard where the *snitz* had boiled its way out between the crimped edges, leaving a dark, brown gluey covering along the crust.

When a crust was too inedible, it was usually hidden discreetly beneath the lip of a saucer. In some cases, it was left boldly on the saucer and dumped unceremoniously into the waste can. Then the saucer was handed to the dishwashers, who usually asked what was wrong with the crust. Eyes rolled or eyebrows raised, but never a word was spoken.

The men ate at one table; the women at another. They usually filled a second time with younger men and boys, young women and girls. The men always filed into services by age, as did the women, an orderly routine that was copied at the tables where dinner was served.

It seemed a bit unfair that the hungry boys and girls had to wait until their elders had eaten, but with their hungry children in mind, the older folks ate their meals quickly, without loitering or negligent conversation.

Sarah did not wait on tables. She remained in her chair, away from prying eyes, watching the swish of skirts, the colorful children dashing to and from the tables to snitch a salty seasoned pretzel if they could get away with it.

Sarah watched a two-year-old boy climb up on a bench, lean his rounded little body across the table, and grab a handful of bologna, knocking over a tumbler of water in the process.

Gasps went up as Anna dashed to clamp her capable hands around the errant little boy's middle and whisk him efficiently off the bench, the color in her cheeks giving away her impatience. The little boy stuffed a slice of bologna in his mouth, glared up at his abductor, and ambled off indignantly.

"People that don't watch their children!" she hissed to Sarah.

Rachel came scurrying with a tea towel extended, clucking and wiping, leaving Sarah in awe of these rounded women who moved with the speed of lightning, more or less.

She wondered if Lee would ever gain weight. Well, it was nothing to her, now that he was going to Alaska, if such a thing was possible.

She was summoned to the table, sat with eyes averted, enduring the open stares of the young children around her.

Rosanna, her former student, slid onto the bench opposite Sarah and smiled. She noticed the open stares of the children, Sarah's apparent unease, and spoke firmly, "Stop staring, girls. It's not polite. She can't help she was in an accident."

The response was immediate. Faces lowered, with color rising in their cheeks. The girls mumbled apologies, their eyes blinking.

Sarah immediately felt sorry for the girls, especially the ones that had been her pupils at Ivy Run School.

"It's okay, Rosanna. It really is. I know I look like a monster."

That brought a giggle from Katie Mae, a third grader, who shook her head and told Sarah she looked like a nice monster.

"When I go back to school in the fall, I'll look better, and we can really have an amazing health class with everything I learned about burns, right?"

Rosanna's eyes stayed intently on Sarah's face until Sarah met them. The two raised eyebrow and exchanged knowing smiles.

A feeling of peace enveloped Sarah, a gradual sense of quiet, knowing she would go back to school, back to her teaching job, perhaps enabling her to help Rosanna find a sense of direction in the process.

There was so much more to life than finding a husband. First, she must heal, from the scars and burns, as well as the knowledge that she and Matthew were not to be. Not now, not ever. She knew it in her mind, but had her heart accepted it?

If Lee actually did go to Alaska, then she guessed that spoke of his character. Who did he think he was, anyway?

Sarah chomped down on a wedge of pie, and the sweet *snitz* filling fell to her plate. The girls opposite her covered their mouths with their hands to keep from laughing.

Chapter 10

It was on a hot summer's evening that Lee rode down to Widow Lydia's for the last time, his schedule prepared, his Amtrak ticket bought, his future life as an Alaskan mapped out.

He wouldn't be back for the wedding, but it was

lright. Melvin and Lydia could be married vithout him. He was sure they would have a 'ery nice wedding, and the children would be ιappy to have a father again.

The hardest part was explaining his plans to Ɔmar, without disclosing the truth. He tried to tell ιim it was a dream he'd always had. And now hat Omar was old enough to take responsibility vith the Belgians and his mother and Melvin vere getting married in the fall, things would be ust fine, Lee said.

Omar had squared his shoulders, believed him, ιnd remained stoic, his young face showing strength, having weathered so much in his young life. He had survived the death of his abusive father, Aaron, two barn fires, and his mother's mental anguish. Lee believed his leaving was only a small thing, and Omar would accept it. He'd have Melvin now.

His horse raised his head, then lowered it, as Lee slid from the saddle. He led him into the newly finished horse barn, almost identical to the last one. The hooves clopped on the clean, white cement as Lee eyed the fresh lumber apprecia- tively. He'd have to tell Melvin to build a closet for the harnesses.

He tied his horse and turned toward the door. He leaned against the side of the barn, watching the insects wheeling and darting through the still, hot air. It wouldn't be long till the bats appeared, gobbling up their evening smorgasbord on wings

The willow tree in the pasture was completely still, with not even a small shiver of the long thin leaves. Must be a thunderstorm brewing somewhere, as heavy as the air felt tonight.

Far away, the wail of a siren began, low at first then more distinct. Likely a cop chasing someone out on the Old Philadelphia Pike. He'd miss this life, the hustle, the hurry.

Lee raised a hand to swat at a mosquito that was whining at his ear. The kitchen door opened and Omar dashed across the porch and down to the barn waving.

"Hey!"

"I thought you might have gone to bed."

"Me? Why would I go so early?"

"Sleepy? Tired?"

Omar cuffed Lee's elbow.

"I am eighteen, not eight months old."

Lee laughed with genuine pleasure.

"Think it will storm?"

"It could. It's still."

"Yeah."

A comfortable silence lay between them, an easy, velvety feeling, like the evening with the heat, the quiet of the willow tree.

The wailing siren grew in magnitude and was joined by another.

"That sound will never fail to give me the creeps."

159

"Yeah."

"Think the fires are over, now that someone's n jail?"

"I doubt it. I don't know."

Lee scuffed a heel against the edge of the cement, then lowered himself to sit on the edge, esting his arms on his knees.

Omar followed suit, and Lee looked at the youth's profile.

"How's your mam?"

"Good. Happy. Melvin makes her laugh."

"That's good."

"Yeah. She had a tough time of it, before."

"Did she?"

Omar nodded.

"Dat was not a nice person. I wouldn't know what a kind father is like, except for you."

"I'm not your dat."

"Closest thing to it."

Lee laughed, a derisive outburst, a mockery.

"Yeah, well, I'll never be a father. That's for sure."

"What? Why are you saying that?"

Lee shrugged his shoulders.

"You could be, if you weren't running off to Alaska."

"You can't change my mind, Omar."

"I know."

Suddenly Omar turned to face Lee and exclaimed loudly, "Why are you going? Really. If you want to see that state so bad, I'll get you a book."

"Omar!" Lydia called from the porch, her thin form upright as she leaned against the white post, her arm encircling it.

"Hey!"

"Come on up for mint tea and soft pretzels!"

Immediately, they were on their feet, moving toward the porch. Few things were as tempting as homemade soft pretzels, hot and buttery from a 500-degree oven. They were delicious dipped in warm cheese sauce or laced liberally with mustard, especially when there was ice-cold mint tea to accompany them.

They clattered onto the porch, joking, opened the screen door, and stopped short.

Sarah stood by the kitchen table, dressed in a soft shade of blue. She was wearing her covering all the time now, her hair growing fast, and a black bib apron covered her blue dress. She was pouring the tea in tall glasses filled half full with ice cubes.

She looked up, her eyes dancing, her wide mouth turned into an eager smile for Omar.

When she saw Lee, every attempt at self-control failed. She lowered the pitcher with a clunk, leaving two glasses unfilled. As the color left her face, her eyes became dark, as they did when she was confronted by surprise, or fear, or sadness.

Lee stopped, uncertain, as he struggled for composure as well.

"Lee!" Lydia broke the awkward silence with genuine welcome in her voice.

"Hello, Lydia. Sarah."

"You are just in time. Come, let's sit outside. Grab that tray, Sarah. You can put the tea on it."

Little Aaron toddled along, dodging feet. The two older girls, Anna Mae and Rachel, hung shyly in the background as Sarah resumed filling the tall glasses, her hands shaking so that she needed both of them to steady the pitcher.

Why had he come? How could she survive this evening? She'd go. She'd tell them she was needed at home. She would not sit here and listen to Lee bragging about his upcoming Alaskan adventure.

But when she saw him leaning back in the wooden Adirondack chair, his golden head shining in the evening light, she hesitated. His wide shoulders exuded strength, the yellow shirt he was wearing a perfect backdrop for his tanned face. Her knees felt a slight loss of muscle tone, and she quickly set the tray of glasses on the wooden table, the ice clinking, the tea sloshing over the sides.

Lydia looked at Sarah's face, then dabbed at the spilled tea with a corner of her apron. She passed the platter of pretzels and small dishes of cheese sauce, noticing immediately when

Lee waved them away and Sarah shook her head.

Lee was talking.

Sarah shrank back against her chair, her arms folded tightly around her middle, her knees pressed together, tense.

"I'll be back. I just don't know when. Six months, maybe a year. I came to say good-bye. I'm leaving Thursday."

Five days. This was Sunday evening. No. Three days. Four days.

"Where's Melvin?" Omar asked suddenly.

"He's late. Way late. You know, he's with the fire company, and I heard the sirens, so perhaps he's out on a call."

"Could be."

Sarah could only sip her tea, raising and lowering her glass, as if her arms were programmed like a robot, mechanical. As the twilight moved across the yard, enclosing the porch with a graying aura, she watched a light blink on in Elam's house, upstairs. Matthew must be home early.

As if Lydia had read her mind, she inquired about Matthew Stoltzfus. Was he dating yet? You'd think it was too soon, but someone had seen him down at Rockvale Square with Rose Zook.

Omar said people jumped to conclusions. Maybe she'd just needed a ride, and there wasn't a thing to it.

Lee said nothing, as the wall of tension between him and Sarah built itself up in the silence, sitting heavily, unseen, unspoken, but felt keenly.

"Aren't you going to say anything, Sarah?" Omar asked. "You surely know what's up with Matthew."

Sarah choked on a mouthful of tea, coughed, and wiped her mouth with a napkin. She shook her head.

"I haven't spoken to Matthew since I was at Crozer-Chester."

The silence exploded as Omar pumped his fist into the air, yelling something about I told you so, you big old skeptic, you. He jumped sideways, slamming a fist into Lee's arm with a smack. Lee grabbed his arm and grimaced in pain, before leaping to his feet as Omar took off down the porch steps and across the yard. Lee shot after Omar and easily overtook him, grabbed the waist of his trousers, and pulled him to the ground. They tussled a bit on the grass and then returned to the porch caught up in a new discussion about the Belgians.

As night fell, Sarah said she must be going. Everyone protested, saying the night was still young. They'd go inside and play a game, but Sarah shook her head, remaining firm.

Why sit here on Lydia's front porch and prolong the torture of Lee's leaving when all she wanted to do was pound him with her fists? She just wanted tell him how disagreeable he was, how stubborn.

She was just getting up to return her glass to the kitchen when a team came up the driveway. It turned towards the horse barn, the blue LED lights raking across the porch, the glare invading their privacy.

Melvin.

Lydia, clearly relieved, began babbling senselessly and begging Sarah to stay, but Sarah was afraid. She feared Melvin's lack of restraint, his honesty, when she just wanted to cling to her pride, her silence the only hope of redemption.

She said goodnight, stepped down from the porch, and was ready to open the gate when she heard a frantic call.

"Sarah! What do you think you're doing? Get back there!"

A wide smile immediately spread across Sarah's face. He really meant it.

Hurrying up the slope from the barn, Melvin met Sarah at the gate.

"Just give it up, Sarah. Turn around. I'm here."

"I have to go," she answered.

"Why?"

"Because. I just have to."

"Sarah, I haven't seen you in ages. Come on. We'll play Upwords. Just for you."

She hesitated, weighing her options, but suddenly she had no choice as Melvin grasped her upper arms, turned her, and steered her back up to the front porch.

In the semidarkness, Melvin strained to see the occupants scattered along the width of the porch. He warmly greeted Lydia, his bride-to-be, then shouted overenthusiastically, "Lee! Long time, no see! What's up?"

"Not much."

"I hear you're going to Alaska! Boy, I envy you. Why don't you wait till we're married, and we'll go with you on our honeymoon?"

Lydia laughed and protested, while Omar yelled with delight. No one heard the telephone in the phone shanty when it began its incessant ringing—no one except little Aaron, who finally shouted, "Phone!"

"Let it go. They'll leave a message."

"I'll get it."

Omar made a dash for the phone shanty, slapped open the gate, and yanked the door open, catching the caller on the last ring. There was no sound from the phone shanty, only another siren wailing in the distance, then another.

When Omar stepped out of the shanty, he did not dash up to the porch. He walked, lifting the gate latch heavily, his steps leaden as he came. He leaned heavily on the porch post.

"Lee. It was your sister. You need to go home. I'll come with you."

Lee was out of his chair immediately.

"What happened?"

"It's Ben, your brother-in-law."

"What happened to him?"

"She didn't say how bad it was."

Lee leaped off the porch, ran down to the barn, loosened his horse, and was out the drive in less than a minute.

Omar followed on his horse, as Lydia and Melvin soberly cleared the wooden table on the porch. The children pitched in to do their share, but Sarah sat, immobile, unable to tell herself to do something, get out of her chair.

What had happened? She shivered. Surely not another fire, with the suspect incarcerated.

They sat together in the kitchen without speaking, the inability to understand robbing them of the will to make small talk. Lydia sat close to Melvin, his presence enabling her to get through this—whatever it was. It was a significant gesture she would likely incorporate repeatedly over the years, with her husband as the rock she needed when adversity emotionally disabled her.

After an hour had passed, they checked the phone messages to find nothing. They resumed their quiet vigil, until Sarah decided to check for a message again.

There was an ominous rumble in the distance. Heat lightning skittered across the sky, but the air remained heavy and still. Traffic could be heard plainly, the cars stopping and starting, changing gears, a horn tooting, then again.

There was a message this time. Sarah could tell by the beeping on the line, but she did not know Lydia's pin number or how to access her voice mail, so she called for her repeatedly.

Lydia came quickly, pressed the buttons, then listened, her head bent.

"No. Oh no," she breathed.

Sarah waited, frightened, afraid to know, afraid not to.

"What is it?" she whispered.

Lydia pressed the 3, then slowly replaced the receiver, a sob catching in her throat.

"A bull. A bull got Ben."

Sarah would never forget her friend's words. They did not convey the final outcome, only the immediate accident, but everything they had shared together already had schooled them in the art of acceptance.

Blindly, they clung together. Blindly, they broke apart and stumbled into the kitchen.

They told Melvin but could not remember, later, who had actually related the message. Melvin held Lydia in his arms and comforted her. Then he asked Sarah to stay with Lydia. He was going over to the Zooks' place. They sat side by side, the children around them, and stared unseeing at the opposite wall, jumping and afraid when the refrigerator hummed and clicked.

When a flash of bluish white lightning illuminated the kitchen, they squeezed their eyes shut like small children and cowered at the following clap of thunder. They allowed the children to pile a heap of sleeping bags and blankets on the living room floor, so they could stay close together as the storm approached.

Sarah closed windows upstairs, guided by the glow of the LED lamp she carried. When she went to close the downstairs bedroom window, a startling streak of lightning made her step back, stifling a yelp.

The rain came down in hard-driven sheets, sluicing down the west side of the house. It filled the spouting with heavy gushes of water that clattered against the inside of the downspouts and shot out the bottom, where it tumbled over the small path of rocks Lydia had built for just this purpose.

The wind howled around the eaves, and rain pounded against the windows as thunder roared and clapped overhead. The lightning flashed brilliantly, but the air became stifling in the kitchen with the windows closed to the only available breeze.

They sat around the table and comforted one another with words of hope, but they were unable to rest or relax. Lydia leaped to her feet repeatedly, searching wild-eyed for Melvin, but Sarah knew she was also in constant fear of lightning striking the barn. She ran from window to window, lifting, then lowering the sashes, always alert for any strange light from the barn.

As the storm slowly left, the lightning became weaker. The thunder grew muffled, and the rain fell gently instead of being pelted against the side of the house from the force of the wind. Lydia took a deep breath, sagged against the back of the couch, and said bluntly that she was so glad to be getting married again. She was eager to have a husband, a protector, a person stronger than herself.

Sarah nodded, a wave of longing taking her by surprise.

When Melvin finally came back, he found Lydia and Sarah, one at each end of the couch, asleep. When he woke Lydia, she sat straight up, her eyes wide with alarm. She shook Sarah to waken her, wanting her to hear what had happened.

Anna had done the supper dishes. Then they had worked together, she and Ben, weeding the watermelon and cantaloupe plants.

A cow was due to freshen, so Ben went to the pasture to bring her in, never thinking about the mild-tempered Holstein bull grazing with the herd.

When Ben did not return, Anna went to find him, calling and calling. She became alarmed when she saw the cloud of dust the bull was pawing from the earth. That was strange. He had never shown aggression.

Afraid to enter the pasture, she dialed 911. The dread washed over her repeatedly, yet she clung to the hope that Ben had not gone to the pasture at all.

They had to tranquilize the bull in the end.

They gathered up Ben Zook's broken body and carried him to his wife on a stretcher, these men dressed in navy blue outfits with EMT emblazoned across their backs in silver letters, with kind eyes and hands to help her sit down. Anna sat, but she did not faint. She remained alert as she gathered her children around her soft, ample body and wept endlessly into their clean, straight hair.

She was so glad they'd worked in the garden together on his last day on earth.

When Lee arrived, he was shocked, but they said his shoulders heaved with the force of his weeping.

The news spread like wildfire.

After hearing the details, Sarah went home to her bed, but she lay sleepless, wondering, her thoughts running rampant. What had God wrought? The taking of Anna's husband. Why? She was so lively, so full of life and energy and hope, no matter what the circumstances.

In the morning, a bit of sleep had been enough, and Sarah stumbled down the stairs at the first stirring of her parents in the kitchen.

She broke the news, which was received in a typically restrained manner. They wept, but acknowledged that the Lord giveth and the Lord taketh away, and blessed be the name of the Lord. Thy will be done, they said. The backbone of their faith was that highly esteemed acceptance of a higher power, and what God does, He doeth well, even in times such as this.

Sarah and Priscilla did the milking, knowing Dat would be expected to go immediately to the Zooks' and Mam would accompany him.

Mam gathered a bag of potatoes, a container of Jell-O from the refrigerator, a stack of white American cheese, and eggs. She filled her sixteen-quart kettle with bags of frozen corn. She had plenty, and this would come in handy, feeding all the relatives and friends during the three days before Ben would be buried.

She dressed in her black dress and pinned a fresh white covering to her head. As she sat beside her Davey in the buggy, she was thankful he was alive and well.

Sarah worked with Priscilla, milking the cows. They swept the aisles, fed calves, washed milkers, and hosed down the milk house. Sarah was grateful for her returning strength. When the milking was done, they returned to the house, just as the clock struck half past six.

Sarah missed Mam's breakfast immensely, but she got to work in the kitchen immediately, frying bacon, while Priscilla woke Levi and helped him get dressed and into his shoes.

As Sarah flipped the eggs, she heard a great shout from Levi, who did not want to wear his shoes.

"Levi, come on. I'm starving. You have to wear your shoes!"

"I'm not going to."

"I'm going to tell Dat."

"Dat does not care if I don't wear shoes. It's too hot."

"Alright, then. You're not getting any breakfast."

Levi lumbered into the kitchen in his bare feet and stepped on a pen that Suzie had left on the floor. He became so irritable that he threw the pen at Priscilla. It bounced off the side of her head and against the refrigerator.

"Levi! Priscilla!" Sarah scolded.

"She needs to sit down and read her Bible," Levi said.

Sarah told Levi about the events on the Ben Zook farm, blinking back tears of pity for her friend Anna, who would now be a widow with three fatherless children.

Levi could not fully absorb this awful news. He told Sarah that Ben wasn't really dead, that Dat said dead people went to heaven after they were viewed in *die laud* (casket). Did Ashley Walters? Did Mervin? If Ben Zook went up there with Ashley and Mervin, he was afraid there would be no room for him after he died.

Sarah assured Levi that heaven was very, very big.

"Bigger that Pennsylvania?" he asked.

"Oh my, yes."

Levi pondered this bit of information, then nodded his head, agreeing with Sarah. He was glad to be able to think of his own place up there.

"Did they shoot the bull?"

"I don't know, Levi."

"He should be ground into hamburger."

"He probably will."

Levi sat down to his breakfast and lowered his head with the girls for the usual silent prayer. When they lifted their heads, Sarah was surprised to see a trickle of tears falling slowly down Levi's cheeks.

He pulled out a red handkerchief, blew his nose, and shook his head solemnly.

"I wish Ben would have waited on me. It's not fun here anymore," he said. "Since you were burned, Mam never makes shoofly."

Chapter 11

When their parents returned, Sarah and Priscilla were sent to work in Anna's yard, mowing grass, raking, tilling the garden. The women had cleaned the house and prepared the basement as a cooking and eating station. They would be feeding dozens of relatives, refilling the long tables over and over.

The girls were expected to wear their black dresses, with capes and aprons pinned over them, their white covering strings tied. They also wore their black shoes and stockings, even with the temperature hovering around 90 degrees.

Fred was lethargic. He was clearly displeased at the thought of returning the way he had just come. He would have preferred being turned loose into the green pasture to stand comfortably beneath a maple tree, swatting flies with his tail.

Sarah slapped his rump with the reins. Fred's ears laid back, flicked forward, and he broke into a halfhearted trot, allowing a cool breeze to flow into the buggy. At the slight incline on Old Leacock Road, he ambled into a stiff-legged walk, eliminating any hope of a breeze.

"Seriously, Fred. Make him go, Sarah. Fred! Come on!" Priscilla grabbed the reins away from Sarah, giving Fred a smart rap on his haunches.

"Come on!"

Fred lunged dutifully into his collar, and the breeze resumed.

"It's so hot," Priscilla groaned.

"Just wait till we have to start working in the yard in all this black," Sarah said.

"I don't think we should have to go help. We're not in Ben's, uh, I mean, Anna's church."

"So? We're friends. I used to work for her. Besides, lots of people came to help after our fire—church members or not."

"Whatever."

Priscilla leaned back against the seat and crossed her arms defiantly.

Fred slowed to a walk.

"Fred!" Priscilla shouted.

"How would you like to be hitched up in this weather? He's probably thirsty."

"I don't like viewings and funerals. Everyone is always crying and hugging and looking so awful and sour. I don't have to cry. I hardly knew Ben," Priscilla complained.

Sarah said nothing. She had been unable to share her deepest feelings with Priscilla since she had been burned. Sarah never even mentioned Lee's name to her sister. She was afraid Priscilla would think her too sure of herself.

How could she tell Priscilla about the anticipation of seeing Lee? She couldn't. So she looked straight ahead, stopped at stop signs, turned the buggy, and prodded Fred some more. She wondered what Lee would be doing now—if he'd be there, if he'd see them drive in, and if this unexpected turn of events would prove his undoing.

She did not have long to wait. When they drove up to the house, Lee appeared, dressed in his Sunday clothes—a blue shirt, black vest, and black trousers. He stopped when he caught sight of them. "Want me to take him?" he asked reaching for the bridle.

"You may."

Priscilla smiled widely. Sarah became painfully aware of the discoloration on her right side. The angry, red scars had ruined her creamy complexion and the perfect symmetry of her face.

The realization stung. Priscilla's smile was the most irritating thing she had experienced in a long time.

Sarah didn't look at Lee. She imagined her stubby lashes, the dark scars, the skin taut like red Saran Wrap pulling her cheek and slanting her right eye down on the outside.

She walked away.

Lee spoke to Priscilla, who gazed up at him and then came running after Sarah, gushing on and on about his blue eyes. And what in the world was up with her, she wondered, walking away from him like that.

"Pris, hush. This is a viewing. Or going to be."

Meeting Anna was almost more than Sarah could manage, but she held the short, soft woman in her arms as tears of sympathy coursed down her face.

"I am so sorry, Anna. He was a good man."

"Oh, he was, Sarah. He was."

Stepping back, she swabbed viciously at her swollen eyes, blew her nose, and shook her head from side to side.

"He was never the same, though, after the fire. Remember how he had to take anti-depressants, the Zoloft? It seemed as if my Ben never quite returned. He had his struggles, and I was the only one who really knew."

Suddenly, she grabbed Sarah's hands. "But who am I to stand here and pity myself? You have gone through so much."

"But I am here, disfigured maybe, but grateful."

Sarah stepped back, allowing others to shake Anna's hand and offer condolences as she moved on to talk to Rachel and Anna's sisters. Then she set to work, mowing grass, weeding, working side by side with girls from the church district where Ben lived. They were not strangers, only acquaintances, but they were all united now because of the death of a young husband and father.

The sun beamed down, its strength like an oppressive hand, large and heavy with the heat. Admitting defeat, Sarah leaned against a tree, lifting her apron to mop her brow. She had regained a lot of her strength, but she still couldn't do everything she had been able to do prior to the fire.

When she became overheated, her scars thumped painfully, and she knew it was time to stop. Lifting a hand to her cheek, she was shocked to feel the heat.

"I probably look like a tomato under the broiler, so hot it's ready to pop," she said ruefully.

There was a deep, masculine chuckle behind

her. She recognized Lee's laugh, so she kept her back turned, hoping he'd go away.

She sighed with relief when he did.

The day of Ben's funeral was not quite as humid. The black clothes were much more bearable, and the tall, green corn stalks waved in a perfect summer breeze.

Priscilla did not "have word," meaning she was not invited to attend funeral services, so Sarah rode with her parents, dressed in her lightweight black outfit.

Why was it that sewing a new dress, cape, and apron made her feel so much better about herself? That morning, she had discovered the unscarred side of her face matched the scarred side better now that it was tanned by the summer sun. Her hair was sleek and neat for once, in spite of being thin, and the covering she wore was brand new and very white. For the first time since she had been burned, she felt a real sunbeam of hope.

The large shop was filled to capacity. The mourners endured the heat stoically. Heavy women flapped crocheted handkerchiefs for the slightest whisper of a breeze, while men's faces turned ruddy as the shop's temperatures escalated. The sea of people dressed in black endured together, for Ben.

After the short service, they filed respectfully past the wooden casket. The tradition was expected of them, and they turned their faces for one last look at Ben Zook.

Many spoke of the disfigurement, the likeness not even close to the friendly face they remembered. But they must have done the best they could, considering the circumstances. They just hoped he hadn't had to suffer.

The bull probably caught Ben in the right side, the way every rib had been broken. His chest had caved in, they said. Perhaps the bull crushed his heart instantly, and he felt no pain after the first pounding to the ground.

His face was a mess, though, so they couldn't bear to think too much about Ben's death—alone in the deepening twilight on a midsummer evening, a thunderstorm rumbling in the distance, the fear of the charging bull.

Like a magnetic force, the death of Ben Zook drew the local farmers to face their own livestock and the dangers on their properties. It was not just a seemingly docile bull in the pasture, but also the uncovered squares upstairs on barn floors, broken gates, and loose ladder rungs. Many repairs were completed in the following month, and more than one massive two-thousand-pound Holstein bull was sent to auction.

They all said it was time to sell—the bull was too heavy. However, in the back of their minds, they cringed as they pictured the lowered, wide, hard head of the angry creature, coming at a terrible pace. They envisioned the impact, the crushed bones as poor Ben was ground into the dry earth of his own pasture, and they were relieved to sell.

Halt uns, *Himmlisher Vater* (Keep us, Heavenly Father). Ben's death just after the Widow Lydia's second fire and the Beiler girl getting so burned —what was God trying to tell them? Everyone had better sit up and take notice. It was the end times, for sure. The fires, the danger still among them—where would it end?

After the service, a giant circle of buggies stood waiting. Numbers had been written in white chalk on the gray canvas of each buggy. Solemnly, the plain wooden casket was loaded into the carriage designed for that purpose, and the driver was seated on a plain wooden chair. Anna and her children rode in the buggy marked with a large number one and followed immediately after the carriage containing Ben's coffin. Lee drove the horse. Relatives of Ben's—his parents, brothers, and sisters followed—then Anna's family and then their uncles, aunts, nieces, and nephews.

Slowly, the first carriage started, followed by the buggy Lee was driving, then numbers two and three. One by one, they fell into an orderly line, wending their way down the drive, turning onto the road as the director from the funeral home signaled for the traffic to stop.

After the buggies had all gone, a flurry of activity resumed as the church members prepared the traditional funeral meal and set up the long tables made with benches.

Sarah did not go to the *begrabnis* (burial). She opted to stay and help, filling the tables with great platters of cold, thinly sliced roast beef, slices of Swiss, Longhorn, Farmers, and Provolone cheese layered beside it.

Bowls were heaped high with mashed potatoes, and silver gravy boats filled to the brim with thick, savory beef gravy.

Pepper slaw, chilled and pungent, applesauce, and dinner rolls completed the meal.

Dessert was cake and fruit. The women of the district each baked a cake and brought jars of canned peaches or pears, applesauce, or whatever they had on hand.

There was plenty of chatter as the members of the church and Amish community worked together. Everything ran smoothly, the way they had been taught. Their parents and their parents before them had done things in the same manner.

There were always the older ones, with bent backs and graying hair turned mostly white, who would have their say.

"We didn't used to have cake."

"Prunes. We always served prunes at a funeral."

"Should still be that way."

"Ah well, changes come. May as well enjoy the cake."

"Sure tastes better than *gvetcha* (prunes)."

Younger women would stop to listen and ask, why prunes? Shoulders were shrugged, eyebrows raised, hands lifted. A mischievous smile played around a stout little grandmother's features, her round shoulders shook.

"Maybe to offset all the cheese?"

Yes, if they took time to *unna such* (search), these traditions had reasons, usually based on common sense. Yes, indeed, prunes were a wise choice, they thought, eyeing the mounds of sliced cheese.

They assigned each person to their tasks. Three couples cooked and mashed potatoes with mounds of butter, gallons of milk, and plenty of salt and cream cheese at their elbows. The men, dressed in traditional Sunday garb with white aprons tied about their waists, straddled benches, kettles of steaming hot potatoes in front of them. Their sturdy arms were put to good use, as the women stood by with the hot milk, salt, and butter.

As the potatoes were beaten to creamy masses by the potato mashers, piles of cabbage were grated across hand held graters. But no one thought of the hard work. The companionship they shared was a labor of love.

Sarah leaned against the cupboard in the basement, her eyes filling with tears as she watched Anna return from the graveyard. Her face showed the strain of the trial laid heavily on her ample shoulders, but she was brave. She was holding up the way Sarah knew she would, her pleasant, can-do attitude serving her well at a time like this.

Sarah caught her breath, watching Lee follow his sister. She groaned within herself, etching his profile in her heart, remorse taking away all ability to breathe, to go on living.

Where had she been? What had possessed her? It was too late now. He really was leaving for Alaska tomorrow. Tomorrow. He had changed his tickets to stay for Ben's funeral, but now he was really leaving.

Lee bent, picked up Anna's youngest, Elmer, and set him on the bench beside him. When Elmer couldn't reach his plate, Lee picked him up and set him on his knee. Immediately, one of the girls that was serving rushed over with a booster seat, and Lee placed Elmer on it carefully. He looked up at Lee, a bright smile spreading across his handsome face.

"*Konn do sitza* (Can sit here)?"

Lee nodded, smiled back.

When the table was full, heads were bowed in silent prayer, and the meal began in earnest. Anna filled her plate well and ate hungrily. Sarah filled their coffee cups, consumed with longing to touch Lee's shoulder for just one second, his nearness sending her into despair.

Numbly, she served, washed dishes, and served another table, feeling as if she had one more day to live. It was a hard sentence, flung rudely in her face.

Her future stretched before her, a hot, gritty, windblown desert devoid of joy or purpose. Her spirits plummeted down and down, until she knew if she kept this up, there would, indeed, be consequences. Depression would rear its ugly head, crippling her life.

Gepp dich oof (Give yourself up). Mam always said those words, regardless of the dilemma. They were her mantra, a cloak she wore like a royal garment, enabling her to face life unafraid.

Sarah knew she must do this, deep down, in her spirit. But oh, why was it so hard?

Because it's my own fault. Now I'm all messed up, my face hideous. Who will ever look at me or want me for his wife?

You're beautiful, Lee had said. That was before he knew Matthew had been to visit her.

She went upstairs, suddenly filled with purpose. She'd stay.

Grabbing the hamper in the bathroom, she lugged it to the laundry room and began to sort clothes. She closed the drain on the wringer washer and turned on the hot water, then hurried upstairs for Lee's hamper.

She had never been in his room.

The afternoon sun shone through the sparkling

windows. A warm breeze toyed with the beige linen panel curtains at each window.

His bed was high and wide, made up neatly with a brown plaid quilt and extra pillows. She touched it with her fingertips. On his dresser, there was an expensive-looking world globe, a chest, and some carved shore birds.

She reached out a hand to straighten the red placemat beneath the small, wooden chest, irritated when a square, white paper fell to the floor.

Bending, she swooped it up, the glossy feel of it a realization. A photograph.

She had to hurry. She had the hot water running in the wringer washer. A gaggle of noisy girls was coming up the stairs, brooms and dust mops thumping. Quickly she flipped it over. She gasped. A younger version of herself smiled up from the glossy photograph, her skin tanned, her hair disheveled, as usual.

When she heard the girls coming down the hall, she slammed the photo beneath the mat, turned, and grabbed the hamper as the girls reached the doorway. Just in time she turned to face them guilelessly. She smiled and said quietly, "I'm washing."

"Good!"

"Good for you."

"This must be Lee's room."

Giggling, they all voted to clean it. Sarah gritted her teeth and lunged towards the stairs heading for the laundry room at breakneck speed.

Well, the despair would have to go. She'd stay until the last chore was completed. If God gave her one last chance before tomorrow, she'd take it. If not, she'd go home, prepare for a new school term, and settle in for the wait.

Gepp dich oof. Alright, Mam. I will.

Opening the lever on the air hose, she was rewarded with the loud er-er-er-er of the air motor turning beneath the machine, swirling the water as the agitator swished steadily back and forth.

On the shelf, instead of Mam's Tide with bleach, there was an odd-looking white Melaleuca box. So, Anna was one of those women who stuck like a determined leech to her choice of off-the-wall products like Amway or Shaklee or the new eCosway. Everyone who was someone had to be introduced to the cheaper and apparently far superior products, which, in Mam's opinion, left the men's socks gray, but she told only Sarah.

Mam would listen with great interest and pour over the literature. Then she would smile, give back the catalogue, and never order a thing. Absolutely nothing could beat her Tide.

Well, there was always the possibility of trying to beat Mam, Sarah thought. She carefully measured white soap powder into a rather small plastic cup and dumped it into the steaming water, followed by a load of white tablecloths.

"Sarah."

Turning, her face flushed from the heat of the swirling water, she looked up into Lee's blue eyes.

"Oh. Oh. You sc . . . surprised me."

Flustered, she reached for the corner of her apron to dry her hands.

"Do you need the diesel started?"

Sarah checked the pressure gauge on the air line.

"Eighty pounds. Yes, you'd better."

She met his gaze. The blue eyes were pools of kindness that washed over her, erasing every thought of despair or remorse. She did not want to look away, but the intensity in his eyes was almost more than she could manage without flinging herself into his arms and begging him to stay, to reconsider.

She must have been leaning toward him, when Marlin came into the laundry room. Sarah was embarrassed to find she had to grasp the edge of the washer to catch her balance. She got her hand wet and had to dry it all over again.

Lee left, and Marlin got a pair of boots from the closet.

She'd stay. She didn't care if the whole place was put back in order, every piece of laundry hung on the line, the driveway raked, the cows milked. She'd stay.

She had one day. One evening.

Humming under her breath now, she counted

her options, bolstered by the photograph, and . . . She smiled. She'd call it "the look."

How was it possible? Perhaps he was just happy to find her doing laundry, sparing his grieving sister the mundane chore.

Going to the mirror above the small sink where Ben had always washed his hands, she turned her face slightly to the left and tentatively ran the tips of her fingers across her neck and cheeks. The red Saran Wrap had definitely turned to pink. A bit better.

Turning, she began to feed the sweet-smelling tablecloths through the wringer. She watched as they sank into the rinse tubs and settled in the blue water containing the odd-smelling Melaleuca fabric softener.

She added a load of towels to the washer and put the tablecloths from the rinse water through the wringer. Then she took the laundry basket through the door to the back porch to hang them on the wheel line.

The afternoon sun was headed towards the western horizon, the heat shimmering from the macadam drive and the tops of the gray and black buggies. Men stood in huddles, their identical black felt hats reflecting a sameness that spoke of contentment, of unison and brotherly love.

Women clad in black, their white coverings bobbing, moved across the lawn. They bundled boxes of leftover meat and cheese, pepper slaw, and plastic containers of gravy into the buggies of the Zooks' relatives, gifts to take along home.

They would be told that they could "make use of it" and given a kind pat of sympathy on shoulders drooping with grief.

Sarah hung the last white tablecloth on the line, secured it with wooden pins, and pushed on the bottom cable, sending the tablecloths flapping high across the lawn. A pulley wheel attached to a steel post at the other end served to pull out the loaded lower line and return the empty upper clothesline. The wheel line was really an ingenious device, allowing busy mothers to stay on a protected porch and send laundry high across the lawn, without lugging heavy baskets of wet clothing into the blazing sun or through a foot of snow.

Sarah watched Lee emerge from the door of the diesel shed and experienced a strange thrill, an intuition, or was it only her imagination? Would he feel it, seeing her there by the wheel line, hanging out his laundry?

As if he read her thoughts, he looked her way. He lifted a hand and gave a thumbs up to signal he had started the diesel.

She lifted her own thumb for only a second, then turned away. She picked up the basket, overcome by shyness, feeling the blush spread across her face. She hoped no one had seen them.

Then, a wild thought. What did it matter? Who would care? They were two mature adults, no longer silly teenagers shamelessly flirting.

She had only tonight.

Chapter 12

The dirty water swirled down the drain and gurgled in the pipes of the sink as the last pair of denim work trousers squeezed out from between the rollers of the wringer. Reaching across the washer, Sarah turned the lever, shutting off the air valve. Silence reigned as she lifted the heavy basket holding the last load.

She tried to imagine how Anna would feel later today as the sun slid its way toward darkness. Night would arrive, and with it, the necessary act of going to bed. Now, Anna would sleep so completely alone. Tears stung in Sarah's eyes as she imagined Anna's mourning. Surely a mother or a sister, perhaps both, would stay.

On her hands and knees, she wiped the laundry room floor clean, hung up the rag, and went in search of her friend Anna. She found her sitting on the living room sofa, her head on her mother's shoulder, crying quietly, a group of sisters and sisters-in-law crying with her.

When she saw Sarah, she sat up, dabbed her eyes, and honked furiously into a sodden Kleenex.

"*Komm*, Sarah."

"Is there anything you need done yet?"

Was it only her imagination or were there a few knowing looks being exchanged, a thread of cunning glances she thought she was seeing?

"They're going to be starting supper and the milking soon. I was wondering if you'd like to take leftovers to Old Mommy King. Maybe Lee could take you. I asked Benuel *sei* Rachel to take them along, but they already left. It's about six or seven miles. Do you mind?"

Warily, Sarah was slow to answer.

"Could he do it on his own?"

"No. He . . . Well, no."

Their faces were poker straight, their noses red from weeping, their eyes blue and guileless, devoid of strategy.

"Where do I find him?"

"In the basement."

Anna immediately turned and began to show her mother the angry red rash on the back of Marianne's knees, thereby abruptly excusing Sarah. There was nothing to do now, except head for the bathroom with its mirror and all the demons of insecurity and fear that lurked within its frame.

A cool washcloth. Some soap. With shaking hands, she washed her face gently, swabbing it clean. Then she opened the vanity drawer to search for a bit of face cream.

She unpinned her covering, took her hair down There was only a bit of it to make up the tiny bot on the back of her head. She found Anna's hair gel, her hairspray, and thanked God for allowing these wonderful supplies. It was necessary that her hair looked okay.

She smiled to herself, her eyes bright with wondering, longing, and something else.

There. That would have to do.

Her knees threatened to buckle as she ran down the basement stairs, almost bumping into Lee as he carried a box away from a plastic folding table.

"Oh, there you are."

"You going?"

"I guess. Anna says I should."

"Yeah. Mommy King will be more at ease with you."

He smiled, and his smile stayed for a long time, which was a good sign that he was actually pleased that she had agreed to accompany him.

The buggy was clean, the horse spirited. Sitting beside him, the late afternoon sun's rays had no mercy through the opened window. Sarah withdrew into the corner, attempting to wrap a protective shell around the right side of her face. All the words she had wanted to say slipped out of her mind and disappeared, leaving her mouth dry, her tongue thick with anxiety. Now she wished she had not come.

When Lee guided the horse out on the main road, he asked if she wanted to go the long way around, since it was such a gorgeous evening. They could stop at the park on Buena Vista Road and feed the ducks.

"I will if the sun isn't too bright."

She had nothing to lose, so she figured she may as well tell him exactly what she felt.

Astonished, Lee looked at her.

"Whatever is that supposed to mean?"

She did not meet his eyes.

"My face."

"Your face. What about your face?"

"It's—you know, Lee. Don't make this hard for me."

When there was no reply, she stared miserably out the window, to the left, away from him. When the silence continued and stretched out before her with painful intensity, she caught her breath when he suddenly picked up her right hand and held it very lightly in his own. Still he did not speak.

Barely daring to breathe, Sarah turned her head slightly to the right and was shocked to see a wet trickle of tears washing over Lee's tanned, chiseled cheek.

Well, yes, of course. It had been a tough day. He had buried Ben, his beloved brother-in-law, and soon he would be leaving his dear sister Anna. He needed a hand to hold. The human touch has great power, she had read. Her hand was just that a comfort on this troubling day of mourning and anticipated farewells.

He pulled his hand away then, and Sarah left hers in her lap. It lay there, feeling obsolete, helpless, cast away.

Lee had to use both hands to guide the horse down a gravel road. A pond stretched before them, with geese and ducks of different colors swimming and milling about on the freshly mowed grass.

There were trees and rustic pavilions with weathered picnic tables. Several cars were parked in a designated area, and children played on the swings as mothers watched from their perches on lawn chairs.

To Sarah's surprise, Lee drove to the far end of the park before he stopped the buggy. The horse immediately stretched out his nose, raising, then lowering his head, attempting to relieve himself of the neck rein that kept him from stretching his neck comfortably.

Lee climbed out of the buggy and loosened the rein. Then he stood facing her, a hand draped across the shaft.

Hesitant, Sarah was unsure what he wanted to do, so she remained seated.

"Would you like to walk for awhile? We'll stay out of the sun."

He smiled. Sarah would not look at his eyes.

When she alighted from the buggy in her black funeral garb, Sarah moved in one swift, graceful movement. She was unaware of her elegance, the ease of her movement. Lee imagined many girls had to train themselves to move like that.

He stood very still, and Sarah hesitated, wondering at his stillness. Throwing the reins across the horse's back, he led him to a tree, then got the neck rope from beneath the seat, tied him securely, and turned to look at Sarah.

"Ready?"

She nodded.

The park was a lovely place, but the small adjoining woods was far more restful for her, the leafy, green shadows giving her more confidence.

Crickets and cicadas were noisily lending their voices to herald their walk, creating an uninvited, deafening harmony of clamorous sound. Sarah remembered the woodland insects from her childhood, when she and her siblings had played on the wooded hillside at her grandparents' home.

Sarah wanted to tell Lee about these sounds from her memories, but he seemed so aloof and remained so stone silent that the words would not come.

They walked toward a small, decorative bench made of cement. The seat was wide, comfortable, inviting. He stopped, looked down at her.

"Do you want to sit for a while, to talk?"

"Yes."

Sitting side by side with her shoulder touching his, but barely, she was completely aware of him, and her speech left her again.

She knew then, that she could not do it. She should have gone home the minute everyone was fed. Instead she had come up with all these grandiose presumptions about the possibility of Lee staying here instead of going to Alaska, when in reality that was a dream swiftly coming true for him.

Overhead, the leaves fluttered and rustled, the sound accented by the chirping birds, heralding the evening as they called their offspring to bed, or at least for an evening snack.

A goose honked on the pond, and another answered. A child's high squeal came from the swings.

It all seemed unreal. Here she was with Lee, on his last night, and the longer she remained seated beside him, the less she could think how to go about asking him to stay.

Lee cleared his throat and turned to look at her. "Sarah."

The word was woven through with so much kindness, her throat tightened.

"Look at me."

The courage to do his bidding came slowly, but finally she turned her head and lifted her eyes to his. Always, the color of them amazed her. There was sheer pleasure in the blue depths, but now, in the shadowy green of the trees, they were electric with emotion.

"Sarah, you know my tickets are bought, plans made. You know—Alaska, new life, here I come."

He laughed derisively.

"Can you figure out my life for me?"

Sarah's hands were in her lap, the fingers twisting, turning. She clenched them together to still them, straightened her shoulders, drew a deep breath, and opened her mouth, but her courage fled.

She closed her mouth again, bent her head, and said nothing.

Lee waited. He thought he heard something, but he wasn't sure. He turned again to look at Sarah.

"Don't go," she whispered again.

He heard.

"Did you say what I thought you said?"

Sarah nodded.

"You don't want me to go?"

She shook her head.

Then he did something she would never forget. He reached across her lap, picked up the scarred hand, and pushed back the sleeve. He let his fingertips trace the scars and the ridges where the sutures had been. Softly, he stroked her arm, then stopped and looked at her, tenderly.

"I can't go. Every bit of my conscience, every pore of my body knows I have to stay here on

Ben's farm. It's a moral obligation, the only right thing to do. Ben was in debt, of course, as every young farmer is, and now that Anna is alone, the place will have to be sold. It's a shame. I am attached to the place."

Lee paused but kept Sarah's hand in his. Then he continued, "I could sell my roofing and siding business—I think I could swing it—to buy the farm. Anna could stay. We could add an addition for her living quarters maybe. Or else we could just live together. She's so easy to get along with."

Lee was talking quickly now, the words tumbling over each other.

"I think I could be happy as a farmer, but I'm not too sure about being a bachelor. Anna's a wonderful cook, but there are things in life I need other than just food. You know, Sarah, I get the feeling that you and I are two people with the same mind set. We want what we want, and nothing is going to change our minds."

Sarah listened to the beauty of his voice, his words, and tried to grasp the true meaning.

"Then God comes into our lives and says, look here, it's time you sit up and take notice."

Sarah nodded.

"After I was burned, I knew what Matthew had become."

"You mean, what he always was. You just looked at him through rose-colored glasses before."

"Yes. I was kind of stuck in tunnel vision."

Lee laughed.

"But Sarah, are you sure this time? Are you certain no love stays in your heart for Matthew?"

Sarah shook her head.

"No, Lee. My eyes were opened, after I went through all the pain of my burns. There was nothing I needed, as far as Matthew was concerned."

"I couldn't stand it, Sarah. I couldn't bear to think of you suffering. I'd end up pacing my room in the middle of the night. No human being should have to endure what you did. I'll never know how you came through it."

Sarah shrugged her shoulders.

"You do what you have to do."

"And now, Ben is gone. And it torments me. Did he have to die so my pride could be extinguished? I was going to Alaska because of you. Your sad eyes, your scars. And then Matthew living down the road, asking you to leave your family. I could not take one more week, one more day of it."

"Lee, don't blame yourself for Ben's death. You know the Lord truly does end our lives according to His will. When our time on earth is finished, we're done."

Lee groaned.

"Oh, Sarah. You will never know what I've gone through. I tried to give myself entirely to God's will, but I could not bear to think of the possibility of you drawing your last breath, never to have you as my own."

Sarah couldn't move. Was she hearing Lee correctly? Was he speaking from the heart?

"But I'm burned, scarred," she whispered.

In answer, he stood, reached for her hands, and pulled her to her feet. Slowly he let go of her right hand. His fingertips explored every fissure, every riddle of her scars, along her cheek, her ear, the side of her neck. He stepped back to smile at her. He looked deeply into her eyes that changed color with the rustling of the leaves overhead, stormy with her own discovery of this new and certain love.

He bent his head, his cheek brushing hers, as he placed his lips delicately on the side of her jawline where the scarring was worst.

"I love you with all my heart. I have always loved you, this way and before. I love you, Sarah, your scars, your burns, everything. These scars are a testimony of God's will for our lives. I believe in my soul we are meant to be together, here on earth and in eternity."

When Sarah's tears overflowed, he kissed them away. Then he pulled her into his arms and crushed her painfully against himself, shocked when she let out a soft cry.

"I'm sorry, Sarah. I didn't mean to hurt you. Can you forgive me?"

Sarah laughed.

"No, no, it's okay. It's just my shoulder. It's the worst. I'm . . . Well, Lee, are you sure you want me? I'm probably scarred worse than you know."

Lee searched her eyes. He saw the anxiety, the genuine doubt, and he wrapped his arms around her gently this time. He lowered his face, inches from hers, and whispered again, "I love you."

From the depths of her heart, Sarah replied, "Lee, I love you more."

He kissed her then, softly. It was a pact, an agreement of a budding consent, cementing a love between two people that would stand the test of time. The years would bring changes, more trials, days of happiness, sorrow, and shared concern, but their love would see them through.

This knowledge flowed between the sweetness of their lips, the wondrous sense of having found the good and perfect will for their lives.

Lee sighed, trembling, his hands on her shoulders.

"Do you think you can stand to be a farmer's wife?"

She gasped.

"What?"

"I'm asking you to be my wife."

"But we never dated!"

"I dated you a lot—in my head."

Sarah's laugh rang out, and she reached for him, put her arms around him, and said, "This year?"

"Sarah, oh yes. This fall. I will have a whole

herd of cows and the harvest, and, well, everything."

"You won't have time to get married."

"I'll make time."

Smiling up at him, Sarah breathed, "Yes, Lee, I will be your wife."

His lips sought and found hers, and they became part of the wonder of the nature around them, created by God, designed so that man should not live his life alone.

Darkness was falling as they walked out to the pond. The mowed grass, the pavilions—everything took on a new appearance as the grayness descended.

They found the horse, patiently snoozing by the tree where he was tied. He lifted his head when he heard their approach, ready to go home to his stall and box of feed.

"Oh, Lee, what about Mommy King's leftovers?"

Lee stopped short.

"We forgot."

"She'll be in bed."

"What should we do?"

"Have a picnic?"

The horse had to wait another half hour, and Mommy King told Anna's mother, Rachel, that it was a shame the way these old practices were becoming lost. Since she had been unable to attend Ben's funeral, she should absolutely have gotten some cheese and sliced roast beef. The older generation did not get the respect they deserved.

Rachel bought a nice pound of meat and cheese and told her they had saved it for her, which repaired the rift quite nicely. Especially since Rachel sent along some cupcakes as well.

They would wait to tell their parents, but only for a few short weeks. They had to think of Sarah's mother, the one who would be organizing the wedding.

Lee told Anna that very night, after he took Sarah home. His sister hadn't been able to sleep. She was lying on the recliner, weeping, her poor face blotched with the depth of her grief.

"Anna, is it a help to you to know that I asked Sarah tonight?"

"You're not going?"

"To Alaska? Oh no. I can't, Anna. Not with Ben gone. I'll buy the farm. We'll build an addition. Don't worry, Anna. I'll *sark* (care) for you."

A storm of weeping ensued, but it was a relaxed, gentle crying. Over and over, she thanked her brother, told him it was a dream.

How she had dreaded having to leave the farm, and now she wouldn't need to. She wished she could tell Ben.

"When is your first date?"

"No, not dating. I asked her to marry me."

"But what about joining the church? Lee, you

can't get married this year. What are you thinking?"

Far into the night they talked, planned, and remembered Ben. Lee got up to do the milking and felt as if he hadn't slept at all, which didn't make much difference. He could live on fresh air and the thought of being Sarah's husband.

When Sarah did tell her parents, they were shocked, then ecstatic, unable to hide their wide grins of approval. The anticipation made their faces young, the surprise proving a veritable fountain of youth.

It had been a long time since Anna Mae was married, almost five years. Having a wedding would be something to look forward to.

Over at Elam's, the news was received with far less enthusiasm. Hannah stated the news, said she was supposed to keep it a secret, and they better not say anything.

Elam grunted behind his paper and said he'd not tell. He was one hundred percent trustworthy, as everyone knew the length of time that elapsed between him ever opening his mouth about anything. A cow could be dead for a week before he'd bother telling his wife. The time the milk tested for high bacteria, he silently and sourly let it run down the drain and never said a word.

Hannah fussed for weeks about the pathetic milk check, but he told her the hot weather was hard on milk production. She clamped her mouth into a solid line and didn't believe him.

Matthew, however, lay in his bed, full of frustration. He could guarantee Sarah didn't love that Lee. He knew she had always loved him. She still did.

Suddenly, he knew without a doubt that he wanted Sarah for his wife. Who else would he marry? Her scars would improve.

Knowing she was betrothed to another man made her twice as desirable. He lay on his back, his hands clasped behind his head, and schemed, his heavy black brows drawn down, his mouth curved in the same direction.

He'd go Amish again, if that's what it would take. He'd tell her that for now, and perhaps after they were married, she'd again agree to leave.

The thing was, he didn't think Rose would take him. She was starting to act the way she always did—grouchy, bored. Yes, Sarah would be just right for him.

Thinking of the challenge, he smiled. All it would take was to announce his desire to be Amish again. He'd do it.

Down in the kitchen, Hannah berated her husband for just sitting behind his paper. She thought he should be admonishing Matthew, the way other fathers did. It was no wonder he wasn't Amish, and now it was hard to tell who he would marry.

Elam harrumphed behind his paper and rustled the pages. He crossed one stockinged foot over the other, snagged the hole in the sock with his big toenail, and resigned himself to the fact that his toenails needed clipping.

Getting up, he headed for the desk drawer and began his task as Hannah stood over him and finished her tirade. She went to bed without him, so upset about Lee and Sarah.

Elam finished his toenails, shook his head, and was glad for Sarah.

He'd hate to be married to Matthew.

Chapter 13

Michael Lanvin was released on bail, his court appearance not yet announced. He maintained his innocence, and since there was no proof and no one willing to testify, the case was left undecided, likely to be placed on the back burner. For one thing, Michael had no money. He was assigned a public defender, rendered helpless for lack of prosecution.

David Beiler, one in a group of ministers, stayed true to his convictions, despite the visitors who entered the house on many week nights, quietly assuming Levi and the girls would be in bed or at least out of ear shot. One late-night group of visitors accused Davey of being hard-hearted, unfeeling. How could he stand to see his daughter injured so badly? If he'd use some common sense, they'd be glad to testify and get these fires stopped. Levi had all the information they needed.

Davey argued quietly, sensibly.

This situation could be resolved with forgiveness, he felt—so strongly, in fact, that he quoted Scripture to justify his actions. And that was something he did not condone, depending on the circumstances.

Davey's eyes became weary, underlined by dark circles, as he lay sleepless night after night, endlessly pondering the viewpoints of his distraught laymen.

Sarah moved through the remainder of the summer on wings, her feet skimming the ground as she ran to the barn, skipped across the yard, or swung on the tire swing attached to a limb of the maple tree. She was full of life, nearly fully recovered despite her lasting scars.

Matthew began to show up at the most inopportune times, cheekily rapping on the screen door and asking for Sarah. Sometimes, he simply spent time with Levi, who promptly produced a checker board, proud that his English friend Matthew wanted to stay.

One evening, the leaves on the maple tree stirred restlessly as an east wind bore smells of an oncoming rain. Dat asked if all the girls could help unload the remaining bales of hay stacked on the wagons by the barn.

Mam said she'd clear the table and do the dishes, so the girls went out to the barn and watched as Dat started the engine on the elevator. It would carry the bales to the bay already stacked high with hay for the horses and cows.

When it popped to life, the belt on the long elevator began to move. Sarah hopped up, grabbed a heavy bale, and heaved it onto the moving belt. She watched as it righted itself and began its slow ascent to the top, where Suzie and Priscilla helped Dat stack the bales tightly, making a good solid pile.

Steadily throwing the bales, she stopped to scratch her shoulder, the healing places itchy so much of the time. Shrugging her shoulder, she shifted her apron strap into place, bent to lift another bale, and looked up to find Matthew staring at her, his face uplifted, a half smile playing around his mouth.

Sarah could feel the heat rise in her face, but she kept working. The noise of the rattling engine drowned out the possibility of any conversation, though she was aware of his eyes steadily watching her.

When the wagon was empty, Dat came down to turn off the engine. His face was red, perspiration dripped off his chin, and his shirt clung to his back. It was a warm evening. Up under the metal roof with no ventilation, it was probably well over a hundred degrees.

Matthew shook his head.

"You're never going to change, Davey. Still doing everything the hard way, aren't you?"

Sarah drew a forearm across her face, her eyes burning with perspiration. She could tell by Dat's unhurried answer that he needed time to compose himself. Hot, itchy, uncomfortable, he would have to measure his words.

"Probably," he said finally.

Matthew laughed, a short superior snort.

"I figured you'd say that."

Dat nodded.

"Need any help?"

"Well, we have one more wagon load. If you want exercise, help yourself."

"If Sarah will let me."

Sarah jumped down from the wagon in one swift movement, pushed back her hair, and smiled at him.

"Feel free."

"Aren't you going to help?"

"I'll help Dat in the haymow to give Suzie a break."

Before he could protest, she scrambled up—up to the top and into the stifling heat under the metal roof, away from the sun and Matthew. She knew it was infinitely better there despite the temperature.

There was no avoiding him that evening, however. Matthew was determined to have her alone, so she stayed by the wagon in the fading evening light. She was itching all over from the hay, her legs a maze of scratches, her hair a mess, her face red and dusty and scarred.

Matthew gazed off across the cornfields, the tall stalks rising high above the fertile soil, the yellow ears already formed with the kernels filling out from the heat of the midday sun. He shook his head, solemnly eyeing her with a sad gaze.

"You know Sarah, it's times like this that I want to be about 14 again. We were so young, so innocent, so untouched by the world."

She pushed her bare foot beneath a small pile of loose hay. She picked it up with her toes and let it drop, but no response came to her mind, so she chose to stay quiet.

"You're going to marry Lee, then?"

Sarah nodded.

"Why?"

Why, indeed. Good question, Matthew. Thoughts filled her head, dissolved, reappeared. Some she understood and let go. Others she examined again in a constant shifting of ever-changing emotions and memories. Why do people marry the ones they do?

All she did was shrug her shoulders.

They stood beside each other, leaning against the now empty wagon, neither one daring a glance at the other.

The scene before them had remained greatly

unchanged from the time they were teenagers. Seasons had come and gone. Corn and alfalfa and soybeans were rotated. The earth was replenished with manure and lime and fertilizers, and crops planted. Rains came, and the sun coaxed the seeds into high-yielding crops.

What was the final deciding factor in her choosing Lee over Matthew? Did God reach down from heaven with His great, unseen hand and set Matthew in Haiti with Sarah away from him, now with Lee?

Matthew cleared his throat, becoming uncomfortable in the quiet that surrounded his question. Taking a deep breath, Sarah lifted her head. She looked out across the cornfields and the trees along the fence rising above the moving sea of green and began to speak.

"All my life, Matthew, I loved you—a devoted sort of worship, a feeling stronger than any love I have ever experienced. I never doubted we would marry, spend all our days together, always. Then, there was Rose. You chose her. Still I clung to the high ideal of you. You left the Amish—you left us, our way of life. I would have been excommunicated for you. I would have left everything I believe is right, for you. But you didn't want me."

Matthew's sharp intake of breath stopped her.

"I did. I was afraid you wouldn't leave your parents."

"I question that, Matthew. You married Hephzibah."

"I wanted you first."

"If you did, you would have waited, obviously. Still, I loved you. I felt God had taken Hephzibah because of our love, our destiny to be together. I clung to my desire for you, desperately willing us to be together, just the way I had always imagined. Then . . ."

Sarah spread her hands, palms up.

"There was the fire. I was burned. I endured pain that I didn't know a human being could take and live through. I feel now that I literally went through the fire spiritually, as well. My eyes were opened to God's will. You were my will, my way. You were a magnet that drew me irresistibly."

Matthew stood straight, took a few steps, gripped her shoulders, his eyes dark with rekindled passion. Without a word, he drew her roughly toward himself, his face lowered, and placed his lips roughly on hers. There was no gentleness.

His fingers dug into her shoulders. She threw herself back, away from him. His touch was offensive to her, repugnant in its power, like a charred beam, dead and black, soaked from the fireman's hose.

The action left him standing awkwardly, his hands slowly going to his sides.

"Sarah."

"Matthew, you have no right. You never let me

finish. I think when a love of such magnitude dies, it is completely dead. Ashes, cold, lifeless. I'm sorry. I really am, but I wish you the best."

"Shut up!"

Sarah gasped as his words rang out, feeling as if he had slapped her. She was caught completely off guard.

Trembling, his breath coming in spurts, he spat out, "If you were any sort of Christian, you would see I am the one you want. But since you're not born again, all spirituality makes no sense to you. You're as blind as you always were."

When Sarah faced him, her green eyes were tempestuous, churning with feeling. The dark colors surfaced, then receded, leaving a yellowish light, a gladness.

"Yes, Matthew, oh yes! I was blind. That's one thing we agree on."

He began to cry, his face crumpling, his features twisting, as he begged her forgiveness. He hadn't meant to lose his temper.

"Just go. Good-bye, Matthew."

Quietly, her words sank in, and with wide-eyed disbelief, he backed away.

"You really mean it, don't you?"

Sarah nodded, her eyes on his, and he could not bear to look at the victory in hers.

He lowered his head.

"Sarah, I'll come back. I'll be Amish for you. I love you. I always have, just like you have loved me. We are meant to be together. You knew that. You still know it."

In response, she turned and walked slowly down the slope, away from the empty hay wagon, away from the power she felt and knew she must resist.

He may do that—return for her sake—but that was pathetic. What a pitiful attempt at redeeming the years of treating her as second best, which is what she would always be in his eyes.

Suddenly, she could see the future with Matthew. She would have to take the blame for everything that went wrong, accept the responsibility as fact. She envisioned a houseful of babies, little children, and her attempting the impossible, trying to keep him happy, be perfect, be what he wanted her to be. He would always expect absolute devotion and perfection, without taking any responsibility of his own.

She slammed the *kesslehaus* door, causing a few clay flowerpots to rattle on the shelf above the sink. She washed her hands and lowered her head to wipe her mouth, erasing any trace of Matthew's presumptuous moves.

Mam was in the kitchen as usual, looking hot, tired, and short-tempered. Her face was a brilliant shade of pink, her nostrils distended, her mouth a straight, thin line.

"Where were you?" she burst out.

"Unloading hay."

"No. No, you weren't. I watched Matthew walk right past this kitchen window on his way to see you, and here you're getting married, and that man is going to mislead you."

"We talked, Mam. He wants to come back to the Amish now. He says he wants me."

Mam's eyes were fiery with disdain.

"He won't."

"Mam, please don't get upset. I am marrying Lee. I love him with all my heart, truly, with the real love that God gives. I'm going to be a farmer's wife, Mam, just like you. And I was never happier, never more sure of anything in my life. Lee is a special and absolutely amazing person."

Mam was not an emotional person. Her feelings were always well contained, her demeanor stoic, as reserved as anyone Sarah had ever encountered. Now, she threw her apron over her head and burst into tears. She let out little girl sobs of fear and worry, catching Sarah completely off guard.

"Mam!"

Sarah was incredulous.

From behind the apron came a muffled wail, as the rounded shoulders shook. A hysterical laugh emerged, and the apron was lowered, producing a red, sheepish face changed by the force of her feelings.

"Sarah, I'm only a human being, and a silly mother, at that. But I think if you would run off with that spoiled . . ."

She clapped a hand over her mouth, her eyes round with shock.

"I almost said brat."

Sarah threw back her head and laughed uproariously. It was an unladylike, belly laugh that was so infectious, it caught Mam and tugged her along. Mam lamented her total lack of restraint but finally conceded to it, sitting down and laughing till she had to remove her glasses, wipe her eyes, and take a deep breath.

"*Ach* Sarah, *ach my.* We mothers are a pitiful lot. We only want what is best for our children, and so often we see it long before they do."

Darkness was falling rapidly, but Mam said it was too hot to light the gas lamp, so they'd sit on the porch. Dat would be in, and he'd want his mint tea and pretzel.

Sarah hadn't seen Levi in the house, so she asked Mam about him. Mam shook her head, saying the warm temperatures were hard for Levi. He had gone to bed.

Relaxing on the wooden porch rockers in the still evening air, a companionable silence settled between them. They watched the bats emerge from under the eaves of the old shed by the corncrib. They wheeled and darted on their wide wings, snatching up the night's winged delicacies.

Finally Mam asked, "Have you decided on the color of your wedding dress?"

"I'd love to wear a rich green—a sage color, because of my eyes. Or maybe brown."

"You know that isn't traditional."

"I know."

"I suppose some girls would wear it."

"Yes."

"But I would like for you to remain traditional. Blue or purple."

"Do you think a dark gray, a charcoal, would be alright?"

"I wouldn't know why not."

"Too dull?"

"I think very neat and very in the *ordnung* (rules)."

"Oh, good. Is it too fancy to have the little girls wear a light shade of teal? Sort of aqua?"

"Plain fabric, no. That would be alright."

Dat came up to the porch, lowered himself on the porch swing, and sighed contentedly. When the silence continued, he spoke softly.

"You didn't have to stop talking because of me."

"Oh, we didn't. Just making sewing plans."

"Sewing? That's right, Sarah. You're getting married! We'll be making a wedding. Is that what Matthew wanted this evening?"

Shamefaced, Sarah nodded.

"I saw everything," her father stated calmly.

Horrified, Sarah glanced at him.

"You didn't!"

"Not everything, but enough."

Sarah was so ashamed. She stared at the floor of the porch, noticed the way the evening shadows painted the floorboards black.

"I'm sorry."

"You have nothing to be sorry about. He owes you an apology."

"Dat, it's okay. I can live the rest of my life without his apology, or anything at all from him, for that matter."

"Good girl, Sarah. I'm proud of you."

Then he asked, "How is Anna holding up? We should visit her again."

"She has her times. She had a close relationship with Ben and can hardly bear the *zeit-lang* (missing him)."

"And the children?"

"They miss him, of course, but children are so resilient. They accept things, without question, much easier than we do. Anna is an outstanding mother, providing so much for them. It's hard, but she's doing her best."

Dat nodded.

Priscilla and Suzie joined them, freshly showered and in their pajamas, chattering happily about mundane, teenage affairs. They plopped down on the porch steps, comfortable being with their parents on the farm on a warm late summer's evening.

"Is Levi in bed?" Dat asked.

Mam nodded.

"He's just not himself. I can't put my finger on it. He hardly says a word, walks around muttering to himself. I think he suffers because of the heat."

"Could be."

From the opened window, Levi's voice bellowed out from the confines of his bed, "You're discussing me. Don't you know we're not supposed to talk about other people?"

"*Ach* Levi, we were just worried about you."

"Well, I'm coming out there. I have my pajamas on. Did you make something to eat?"

"Just pretzels."

Levi shuffled out on the porch, his flat, white feet glowing in the semidarkness, his blue cotton pajamas hanging loosely on his great body.

His hair was still damp, and he smelled of medicated body powder. He loved it, saying it made his skin feel cool and slippery when it was warm. He settled himself on the porch swing beside Dat, his hulking figure dwarfing Dat's thin frame.

Reaching over, Dat slapped Levi's wide knee.

"How's it going, Buddy?"

"Not so good."

"Why?"

"Well, how do you expect me to get a good night's sleep if I have to have *kalte sup* (cold soup) for supper?"

"*Ach* Levi. We go through this every summer. We also had fried chicken. Did you forget?"

"But nothing for dessert."

Mam patiently explained how it was better to abstain from overeating when it was so hot, saying he would stay more comfortable when he ate less.

"We need air conditioning."

Dat's frame shook silently, as he tried to hide his laughter from Levi.

"Now, Levi, if we had air conditioning, you might not hear things—like strange cars coming in the driveway at night. It was a brave thing you did, watching, remembering. And now, you helped catch Michael Lanvin. That was also a courageous thing to do."

Levi shot his father a contemptuous glance.

"That didn't make a difference. I heard Melvin talking to Ez Beiler on Sunday. He said if no one charges Michael, he'll go free. So there are going to be more fires. And don't blame me, Davey Beiler. I did all I'm going to do."

"You did a lot. That was the beginning of the end, mark my words."

"*Vee maynshnt* (What do you mean), Davey?"

"To me, it seems insignificant whether or not Michael is jailed. If he did start the fires and he's living in anger, he'll try it again. Eventually, he'll be caught. They always are. But we really don't have enough evidence now."

"I caught him, though."

"Oh yes, Levi. You did."

Satisfied, Levi squared his shoulders, leaned back. The chain on the porch swing creaked as he pushed one foot against the porch floor to set it in motion.

Priscilla smacked Suzie's shoulder playfully, and Suzie leaped off the porch steps. Priscilla chased her across the dark lawn, caught the tail of her pajama top, and yanked. They fell in a helpless heap of girlish laughter by the petunia bed.

Sarah smiled, remembering to cherish this last summer at home as one of Davey Beiler's girls. Soon she would be Mrs. Levi Glick. His name was Levi, a traditional name from the Bible, just like hers. A generation before them, there had been a Levi and a Sarah. Would they continue the tradition, or would there be a Justin or an Abigail or a Caitlyn, a "fancy" name?

Sarah wanted a whole houseful of children to run up and down the stairs, swing on a rope swing in the haymow. They would play with calves and kittens and baby goats and run barefoot along field lanes lugging a red and white Rubbermaid thermos filled with the spearmint tea she had learned to make from her mother. They would take it to their dat, who was mowing hay in the alfalfa field, hot and thirsty, just like her dat.

She wrapped her hands around her knees, rocked back, suddenly ecstatic now.

She didn't hear the first part of Levi's unhurried

speech, but his words penetrated her thought eventually.

"That Michael Lanvin needs a haircut. He'll have to get one when he goes to jail, right?"

Absentmindedly, Dat said he would likely get one.

"Yeah, Michael told me that night. He told me he's not the one starting the fires. He told me that. He said he knows who it is, but he was afraid of him.

"He said the real arsonist is not him, but if he told me, and I told someone, he could get shot. What did he mean by that?

"Then he said this. He said that years ago that man of Widow Lydia's, what was his name? Her husband?

"Michael said he didn't pay this man for a lot of money. Did he mean Lydia's husband didn't pay? Or what?"

Dat stopped the porch swing, his body tense as his breath whooshed out.

"Levi."

"Hm?"

"Are you positive you're not making this up?"

"Why would I? Michael would not want me to do that. He said he thinks Ashley Walter's father is the arsonist."

Dat gasped, and Mam said sharply, "Levi!"

"Well, what?"

Sarah said very quietly, "Harold. Harold Walters."

The man at the leather goods store, the stand at he farmer's market. He had been in a dispute about money. Apparently with Lydia's husband, who had not been a stable person. He had struggled with old grudges and a mental instability and sometimes became quite violent.

Sarah knew Harold Walters as a friendly man hough brusque, a good business person. But hen, there was the suspicious mistreatment of Ashley.

Dat said, "We'll wait and see what happens, alright?"

"Why?"

"We have no proof. Even if we summoned the police and Michael spilled everything, they could both deny all of it. There were never any fingerprints."

Levi shook his head and said Michael hadn't spilled a thing. He drank the whole glass of water Levi had given him.

Chapter 14

When Lee came to pick Sarah up and whisk her away to Anna's house, in Suzie's words, she was ready, her cheeks flushed with anticipation, wearing a new green dress the color of a cornstalk. She remained barefoot, the heat stubbornly draped across Lancaster County, a stifling bubble of high humidity creating uncomfortably warm nights and sending daytime temperatures to a high of 95 degrees or more.

Lee greeted her from the buggy, dressed in a cool, white short-sleeved shirt, his teeth flashing as white as the shirt, his tanned skin a dark contrast. She climbed up and seated herself beside him before he had a chance to step down and help her up.

Their eyes met, and they smiled and continued smiling, both unable to wipe the ridiculously happy emotions from their faces.

He reached for her hand and said, "Sarah, tell me I won't wake up from the best dream I have ever had."

In response, Sarah squeezed his hand, laid her head on his shoulder, and said happily, "You won't."

Few things can compare with driving along country roads in a horse and buggy, she thought. Especially on a night like this. Both doors were pushed back, both windows held to the ceiling of the buggy by a metal clasp, allowing the air to circulate freely. The horse trotted at a brisk pace, knowing he was going home.

She breathed in the aroma of summer as they passed a field of tomatoes, one of corn, and yet another with freshly cut alfalfa, infusing the air with its heady fragrance.

Oncoming traffic was heavy, so the train of cars

behind them grew increasingly longer, until one revved its engine with impatience.

Lee looked in the rearview mirror and pulled steadily, easily, on the right rein, drawing the buggy off the main road and onto the wide shoulder beside it, allowing the cars to pass, one by one. Sarah smiled.

"Lee, pulling off to the side of the road and allowing cars to pass—that puts you in the same highly-respected category as my father. Thank you. Not all men will do that."

Lee grinned at her.

"So you think you made a good choice?"

"Definitely."

Their smiles became slightly idiotic once more, and they stayed that way as they pulled up to Ben Zook's farmhouse.

Not Ben's anymore, Sarah corrected herself. Anna's. And not for long. This farm would be Lee's. And hers. She could hardly bear to think of it. The disbelief, the joy of this great and perfect gift was almost more than she could contain.

Anna greeted her at the door. She threw her soft, ample form into Sarah's arms, laughing, then crying and becoming completely hysterical, as Sarah held her, laughed, and cried with her.

"Sarah, oh Sarah! I told Lee we have to build a patio between our two houses, so you and I can meet every summer morning to talk and drink our coffee. Do you think we'll get along? I promise you, I will mind my own business. I will not meddle in your affairs. Ever. I can't believe you're going to be my sister-in-law."

Sarah was drawn into the kitchen, and for the first time, she viewed the house with eyes of ownership.

The walls were painted a soft white, and the trim and doors, as well as the kitchen cabinets, were a softly gleaming golden oak. There were double windows above the sink and behind the table, allowing plenty of light and air into the large kitchen.

The linoleum mimicked dark ceramic tile. Sarah thought it was very tasteful, as was the hidden alcove containing a small sink and a round ring to hold a hand towel.

The cabinets contained a large number of deep drawers and doors that contained evenly spaced shelves. The large EZ Freeze propane gas refrigerator was built into the cabinetry, as was the gas stove beside the double sink.

Sarah had been in this house many times, but never like this. Her mind tumbled with possibilities—furniture, colors, things she would have on her countertop or her table.

She did not want to be materialistic or greedy, but she overflowed with ideas, thinking of things she wanted to buy, items she would need.

Anna's three children, Marlin, Marianne, and little Elmer, all clamored about her now, asking for attention. She had to focus on the needs of the fatherless children, her heart aching for them as she gathered them on her lap and around her on the brown tweed sofa.

She stroked Elmer's squeaky clean hair, answered Marlin's rapid fire questions, listened patiently as Marianne talked about her new kittens in the barn. She showed Sarah where she had been scratched, and Sarah clucked properly over a proffered hand, which Marianne held to the light, the Band-Aid removed, so the scratch could be examined and fussed over.

She was not aware of Lee's entrance or of the light in his eyes as he stopped, watching Sarah with the children.

Anna was perspiring freely, mopping at her face with a clean washcloth, complaining about the intense heat.

"You know, Sarah, there's hardly a nice, Christian way of complaining about the weather. But what's the difference—that or snapping at everyone all day because you're so hot and tired of it? I can hardly take one more day of this stickiness."

"I think a thunderstorm is on its way, later tonight," Sarah said.

"Yup, paper says that," Lee agreed.

"Well, good. I hope it's a doozy. It better clear the atmosphere and lift this humidity. Did you know it was ninety percent yesterday? It was so humid. I had a glass of water setting beside me on the sewing machine, and it condensed so much there was a puddle all around it."

Sarah smiled. She knew exactly what she meant, having tried to sew and given up herself.

They talked for over an hour, remembering Ben and making plans for the future. Then Anna went to the pantry and refrigerator, producing armloads of food, enough for a dozen people.

There was cold, freshly squeezed lemonade that was so refreshing the temperature seemed to drop ten degrees, Sarah told her.

There was cold, chunked watermelon, red and seedless and mouthwatering, squares of golden cantaloupe, piles of cheese and ham and sweet Lebanon bologna, mustard and dipping sauces, stick pretzels and potato chips. She'd coated strawberries with a combination of milk and dark chocolate, and there were two different kinds of whoopie pies individually wrapped in plastic wrap, moist and soft with a heavy layer of vanilla frosting in the middle.

Sarah had never tasted better whoopie pies. Never. She told Anna, who laughed heartily.

"I bought them, Sarah. You won't catch me baking when the whole house is like an oven. Forget that."

Sarah eyed Anna's plate, then Lee's, and wondered if she would be Anna's size in a few years. Their appreciation for food was contagious.

She found herself chiming in with praise of the texture of the watermelon, the chocolate, everything.

They took food very seriously. She was alarmed at the amount Lee consumed. She eyed his wide shoulders, muscular arms, his flat stomach, and decided he likely had a terrific metabolism, plus he did an enormous amount of physical work each day.

As if he read her thoughts, he smiled.

"We Glicks like to eat, Sarah. I can hardly wait for you to get to know the rest of the family."

"I met your sisters at the funeral and your mother before. She's terribly nice. So friendly."

They all sat up, silenced, as the rustling of leaves began and quickly turned into more than a rustling. An opened newspaper lying on an end table flapped, then slid to the floor, blown by the increasing force of the sudden gust of wind.

Anna ran to the window, flapping her round arms as she went.

"Air! Air! The wind is coming!"

The children were trundled off to bed, and the table was cleared before the faraway rumbles of thunder began.

"Nothing to worry about yet," Lee announced, returning from a short vigil on the front porch.

Anna produced a pink spiral bound notebook and wrote across the front cover in bold, printed letters: Levi and Sarah's Wedding.

They sat together at the kitchen table and planned, writing names of grandparents, uncles and aunts, cousins, friends, co-workers, an endless stream of relatives and acquaintances until Sarah's head was reeling with the immensity of it all.

Who would be the corner waiters to serve the bride and groom's table? Who would be *fore-gayer* (managers)? Who would have the *babeyly* (paper)? Where would Levi sit? He might be better off in a wheelchair that day.

Lee was too easy, saying anything they decided was okay. Anna told him he could say that now, but he'd come up with a few clunkers later. He always did. He'd just wait till a few weeks before the wedding, and then he'd throw a monkey wrench into the works.

She assured Sarah that Lee was bossy. Look at him, running his own roofing crew. He was used to being the boss, and she'd better start preparing to live a humble life of servitude. This thing of sitting there saying anything was alright, was just till Sarah married him and she couldn't get away; then the real Lee would show his true colors.

Lee grinned, relaxed, completely unruffled, as Anna's harmless banter continued.

Sarah watched him, as he raked a strong, brown hand through his sun-streaked blond hair. She noticed the way his shoulders were propped against the chair, took in his steady, smiling blue eyes, and her knees became quite weak, her heart accelerated. The love she felt for him was growing into a steady, consuming flame.

She was grateful, humbled, to have this man in her life. Only God's infinite mercies could have enabled her to safely make this choice. Deep in her heart, she knew Lee would be the kind of man that would never cause her a moment's grief. Like Dat, he existed on a bedrock of kindness.

Dat's description of others was almost always, "He would do anything for anybody." That was his way of relating the goodness he saw in most people. This phrase could truthfully be applied to Lee, she knew. It showed in how he had worked for Ben, became a mentor for Omar, and all while he ran his roofing crew during the day, working long, wearying hours to help others.

In his heart, Lee felt he didn't know much about God or the Bible, choosing to remain quiet when others had long, heated discussions about theology, Scripture, whatever. But the fruits of being inhabited by the Spirit were all there. Lee knew God, or how could he have had this natural inclination toward kindness?

Dat said that was a great mystery, but it was all around us, every day, in mundane things, often unnoticed by others, but very important.

She wondered if Matthew had found a job, or if he would be returning to Haiti. She didn't think he knew what he wanted. He really didn't. Right now, he wanted her, she knew. But wasn't he just acting like a spoiled child who wanted a toy only because it was held by someone else?

And yet, she would always remember Matthew as someone who had flavored her life with sweetness, the first stirring of young love, the reason for living at times. She would always be grateful for him, for his friendship. But that was all.

"A penny for your thoughts."

Lee smiled at her, and she returned it gladly, but chose to keep her thoughts to herself. Someday, she would tell him.

The thunder rumbled, louder, closer, and Lee turned to watch out the window as another streak of lightning cut across the night sky.

"Think it'll be hard this time?" Anna asked.

"I don't know. Seems pretty powerful all of a sudden."

The wind tore at the trees surrounding the house and ripped across the lawn as lightning illuminated the landscape around them. There was a particularly loud boom. Anna grasped her head, her hands clapped across her ears, her eyes widened.

Inevitably, the high wail of the sirens followed. Soon a car's headlights came up the drive and stopped. The door opened, and a figure splashed through the rain. The heavy front door was flung open, and a neighbor stepped inside, dripping.

"Samuel Zook's barn!" he shouted.

Instantly, Lee was on his feet, following the neighbor out the door and away.

Anna sat, staring morosely at the remains of her delicious snack, shaking her head.

"I hate these fires. I'm sick of them."

"It was probably the lightning, Anna. That crack had to hit something, didn't it? I don't think the arsonist is loose, at least not doing that anymore."

"You always say that. You know what I think? I think we should have stocks, those wooden things they used to hold criminals, you know, thieves or mischief makers. We used to see them in our history books in school. Men or women were stuck in there, and other citizens, the good people, were allowed to throw tomatoes or eggs at them. That would be perfect."

Sarah laughed.

"In the Bible, they just stoned them, got rid of them."

"That's sick."

"I know. But still, it would be nice to be rid of these fires. I know how it was for us."

Anna's face became hard, rigid, with the intensity of the memory.

"You know, Ben suffered more than you'll ever know. He had days when he could barely drag himself out to do the milking. I milked alone more than once. I can't tell you the fear I experienced, the heart-sinking feeling of knowing my husband was lying in bed, crying with despair.

"I think the night our barn burned was honestly more than he could handle. He tried, Sarah, he tried so hard. He took his anti-depressants, talked to counselors, but I'm not sure he always felt as good as he let on. I'll tell you, Sarah, if you promise to keep this a secret."

Sarah nodded.

"I'm not sure he was thinking as he would have in former times, the day he went to get that calf. He knew the bull was there. He often told me never to trust him."

Anna sighed. She winced at the sound of the thunder and the rain and the wind moaning about the house.

"We never know, the day we get married, how wonderful God's gift of a sound mind can be. Another thing we never know is what God has in store for us. The important thing is that we live fully, trusting Him, and experience all that joy along the way."

Sarah nodded.

"For sure, Anna, for sure."

"I may spend the rest of my life as a widow now, living with you and Lee."

"No, you won't, Anna. You're young. You're attractive."

"I'm short and fat. You know men don't like big women. Besides, I won't talk about it. Ben is still in my heart, and he'll stay there."

They did dishes, listened to the strength of the

storm abating, and read a few articles to each other from a magazine. Then they took off their coverings and stretched out, Anna on the recliner and Sarah on the couch. They closed their eyes and relaxed, but they kept on talking, the way sisters often do, of everything and anything, comfortable confiding life's joys and sorrows, their fears and failures.

Finally, at two o'clock in the morning, Sarah wondered out loud if Lee was alright. Did Anna think he was?

"Oh yes, he's old enough to take care of himself," she said. "He probably just thinks the whole night's outcome depends on him. He takes too much on himself."

They must have dozed off and were awakened by a shrill cry from the bedroom. Elmer was thirsty, so Anna stumbled to the kitchen and got him a cold drink. She crooned and fussed to her baby boy, before settling herself on the recliner, with plenty of grunts and snorts of discomfort.

The night was still warm, but Sarah tried to remain positive, imagining a cool morning breeze to greet her.

Suddenly, the footrest of the recliner slapped down. Anna sat up and announced loudly, "I'm so miserable. I cannot take one more minute of this heat. I'm going to take a shower. It's too hot on this itchy recliner. I guess if something bad happens, you'll have to call me."

With that, she stomped off toward the bedroom. Sarah heard drawers open and shut. The bathroom door slammed, the water turned on, and peace returned.

Sarah watched the remains of the storm, the ripples of blue heat lightning, and listened to the distant rumbles. She was glad the storm had gone through, giving hope of cooler temperatures tomorrow.

Her eyelids became heavier and heavier.

She was awakened by someone softly calling her name. Her eyes fluttered open, looking straight into Lee's blue eyes, his face blackened, his gaze weary.

"Oh."

She sat up immediately, all her senses keenly aware of him.

"Sarah."

Reaching up to fix her hair, her eyes remained on his face.

"They, we, I . . . we caught the arsonist."

Unable to comprehend Lee's words, Sarah looked at him blankly.

"We caught him. We have his lighter, the newspapers, the car, everything."

His voice was hoarse, strained, exhausted.

"Tell me," she said.

Evidently, Harold Walters had taken no precautions that night. The lightning was so sharp, the fire could have been blamed on it handily, so he got bold and drove up to Samuel Zook's barn without trying to cover anything.

In the flashes of lightning, they'd watched. When the barn was hit by a bolt of lightning, it was soon extinguished, most of it saved. But there he was, crouched beside the silo on the barn hill sloping up to the haymow, stuffing newspapers in the door, igniting them.

Lee, the neighbor Amos, and the driver—the three of them jumped him and wrestled him to the ground. They were surprised when they saw he was an older man. It wasn't Michael.

They subdued him, called the police, and spent the rest of the night listening, watching, answering questions.

So now a lot depended on the arsonist's willingness to tell the truth and the Amish people's ability to prosecute. Without pressing charges, they were back to square one.

Sarah listened, then stated that this was not a whole lot different than Michael Lanvin being taken into custody. It still depended on the Plain people's prosecution.

"Dat will not do it."

"Perhaps others will."

"Which one is right, Lee?"

He sat beside Sarah, leaned back against the cushions, and closed his eyes.

"We'll talk at breakfast. I need a shower, then I may as well start milking. Anna's asleep, right?"

Sarah nodded.

"Let her sleep. Poor thing, she minds the heat so much. I can milk."

"I'll help," Sarah offered.

"No way. You hardly slept."

"I want to."

And she did. Secretly, she wanted to see how it would be to milk cows in the stable that would be hers and Lee's. Her feet skimmed the wet sidewalks, she was so excited. She knew cows and could hardly wait to show Lee her expertise. Without any instructions, she assembled the milking machines, washed udders, fed cows and calves, and swept the aisles. She was a regular cyclone of energy, leaving Lee duly impressed.

Afterwards, they washed the milkers together, and Sarah swept the cement floor, carefully rinsing it with clean water. She smiled at Lee and said, "Let's go make breakfast."

But Lee was staring at her with a strange look on his face. And he stood rooted to his position by the bulk tank.

"What?" she asked innocently.

"I am in disbelief. Besides being beautiful and kind and sweet, you're a real workaholic."

"Oh no, Lee. This is the first time I ever helped you do the milking. I was trying to make an impression. It might not always be this way," she laughed.

"But do you like milking? Farming? It's terribly hard work for a girl."

"Oh, it's not. I love it. It's all I know. I've been a farm girl all my life."

He closed the gap between them, folded her gently, with a sort of reverence, into his strong arms, and held her.

The milk house door was suddenly yanked open, and Anna stuck her head in.

"Whoopsie! Sorry! Hey, if this is how it's going to be, and I run into this kind of situation all the time, you're going to have to set up a beeper or something. Like a flare at an accident, some kind of warning."

But she was laughing, and Lee introduced Sarah to her as the new Mrs. Lee Glick, outstanding farmer of the year. Sarah smiled, then laughed, and said, "Oh, come on." But the pleasure of his approval stayed with her all morning, creating a smile that fairly glistened, until Anna said she had never known her teeth were so white. Sarah replied that Anna had just never seen them for such an extended period of time.

Chapter 15

As always, when everyone was least expecting it, a small white car drove up to the house. No one could predict exactly who the caller was, although Levi said his heartbeat was getting heavy—that car was the same one that drove in the lane the night the barn burned to the ground, or would have if the firemen hadn't soaked it.

Dat listened halfheartedly, watching warily. Sarah scraped a residue of meatloaf from the supper plates and leaned over to catch a glimpse for herself. Priscilla said that—sure enough—it was the car Levi had always described, and Suzie said perhaps they should all run to the basement —what if he had a gun?

They all tried to make light of the white car's arrival, but even Dat's face blanched when the car door opened. A gangly, unkempt youth unfolded his long limbs and stood uncertainly, one hand clutching the door handle, as if he would rather reopen the door and fold himself back inside.

He was dressed in torn jeans and an old sweat-shirt of a nondescript color with the sleeves hacked off. A cap sat low on his forehead, stray hair erupting around it like brush bristles.

Levi said this was too scary for him and he was going to his room. But as soon as he saw all the windows in his room, he felt exposed and shuffled back to the safety of the recliner. He sat down solidly, watching with a stony expression.

Finally, when Dat wondered if he should go out and invite him in, the young man began a wary walk up to the porch, his focus mostly on the sidewalk.

At the first rapping sound, Dat went to the door, opened it, and stepped outside, perhaps to protect his family, perhaps for privacy. Sarah couldn't tell. She was surprised when Dat opened the kitchen door and ushered the visitor inside.

Quickly, Mam pushed aside a few empty serving dishes and wiped the tabletop swiftly, murmuring excuses, casting furtive glances at the visitor with the intense black eyes.

But here was Dat, asking him to sit, so if Davey did that, she assumed he knew what he was doing. But Mam still felt so ill at ease that she scrubbed all the pots and pans so vigorously that they shone like a mirror the remainder of the week.

Sarah went to the sink, finding safety in turning her back. She concentrated on the simple task of helping Mam with the supper dishes. Her ears, however, were fine-tuned to words spoken by the two men.

Dat kept up a friendly conversation, until that ran out, sputtered, and died. Mam cleared her throat and cast a sideways glance at Sarah, who coughed involuntarily.

A steady thumping ensued as the youth bounced his one knee in furious repetition, his large gray sneaker steadily whacking the linoleum. He raked his soiled cap off his head and ran a hand through his unkempt hair.

Sarah turned halfway around and observed him closely. Yes. It was. He was the guy at the funeral home. Michael Lanvin. The arsonist?

His mouth was working, painfully. He ran a hand across the back of his neck, tugged at the neck of his sweatshirt. Beads of sweat appeared on his upper lip. He wiped them off with a shaking forefinger.

"Um, yeah, I'm like."

He stopped, searching Dat's face.

Dat remained steady, his gaze unknowing, calm, and unfazed, waiting for the youth to reveal what was on his mind.

Hadn't Davey dealt with many youth, recognized guilt and its unfailing disciple, its lack of trust? So he waited.

"Yeah, um . . ." Again, he stalled, unable to continue. "See, I, like, met you when she . . . Ashley . . . my girlfriend died. It was you, right?"

Dat nodded, a half smile of reassurance evident now.

"That was you, right?" he repeated.

"Yes, it was. I remember you," Dat answered. "You seemed quite upset."

"Yeah, I was, I guess."

Another pause.

"Which one's Sarah?" the youth asked suddenly.

Sarah stopped, motionless, and slowly put down the plate she was washing, watching the suds cover it. Drying her hands on her apron, she stepped forward, smiled slightly, and introduced herself.

"Hi," he responded, "I'm him. Ashley's boyfriend."

Sarah nodded.

"I'm, well, how much did she tell you?"

"About what?"

"The fires."

"Nothing. She was concerned about each family, cared about them."

"She never said nothing about, you know?"

"No."

Suddenly, he slid down in his chair so far Sarah thought he would slide off, but he splayed his feet, stopping himself.

"It wasn't me."

Sarah looked, found Dat's eyes. His face was frozen, a granite profile.

"It was her dad. That guy at the leather goods place at the market. Not her real dad. I drove him around, but he lit the barns. He hates a guy named Aaron. Or he did. This guy died, but he's never gotten over it."

Dat nodded. "They caught him."

"I know. But they think it's me. He'll lie. He

won't care if I go behind bars, as long as he can save his own skin."

"I see," Dat said quietly.

"Will you come to my hearing?"

Dat pondered the question without answering.

"I know you guys don't do court appearances, but would you help me out? I'm . . . I don't want to go again. Jail is not a good place."

Finally Dat said, "I don't know what to tell you."

Sitting up straight, he leaned forward, pleading. "I'm in trouble, either way. What do they call it? I'm responsible as long as I hauled him around some of the time. Look, I got in too deep. I owed him money, lots of it. I couldn't pay him back. I got into trouble, lost my job. It's a mess. I'm scared. I don't know what to do."

"Is this Walters person in custody?"

"I doubt it. He has money."

"Is he dangerous?"

"No. He's a . . ." Michael caught himself, sputtered, and looked pleadingly at Dat. "If you'd just come to my hearing, testify."

"But all I have is your word."

"No! No!"

Desperate now, Michael spoke rapidly. "You gave me a hug, at the viewing. You said God should bless me. Well, He didn't. He can't on His own, the way I figure, but if you were in the courtroom, God would be there, too."

Dat shook his head. "No, Michael. I am not the

go-between you need. There is only One that came to earth, died for you, and is in heaven on your behalf. He's the One you need in the courtroom, not me."

Bewildered, Michael lifted his eyes. "Who?"

"Jesus."

"Oh, him."

Embarrassed, Michael's eyes slid away.

"Yeah, I remember my Sunday school teacher. I remember all that stuff."

"You do?"

"Yeah."

"So all you have to do is ask Him back into your life. He'll come. He'll be there for you."

"Yeah, but . . ." His voice trailed off.

"Are you sorry for what you did?"

"Well, of course. I wish I had never met Walters. Now Ashley's dead, and I . . . I treated her wrong."

There is nothing quite as shocking as the first ragged sob from a man who is truly at the end of his resources, Sarah thought, as the initial battered sound tore from his throat.

"She's dead, and I can never fix it."

He flopped against the tabletop, folded his arms, and dropped his head onto them, his shoulders heaving.

Silent as wraiths, Priscilla and Suzie left the room. Levi began crying, as he always did when he heard the sounds of a distressed person.

Sarah stood, uncertain. Dat laid a hand on the youth's shoulder, his great calloused hand beginning a slow massage, an assurance of his presence.

"You are forgiven," he said softly.

Still, Michael's face remained buried in his arms, and his sobs did not lessen. If anything, they intensified.

"I can never make it right," he repeated between hiccups.

Patiently, Dat explained the plan of salvation, urging Michael to accept forgiveness, share the yoke of sorrow with Jesus. He would carry it for him, relieve him of the shame and guilt. How much of it got through to him, Sarah did not know, but Michael's crying ceased. Mam brought him a clean paper towel, which he accepted shamefacedly, muttering a garbled thanks.

In the end, he accepted the fact that Dat would not come to his hearing.

"You may not have much of one," Dat said. "If the Amish people show their forgiveness, which I believe they will, you will have fines and penalties perhaps, but hopefully, no jail time."

"I will. I deserve it. You know that."

"We'll see."

When he rose to go, Dat did not shake hands, he simply pulled the young man into an embrace and released him. Keeping a hand on his shoulder, he said firmly, "We forgive you. Be a man now, and change your ways. You'll come out of this a better person."

"You think?"

"I think, definitely."

"I need to . . . I don't have a Bible. I used to, you know, read it."

"I'll see that you get one. Stop by tomorrow night."

Unbelievably, he did.

Sarah looked up from weeding the lima beans to find the small white car driving up to the house. She straightened, shaded her eyes with her hand, then laid down her hoe. Walking toward him, she smiled hesitantly.

"Michael. Good to see you!"

"Hey."

"You came for the Bible?"

"Yeah."

"I'll get it."

"Where's your dad?"

"He has a meeting tonight."

"What meeting?"

Immediately, his eyes became hooded with suspicion.

"A meeting about the fires, the arsonist."

David Beiler had known before he hitched Fred to the shining, freshly washed buggy that this would be the last meeting as far as the arsonist was concerned. He was in custody. And it was likely that Michael Lanvin would serve some time as well, although he couldn't be sure.

The meeting would be fraught with argument, he knew. It would be like walking in a war zone, stumbling onto hidden land mines. Dangerous to the hearts and souls of men.

Always, church problems were the same. Maneuvering between the liberals and the conservatives required the wisdom of Solomon. Or more, he concluded to himself.

The leader of the liberals was Melvin, his own nephew, outspoken, charismatic, able to bend other men's wills because of his ability to talk. He could make an expert salesman, selling innocent folks things they certainly did not need.

Melvin and his followers wanted revenge. They called it justice, which was only a nice word for it. In David's opinion, to wish anyone ill, punishment, pain, anything, was a form of revenge. That was an eye for an eye, a tooth for a tooth, the Old Testament teachings of the law.

When Jesus came, He brought a better way, but so few understood or trusted the form of love the ministers struggled to keep alive within the churches as well as without.

To forgive was the epitome of Christ's message. So near to forgiveness, Davey had almost given up the whole gospel when Sarah was injured.

Never, as long as he lived, would he forget the pleading look in her eyes as she begged her father to help her, to free her from her pain. Watching as the doctors scraped the dead tissue from her exposed nerve endings left him weak and drained, completely helpless. That emotion was followed by a bitter wish for revenge, wanting to make the arsonist endure exactly what Sarah had gone through.

It was only human nature.

Tight-lipped men sat on benches around the long table in Sam Esh's shop. They were dressed in colorful shirts with back vests and trousers, their straw hats on pegs along the wall. Some of the younger men wore shirts with a stripe and no vests, their patterned suspenders in stark relief against the distinctive shirts.

Those in the more modern, youthful dress, most of them asking for justice, would gladly enter a courtroom, testify, and press charges.

David was surprised to see Melvin dressed in a plain shirt and wearing a vest, his normally tousled hair combed down over his ears in a modest fashion. He felt a tug of amusement at the corner of his mouth. No doubt Lydia's influence was taking hold already.

Good. That was good. She would be a grounding influence in his life. She was quiet and stable and would bring him back to earth if he went off on a far-flung rant, the way he tended to do.

The meeting opened with a silent prayer, time

well spent as David laid his heart open for God to examine. Thy will be done. Amen.

Sam Esh was the main speaker, having had more interaction with the law and the media than anyone else.

He began quietly, a humble man. It was hard to stand up and face the prying eyes of men who were in disagreement.

He was a man of common sense, and as he spoke, this quality emerged, his voice gained momentum, and assurance broke through as his voice carried well to the far reaches of the room.

"We all want this man behind bars, for our own safety. As of now, he'll go there, whether we testify or not. He was caught, doing the grisly work he's been doing for a couple of years, and there's not much we're going to do to change that. The law is the law. I spoke to the local police, and they're guessing he'll get between five and ten years."

Immediately, murmurs erupted, hands were raised.

"He'd get more than that if we testified."

"Is that all?"

"You know he'll be out in two, the way court cases go."

"Bunch of crooks."

"It ain't right."

David Beiler sat and listened, his heart dropping with a sickening thud. So this was what he'd be up against. This thirst for revenge.

"Two years from now, the barn fires will start again."

Sam Esh stood, silenced by the outrage, his face flaming with discomfiture.

Melvin raised his hand. Sam nodded toward him.

Melvin stood.

"See, this is our trouble. We're gullible people who don't understand the law. Anyone can feed us anything, and we believe it. I talked to a lawyer and got the real deal."

David cringed at his arrogance, his superiority.

"If we testify, he told me, we can change the course of the court's decision."

Melvin paused for emphasis.

David noticed the worshipful demeanors on the faces of the younger men and wondered anew at the necessity of God telling the children of Israel to support the arms of Moses in battle. As long as Moses's arms were held up by his people, their armies had the victory.

Here, tonight, it was the same scenario, but in spirit. When Godly leaders had the support of the people, there was a blessing in the land.

He inhaled deeply, steadied himself, kept his silence, and allowed Melvin to ramble on, using words from his lawyer's book that very few of these simple, Plain men understood. Perhaps this was good.

After Melvin sat down, there were murmurs of agreement.

Samuel Riehl stood and elaborated on Melvin's views.

Old Dan Dienner asked for time, was given it, and David took another calming breath. Dan had never been known for patience and often lacked forbearance. He was a mighty little warrior carrying the spear of his own highly esteemed opinion.

Dan's words were scathing, his bushy gray eyebrows drawn down like angry caterpillars. His mouth snapped open and closed as if elastic controlled his jaws after every hurtful sentence had been released. His words swirled about the room bringing each rebellious nature to fruition.

David watched sadly as a few younger men stood up, grabbed their hats, and strode smartly from the room, angered by Dan Dienner's fiery words.

The meeting stalled when the old minister sat down. Unease crept beneath the chairs. Men settled themselves in different positions, feet scraped fitfully on the cement floor, throats were cleared, and here and there a self-conscious cough erupted.

They called on *Davey Beila*. His limbs were heavy, burdened by the fractious atmosphere. Slowly, like a sorrowful old man, he stood.

"Would someone ask the men that left the room to return, please?"

That was his first concern. They were the church of tomorrow. Personal opinion was meaningless, when it came to *fer-sarking* (caring for) the church of the future.

After a moment of bewilderment, someone nudged Melvin, who hurried out, returning with the young men in tow.

David shared what was on his heart. He could speak no other way. He told of his own fire, the loss, the hard work, but also the overwhelming gratitude in the end, when he viewed the members of the Amish church in a whole new light.

"For we have something. We have an upbringing, a tradition that teaches us to reach out, perform duties born of brother love.

"After the new barn stood in its place, I was as changed as the barn. I have never known gratitude the way I do now. I can never stand in the forebay, throwing a harness on a mule's back, and not be thankful for the mule, the harness, the roof over our heads. I think God wants that gratitude from us.

"So how can He teach us better, besides allowing fiery trials, in this case, literally, into our lives?"

Heads nodded, faces contorted in all sorts of ways to keep emotion from rising to the surface.

"Yes, it was hard sometimes. The hardest by far was when our Sarah was burned. I couldn't forgive then. I couldn't forgive the arsonist. I railed against God. I wanted revenge, any form of torture. I wanted the arsonist to experience debridement, just once. Let him feel what Sarah had endured."

Clearly, Davey had the attention of the liberals. Now he was talking. Sarah was burned so this preeminent minister would stand in the courtroom, his voice carrying well in the great room. What a grand testimony he would have! Their moment of glory was at hand.

"I hardly slept one night," David continued. "Like Jacob, I wrestled with the angel of God. I knew what was right, but just this once, I wanted to be exempt from doing the right thing.

"Toward morning, though, I knew I had to let go. I had to let go of all those thoughts of revenge, of justification and hatred. 'Vengeance will be mine, saith the Lord.' Forgiveness is the only way to peace. The only way.

"Now, before you decide to speak against me, let me finish. The young man who drove Harold Walters to some of the farms where he lit the fires came to visit us. He's sorry for what he did. He wants our forgiveness. He did not start the fires, just drove the car."

"He'll get jail time anyway," Melvin barked.

"Let me finish. He said this Harold Walters held a personal grudge against the Widow Lydia's husband, Aaron. They had some business dealings in the past, not very honest ones, I presume.

"Aaron is dead, may he rest in peace, and it would not be uplifting to speak of his faults now.

But, in a sense, because of the misdeeds of one our brethren, we suffered. In a sense, it was brought on our own heads."

"That's ridiculous!"

The words were harsh, cutting, spoken forcefully by a young man in a striped shirt.

Slowly, one by one, in ripples, heads turned from side to side.

"Yes, I know. It might sound ridiculous, but I'm afraid it's true," David continued. "One bit of spoiled dough will ruin the whole loaf. If we want to live righteously, separating ourselves from the world, then we have a responsibility to live up to what we profess. God sees this long before we do and sends chastening. He *schlakes* (punishes) us, like naughty children.

"After children are chastened, don't they come climb up on our laps and lay their sweet heads on our chests? And we cuddle them, our love for them multiplying and theirs for us. Same with God. We are His children. We have been chastened, and this *schtrofe* (punishment) we will accept, take it upon ourselves. Mind you, the fruits of it will follow. Already it is visible."

Heads nodded, eyes misted, glasses were removed, cleaned. Even the young men understood perfectly the picture of a young child who was punished. They fully accepted the theory, and their heads bowed before the wisdom of David Beiler.

"What about Sarah?"

Like the last sputter from a dying engine, Lloyd Fisher had to throw one more barb.

"Sarah was my Gethsemane, my finish, so to speak. But in ways that are of a personal nature, her outward suffering brought an inward acceptance of God's will for her. I can't call her injuries wrong."

Everyone knew what he was talking about. Eyes twinkled, knowing looks were exchanged.

She'd be published—her engagement officially announced—after communion. That Lee Glick was really something. Good for Sarah.

So Dan Dienner's eyebrows leveled off and smoothed out. The young men acknowledged their leader's wisdom and gave themselves up to it. And Melvin stuck his lawyer's book in his jacket pocket, where it bulged uncomfortably and made him feel lopsided the remainder of the evening.

Chapter 16

As the summer drew to a close, the cicadas and crickets set up their symphony outside Sarah's bedroom window. A breeze billowed the sheer panels at her windows, and she flung her arms above her head and clasped her hands, a sigh of happiness and contentment escaping her lips.

A farmer's wife! Why had she never imagined it? It was the fulfillment of a dream she was never aware of, until it turned into reality.

Beside her, Priscilla was reading a book by the light of an LED battery lamp.

"Pinch me, Priscilla, to make sure I'm real," Sarah said laughing.

"Gladly."

Reaching over, she pinched Sarah's arm between her thumb and forefinger, producing an excruciatingly painful sensation worse than a bee sting.

"Ow!" Sarah yelped, leaping off the bed. "Ow! I didn't say you had to pinch that hard."

Laughing out loud, Priscilla lowered her book, her face lifted to the ceiling, her eyes squeezed shut in laughter.

"It's not funny."

"Uh . . . oh my! Shoo!" Priscilla gasped.

Suddenly, she caught sight of Sarah's shoulder. Her laughter ended abruptly.

"Sarah," she whispered, horrified.

"What?"

"Your shoulder."

Turning her head to the right, Sarah lowered her eyes, then looked at Priscilla, a sad question in her eyes.

"Is it so bad?"

Shaken, Priscilla nodded.

"I just never realized, I guess. My goodness,

Sarah. In this glaring light, it doesn't look very good."

"I know. And I'm getting married. It scares me."

"Does Lee know?"

"I told him. But still. I mean, there's no guarantee he won't be repelled. Priscilla, what should I do? Really?"

"Well, what does he say?"

"He says the scars are beautiful. They remind him of God's answer to his prayers, His will to blend our life into one. After Matthew, he means."

Priscilla's eyes turned soft and liquid.

"Aw. He's so sweet. He's a special guy, Sarah. You're blessed."

"I am. This is first time in my life I can understand that overused word—awesome. Lee is truly awesome."

"Tell me, was Matthew easy to forget?"

"I couldn't let go of him, until I was burned."

"I know."

Sarah lay down on the bed again, and a comfortable silence followed. Finally Priscilla crawled off Sarah's bed, said good night, and padded to her room. Sarah heard her turn off the lamp and sigh. She could soon tell her sister was fast asleep.

Sarah turned on her side, facing the window, thankful for the cool breezes. She listened to the clamorous sounds of summer's insects and wondered at the thought of her upcoming wedding.

They'd chosen December 6, a Thursday. It was smack dab in the middle of the Lancaster County wedding season.

That was fine with Sarah. Everything else in her life would be traditional, being a farmer's wife, living with a relative at the "other end." *S'ana ent.* It was a vague description of a double house, with an addition—the "other end"—built for parents or sisters or brothers on the home place, the family co-existing in peaceful harmony as much as they were able.

Would she always get along with Anna? Already, Sarah looked forward to having coffee with her every morning. Anna was the funniest person she knew. Her sense of humor was outrageous but so deliciously spirit lifting, so light and sweet to the senses, like cotton candy.

With Ben's death, that had changed a bit. Now her grief was a gray shroud that hung about her much of the time, an aura of unbelievable sadness, though her humor still broke through once in awhile. She had loved her husband with a love that was true and strong, in spite of the many ways he exasperated her.

Sarah smiled to herself, picturing Anna canning peaches with the oversized stainless steel bowl balanced precariously on her short lap while she related the story of the calf chasing incident.

In spite of herself, Sarah's shoulders shook, remembering Anna's outrage.

"There I was, big as a barrel, my arms waving, my legs pumping, running as fast as I could to keep that calf out of the peas and onions. What does that Ben do but start waving his pitchfork in the wrong direction, sending the calf straight through the garden, crossways, while he continued waving that stupid fork! Dense!"

That was the typical Anna, who found the humor in almost any situation. Now though, her sunny disposition had begun to fail her as the reality of her situation sank in. She spent whole afternoons lying listlessly on the recliner, getting up only to care for her "littles"—changing a diaper, getting a drink. The immaculate house became cluttered. Little fingerprints were etched on the windows, and dishes lay unwashed on the countertop. Even the laundry piled up, and when she did wash, it stayed on the line till supper-time, as she lacked the energy to bring it in.

Lee's blue eyes became pools of worry about his sister. His mother assured him this was common. She'd seen it before, and they'd just have to do things for her for a while.

True to her word, Rachel came and scrubbed and swept and polished. She stripped the beds and hung clean sheets on the line. She got down on her hands and knees and flipped the switch on the gas refrigerator, turning it to "defrost," then heaved herself back up and proceeded to empty it of its contents.

She cleaned the shelves, the drawers, and the freezer. She made chocolate chip cookies for Lee and graham cracker fluff for Anna. She put little Tom Sturgis pretzels in a huge bowl, dribbled olive oil and a blend of cheddar cheese powder, sour cream and onion powder, and ranch dressing mix all over them. She stirred and mixed and mixed and then ate them, one by one, all afternoon.

She melted white American cheese in milk and butter and made *smear* cheese as a dip for the seasoned pretzels. She made gallons of *vissa tae* (meadow tea) and set it in the spotless refrigerator. Then she kissed Anna's cheek, hugged her and patted her, and said, "My little girl, you'll be fine."

Then off she went, perched all alone on one side of the spring wagon, for all the world like a plump little badger, leaning forward and slapping her slow horse with the reins. She had to get home. She had work to do.

Sarah lay in her bed and thought she could always love Lee's mother. Then she couldn't help comparing her to Hannah with her slovenly sweater, her plodding pace, and the grayish whites on her wash line. Oh, Hannah's heart was in the right place, and her talents were distributed differently, but . . . well, there was much to think about.

Matthew and Hannah.

It was interesting, the way she thought her good-looking son incapable of making one misstep. Pure unconditional love. Sarah couldn't say if that was right or wrong, but ninety-nine percent of the time, Matthew would likely expect that same kind of unvarnished idolatry from his wife. What if he didn't receive it?

Sarah shook her head, remembered his pouting and the stone cold silences that froze her soul, her will, her very being. She had not loved him or approved of him, somehow, somewhere along the line. And yet, if he had remained Amish and married her, could she have had a good life? Some questions are never answered.

Would she ever feel the same kind of love for Lee that she had experienced as a young girl with Matthew? The love for Lee was different. It was slow and steady, comfortable and easy. There were no doubts or heart thumping moments of passion or drama. Within Lee's arms, she was safe, secure, loved, accepted.

Could she include her scars? As a young, innocent bride, would she revolt him? Already, she knew deep in her heart that the answer was no. Lee loved her with a pure and Godly love, and with this assurance, she dropped off to a restful slumber, as the cicadas outside her window kept up their frenzied calls.

The next morning, Mam was in a dither, a fine one. Lizzie Zook's store had only one bolt of the blue crepe fabric they needed for the wedding. They had sent for two more bolts, and it was positively not the same color. Even the shine was different.

Mam hired a driver, fabric sample in hand, and went to Belmont Fabrics. She came home so frustrated she was almost crying and said they might have to start all over again. She could not match Sarah's dress.

"We can't do that, Mam. My wedding dress is finished, and I love it. I found exactly the shade of cornflower blue I want. I'm not going to change it."

Mam tried to put all her good virtues to use. She closed her mouth and attempted serenity, but her eyebrows shot straight up, and she said tightly, "Sarah, now listen to me. You have to have the same color for the other girls!"

"Why?"

"Well, because!" Mam sputtered.

And so they were off to Georgetown, to Fisher's Fabrics and Housewares. They paid the driver an exorbitant fee, as he charged for waiting time, but Mam emerged triumphant, carrying two bolts of the exact shade, texture, and quality she wanted. Along with the perfect blue fabric, she found the black she needed as well.

The white organdy capes and aprons had been sewn a few weeks prior, pressed to perfection, and hung in Mam's downstairs closet. One for

Sarah, one for Priscilla, and one for Rose, who would also be part of the bridal party.

Normally, Rose's mother would have sewn Rose's dress, but Mam offered, knowing she was *fit* (capable). Rose's mother was only too happy to allow Malinda that chore.

They painted the kitchen, the downstairs bathroom, and Levi's room, leaving Levi rocking all alone on the wooden porch swing, dragging his feet across the painted floor, singing dolefully under his breath.

They wouldn't let him paint. He couldn't drive the mules. He felt as if there was not one thing he could do to help with the wedding. He was hungry for shoofly, but no one baked that or whoopie pies or chocolate chip cookies anymore.

Every day they had *kalte sup* for supper, which he refused. He had to eat Corn Flakes or Wheaties, and even if he sliced a banana into his cereal, it hardly filled him up. He sneaked potato chips or Ritz crackers into his bed, but they left a lot of crumbs that made him itchy during the night when he was so tired. Then he had to get out of bed, brush the crumbs off the sheet, and then climb back into bed and settle himself, which was a bit of a chore.

He was hungry for a hot dog with onions and pickles and cheese and ketchup. He lifted his head and listened at the window, wondering if Mam was happy enough to ask her for a "doggie."

Singing at the sewing machine usually rated pretty high, like two cookies or cheese and pretzels, sometimes even a grilled cheese sandwich.

Cleaning windows on a cold day without singing rated only an apple, but maybe he would get some peanut butter, if he was lucky.

Painting meant a pretty slim chance of acquiring anything at all, by the sound of the clipped sentences coming through the kitchen window.

He sighed and flapped a hand in front of his face to cool himself. Maybe he'd be allowed some chocolate milk, if he made it and didn't ask Sarah to do it.

Rising slowly, he lumbered across the porch, letting himself in through the kitchen door.

"Watch it! Watch it!"

Immediately, Mam swooped over, stopping him in his tracks. "Don't step on that pan of paint."

Levi wrinkled his nose, looked dolefully at Mam, and then turned to see what Sarah was doing.

"We're almost finished, Levi. Why don't you go out and sit on the porch a while longer?"

"I'm hungry."

"It's almost suppertime."

"Are we having *kalte sup*?"

"Probably."

"I want a hot dog."

"Wait till supper."

Levi shuffled back out to the porch obediently, flopped on the porch swing, and resumed his mournful singing. His stomach was growling, tumbling about with nothing in it, and he had no hope of anything to eat till suppertime.

A cloud of dust on the horizon slowly came into focus revealing a line of mules pulling a wagon. The steel wheels rattled across the handmade wooden bridge that spanned the small creek by the orchard. It was dried up in late summer, becoming an unhandy little ditch that was no good at all. Levi knew just how the dry creek felt.

Suzie sat on the hay wagon, her skin tanned a dark brown, her hair curling about her face like Sarah's. Her feet were bare and browned by the sun, her pale green dress soiled, one sleeve ripped up the side, exposing her white upper arm. Catching sight of Levi, she waved.

Levi waved back excitedly, cheered by the sight of his youngest sister.

The mules' harnesses flapped, and the chains on the traces jingled. The hoof beats were muffled on the gravel, as the mules' ears flopped up and down, their heads bobbing in time to their foot-steps.

Dat stood on the front of the wagon, his darkened old straw hat pulled low over his fore-head to keep from blowing off in the hot, dusty air.

"Levi!" Dat called happily.

"Hey, Davey!" Levi shouted, sliding off the swing to stand on his bare feet, waving both hands, his broad face wreathed in a great smile.

Dat hauled back on the reins, stopping the team of mules.

"Levi, tell Mam we want ice cream and hot dogs for an early snack. Elam and Hannah want us to come down for a late evening cookout."

Beside himself with joy, Levi moved towards the door at a rapid pace. Dat clucked to the mules, and they continued on their way.

Levi told Mam he could chop onions, but then his burning eyes watered so profusely that the streams turned into genuine tears. Then, because he was so terribly hungry, he began sobbing in earnest, howling and crying and saying it wasn't right that no one allowed him something to eat when he was hungry.

Sarah brushed the last of the paint onto the wall beside the door to Levi's room, hid her smile, and brought him a package of dried apricots from the pantry.

Levi roared with indignation.

"Sarah! Now you know I don't eat dried apricots! They look like earlobes. They even feel like the bottom of my ears!"

Sarah laughed and laughed. She hugged Levi with both arms and smeared paint on his best everyday shirt, but he smiled and was glad for

Sarah's hug. She brought him a Nutty Bar. Oh, how he loved those Little Debbies from the store!

"Don't tell Mam," Sarah whispered. Levi bowed his head humbly, put his hands under the table, and said, "*Denke, Goot Man, fa my Nutty Bar.*"

Sarah told Mam that Levi was getting lost in the shuffle, getting ready for this wedding, but Mam was so hot and so tired, she gave Sarah a look of impatience and told her to go clean her brushes. Why in the world were Elam and Hannah having a cookout on a Wednesday evening when it was ninety degrees, she wondered. And if that Matthew was going to try and worm his way in here again, why, she had a notion to shun him good and proper.

Sarah laughed so hard she had to sit down. She wiped the sweat from her forehead, looked at Mam, and shook her head. "Are you going to be so . . . well, dumb, from here on?" she asked.

"Go clean your brushes, Sarah," Mam said, but there was a smile twitching at the corners of her mouth.

Mam was still a bit abrasive on the walk to Elam's, saying she didn't know why they wouldn't trim those maple trees. They looked so *schloppich aufangs* (sloppy now).

Dat cast a pitying glance in her direction and caught Sarah's eye. They both looked in opposite directions, their mouths twitching. Planning a wedding was taking its toll on Mam's good nature.

Hannah met them at the door, wearing a soiled purple dress. The sleeves had been whacked off too far above the elbow, revealing pearly white forearms with distinct tan lines below the sleeves. It was just about the most unattractive thing Sarah had seen in a long time. She decided it was just like Hannah to cut the sleeves without measuring, creating results that were less than appropriate. But for her, it was alright, good enough.

When Matthew entered, Sarah caught the scent of his overpriced men's cologne before she actually saw him.

He was dressed in a thin white shirt and spotless clean jeans. He was wearing a pair of sandals with his short hair crisp and wet. Sarah had to look elsewhere, the look in his eyes a remembered temptation.

"Good evening, folks!"

His voice was hearty, confident, full of energy. In spite of herself, Sarah's knees turned weaker as she looked at him.

"Ready to start the grill?"

Hannah immediately lowered her head, rambled on about getting the steaks out of the "stuff," and yanked open the refrigerator door, dumping a square Tupperware container of applesauce all over the floor. Putting both hands to her cheeks, she screeched loud and long about the applesauce, then hastily got down to wipe up the mess. Sarah saw that her dress was so old and faded that where the pleats pulled apart in the back, the dress was two completely different colors.

"What did you marinate them in, Mother?" Matthew asked.

Cool and suave, such a man of the world, Sarah observed.

"Well, Matthew, you said French dressing, didn't you?" she asked over her shoulder, straightening and going to rinse the cloth under the faucet.

Sighing in exasperation, Matthew rolled his eyes, shook his head, and said, "Italian, Mother," with practiced patience.

"Well. I don't have any. We don't eat it. It's not good," Hannah said simply.

"Whatever. We're not going to eat these steaks if you have them in French dressing."

"*Ach* now."

But that was the end of the discussion. There were no steaks.

Matthew grilled hot dogs—they'd all eaten one an hour before—but no one said anything. Hannah's scalloped potatoes were amazing, as always, and her green beans laced deliciously with bacon and cheese.

Levi was in his glory. A Nutty Bar and two hot dogs in one evening was more happiness than he could contain. He became so jovial that he turned into the life of the party.

Matthew genuinely enjoyed Levi's sense of humor and laughed uproariously when Levi described the evening snacks that he hid away from Mam.

Sarah sat in a patio chair under the shade of the huge maple trees and watched Matthew's enjoyment of Levi. She thought maybe his self-righteousness was already diminishing. He seemed so much more like the Matthew of old, joking, comfortable, at home here on the farm with his parents.

Elam, as usual, had very little to say. He was quiet, a slow smile spreading across his weather-beaten face and a slight twinkle in his dark eyes. His hand was slow to pass the salt or the ketchup, but he was always friendly.

Sarah thought Elam had to be the most mild-mannered man she had ever encountered. He was completely overridden by his condescending wife but was happy to let her be that way.

Elam knew there was nothing he could do to change the situation with Matthew, so he made peace with co-existence. Matthew lived in the farmhouse with them, doing as he pleased. It made life easier to just go along with it.

They drank cold grape juice and ate Moose Tracks ice cream as the sun settled below the horizon and the heat of the day faded with the setting sun. Robins chirped, calling their children to bed and hopping about on the lawn before flying into the fluttering leaves of the maple tree.

Elam's collie, Lassie, romped on the gravel driveway with Suzie. Sarah sipped her juice, her eyes on Matthew. When his eyes met hers, she looked away hurriedly.

As twilight fell softly, the conversation turned to the two men who were responsible for the barn fires. Elam said, in his slow, wise manner, that the absence of the Amish in the courtroom wasn't going to make much difference, that the Walters man's goose was pretty much cooked either way.

Dat observed Elam, a slow smile of under-standing spreading across his face. He knew Elam well, had lived beside him most of his life, and understood his pureness of heart. There was no hidden animosity, no hatred. He was only stating a fact. He'd forgive the arsonist his mischief, acknowledge the wrong-doing of Aaron, accept events as the days brought them.

Elam watched his wife shoveling ice cream into her mouth and wondered why she didn't get a headache, eating it that fast. He smiled at her and thought she still was the amazing young woman he'd married. He had a heart of gold.

He never could figure out what had gone wrong that Matthew didn't want to be Amish, but he guessed that was his son's business, and none of his own. Matthew was an adult now.

Tomorrow was another day, another chance to plant his late rye seed, milk his cows, and spray the weeds along the fence. He really should get to trimming those maple trees, they looked so *schloppich aufangs.*

Then Matthew got up, stretched, and asked Sarah if she wanted to go for a walk for old times' sake. Maybe they could go visit the Widow Lydia and see if Melvin was there. Elam watched Sarah's face and thought of Daniel and the lion's den. She'd need the courage of Daniel, that was one thing sure. Hannah choked on her ice cream, and Malinda looked as if a thunderstorm had settled over her head.

Davey caught Elam's eye, calm, unperturbed, trusting. It was all that was necessary.

Chapter 17

The twilight turned slowly into a warm summer night as Matthew walked beside Sarah.

He turned to her and said, "Let's not visit Lydia." His voice was husky, breathless. Sarah stopped and looked at him.

"Where do you want to go?"

"Anywhere we can be alone."

"Matthew, listen. I am going to be married to Lee. In two and a half months. I am not going for a walk with you if you are . . ."

Embarrassed, her voice trailed off.

"I just need advice, Sarah. You were always a

true friend. How should I go about winning Rose?"

Taking a deep breath, Sarah looked into Matthew's eyes, those black pools she had gazed into so many times before, when she was always seeking, hoping, wondering. Now here she stood, back to square one, back to the beginning when he had chosen to ask Rose for his first date.

This time, however, there was a difference. Matthew's dark eyes did nothing for her. Instead, she compared them to Lee's blue ones and the purity of the love she found in them. He gave her strength, happiness, an objective for life.

Suddenly she blurted out, "You really want to know?"

"Yes, I do."

"Grow up."

Clearly startled, Matthew drew back and stopped walking. They were in the field lane, between fields of freshly mown alfalfa and waving corn. The dust under their feet, like sifted flour, rose up with every footstep, leaving soft puffs.

"What do you mean by that?"

"Exactly what I said."

"Boy, you're being mean to me, Sarah. Just because you're going to marry someone else doesn't mean you can get all high and mighty on me now."

"Rose is my friend. Or was. I seldom see her now, since I'm no longer at market. Lee and I rarely go to the supper crowd. I taught school, you know, until the accident—when I was burned. I planned to teach again, but Lee asked me to marry him, and I accepted. I feel bad for Rosanna, my eighth-grade girl last year. We had been looking forward to teaching together.

"But that's not really answering your question. I think you could win Rose if you chose to be Amish, and if you had a steady, full-time job, and made a commitment to stay at that job for at least a year."

"You think I'm lazy, don't you?"

"No. Yes."

"What does that mean?"

"Yes."

"Sarah, I'm not. I'm just not interested in farming. It's an endless and repetitive thing, over and over and over. My back isn't good enough to be a roofer, and framing houses is dangerous work. I could landscape, start my own business, but it's too much like farming. I don't have any money saved up either."

Sarah nodded.

"You could always work at McDonald's, flipping burgers, making fries. You always enjoyed cooking. I remember the first barn raising, that whole roaster of French toast you made. It was delicious."

"I bandaged your hand that day." Matthew shook his head ruefully. "I should have taken you when I had the chance."

Sarah saw her life with Matthew. It appeared before her like an empty ship, bobbing on uncontrolled waters. It was impossible to guide and had no destination, no rudder to control it, no way of predicting if it would reach a harbor.

Here was Matthew, twenty-three years old, no job, no money, no goal, no roots. The one single thing in life that he was concerned about was himself. Doing anything he did not want to do was quite out of the question. Every excuse he uttered was rife with the old unwillingness to bend his back and perform the duties expected of him, the one true source of every man's happiness.

At the end of the day, a man or woman who had worked, performing physical labor of some kind, was tired, content. The sun had risen and shone on their labors. When it set, they rested and thanked God for their sound bodies and their blessings.

Paychecks at the end of the week were distributed, used for mortgage payments, utilities, food, clothes, and if there was anything left over, small luxuries. For almost every family, there were sacrifices to make, giving up things they could not afford, learning to live frugally, the sacrifices no big thing.

Matthew had no paycheck. Where was his money coming from? Sarah knew Hannah would try and keep Matthew with them, eagerly handing him cash whenever he required it. Her love for him provided the monetary funds, and what did she receive in return? No respect, none of her feelings taken into consideration. Poor, misguided Hannah.

Without a doubt, she felt superior to Elam. He was too quiet, didn't do his *dale* (share). Why would he even try when he knew any attempt at reining in Matthew would be met by the unyielding brick wall named Hannah?

So they existed peacefully together, but so far out of God's order. They lacked that priceless, perfectly structured family with God at the head, then Elam, and then Hannah in her place below them, the white covering on her head an outward symbol of subjection to God and her husband.

Brought back to earth by the cloying scent of Matthew's extravagant cologne, Sarah shifted her weight on first one foot, then the other, her hands clasped firmly in front of her.

Softly, Matthew spoke again.

"Aren't you going to answer?"

"There wasn't a question."

"No, I guess not."

Matthew gazed out across the dry fields of Lancaster County, his expression unreadable. Sarah looked at him, this man handsome enough to be a model in a worldly fashion magazine, and felt the familiar tug at her heart.

"I should never have broken up with you."

A sadness seemed to erase the evening's light, a melancholy fog settling over them, wrapping them both in the stillness of a mournful remembering.

"But you did."

Suddenly, Matthew grasped Sarah's shoulders, his breath coming thick and fast.

"Sarah, you're just marrying Lee to forget me. It's not going to work. After you're married, you'll wake up and discover you don't even like him. Your future will look long and unhappy, and it will be too late. You know you love me."

Shrugging her shoulders, she stepped away from him.

"Matthew, listen. I love Lee Glick, not you. I told you that before, but you're not giving it up. You don't want me. I am like the carrot dangling from a stick in front of the proverbial donkey. The only reason you think you love me now is because you can't have me. I think there's another old story about the fox that leaped endlessly after a cluster of delicious-looking grapes. After he finally did manage to get them, they were sour, and he spat them out and knew he'd wasted his time for nothing."

"Sarah, stop comparing yourself to carrots and grapes."

"A carrot. Not carrots."

They laughed together, their sense of humor fine-tuned over the years.

It was dark now, their closeness turning into an intimacy. How many evenings had they shared, just like this?

"Sarah, let's sit down, shall we?" Matthew's voice was husky with feeling. "I want to tell you a few things before you marry Lee, okay?"

Realizing the slippery slope she would be descending, Sarah found a soft clump of grass a safe distance away from him. Matthew folded himself close to her. She shrank away from him and the warm, beguiling sensation of nearness.

"I always liked you. Even in ninth grade, I liked you, the way a fourteen-year-old boy does. It was my mother's fault that I asked Rose Zook that first time. She had a fit about what a nice girl Rose was. Then Rose broke up with me, but by then I couldn't have you. It was Mother's fault. She messed up my life, not me.

"And I'll tell you another thing. It's my father's fault that I don't have a job. Everything I did at home was wrong. I could never please him. Mother used to pity me so much."

His martyrdom wrapped securely around him, he rambled on, but Sarah was not listening. She was thinking of Lee, her beloved man. Yes, man. He was a man, so grown up, always thinking of Anna and her "littles," of Omar and the Widow Lydia's plight. He was so busy caring, nurturing, loving others, she doubted whether he ever had a minute to think of himself. And if he did, she thought—oh, if he did!—he would fill that time loving her.

She was the blessed recipient of the love of a man that was so fine and so good, she was sure she did not deserve him, not even for a minute. All his life, Lee would work, till the soil the way his brother-in-law had. They would prosper, endure life's trials, rejoice in the blessings, working side by side, the way their Swiss ancestors had. And then their children after them, and their children after them, on and on, they would hand down the treasured tradition of hard work and love of the land, raising generations in the same order.

Silently, humbly, Sarah bowed her head with this knowledge. She was blessed among women, like Elizabeth and Mary and many other women who came after them. God had granted her the wisdom to make a difference. Blindly, He could have allowed her to marry Matthew.

Why hadn't He? She supposed God was a mystery, and she simply had to hold the goodness of Him to her heart. That was just the way it was.

She sighed.

"Matthew, I don't think it's fair to blame your parents. They did the best they could."

"Who then?"

Should she tell him? Her heart thudding, she said, "Try blaming yourself, Matthew."

"Myself?"

He was completely bewildered, at a loss.

"You make your own choices, Matthew. You are an adult now. You chose to leave the Amish way of life. You chose Rose. You chose Hephzibah. You chose Haiti. You did. Not your parents."

"But maybe I would have chosen differently, if they had acted differently. Parents are a huge influence on their children's lives."

There was nothing to say to this. The futility of her words, the sheer helplessness of them, struck Sarah as being so sad she could not bear it.

Matthew was comfortably held captive in the grandiose imagining of his own martyred state. He was innocent of any wrongdoing, firmly entrenched in this misguided belief.

Born again, in his own eyes, he was oblivious to the fact that he was reveling in life's greatest trap—that of laying blame on others and being comfortable with it.

By your fruits, ye shall know them, Sarah thought. Matthew would learn and would mature. She just wouldn't be there to take the punches in the process.

Inevitably, someone like Matthew would be sent headlong into fiery trials but delivered by God's hand, so that when he was old, he would be a vessel of God's handiwork.

But Sarah was free. Matthew was God's job, not hers.

They parted as friends. This was made possible only by Sarah's ability to stay quiet and allow

Matthew his rants of injustice. He whined about the unfairness of life, and his words fell like rain around them. The sentences started like a soft summer mist, then turned to droplets that came down in earnest, soaking Sarah, leaving her exposed to something she wanted to avoid, but couldn't. She had to give him this evening to unburden himself, she felt. It was all she had to offer.

Bright and early the next morning, Sarah was still enjoying her final cup of coffee. The breakfast table was laden with sticky syrup-covered plates, bits of pancake, and a leftover fried egg congealed on a greasy plate. As Levi was swallowing his vitamins and blood pressure medicine, Hannah burst through the door without knocking, threw herself on a chair, and told Mam a cup of coffee would be *hesslich goot* (awfully good).

Her hair had been freshly plastered to her head, dragged back with a wet, fine-toothed comb. Her round face shone from a washing with the soap she kept at her *vesh bengli* (washbowl).

She eyed the remaining fried egg and cold pancakes and looked at Mam, who nodded and pointed. They knew each other so well, no words were needed.

"*Ach* Malinda, I haven't eaten yet. Matthew often cooks breakfast, but he didn't get in till so late. Then he was restless, walking around, going to get pills. I guess he had a headache."

She turned towards Sarah.

"What happened last night?"

Ducking her head and squeezing the syrup bottle as if her life depended on it, Hannah avoided meeting Sarah's eyes.

Mam choked on a hot mouthful of coffee, got up, and coughed over the sink, wheezing and hacking.

"Malinda, *geb dich an acht* (be careful)," Levi said gravely.

Mam straightened, a hand fluttering to her chest, and smiled. She said she got some hot coffee in her Sunday throat, the way she always said.

"Uh, not much," Sarah answered Hannah.

"Did you talk?"

Hannah inserted a huge forkful of pancake and egg into her mouth. Syrup dripped on her dress but went unnoticed. Sarah watched the gob of stickiness elongate, then drop onto her stomach, where it soaked into the gray fabric.

"Um, yes. Yes, we talked."

"Did he say what's on his mind?"

"Yes."

"So. What's happening then?"

Anger lurched through Sarah. The nerve of her! Assuming that the minute her Matthew wanted her, Sarah would literally leave Lee at the altar and come racing back to him. Knowing she would cause an uncomfortable situation, as she had done before, Sarah opted to keep the fiery retort to herself.

"Probably not much."

"But Sarah, he'd go Amish for you! He said he would!"

Hannah's voice was plaintive, whining, begging.

"Hannah, I am engaged to Lee. He is the one I love. I would never leave him."

What she wanted to say and what actually came out of her mouth were two completely different things, and she spoke in a way that was entirely distinct from the way she felt.

What she wanted to do was to tell Hannah to heave herself off down the road with that syrup all over herself. She would tell her to go let her husband raise that spoiled son of hers (or at least help), and if she had an ounce of insight, she'd remember every painful day Sarah lived through with Matthew's rejection of her.

Delighted with Sarah's deliberate stand, Malinda's face shone with the sheer relief that flooded through her. Immediately, her hospitality increased fourfold. She hovered over her neighbor with the coffee pot and brought the leftover bacon she had put back to use in a salad, placing it at her elbow.

She touched Hannah's shoulder and said, "Hannah, let me make you some toast. I'll heat up these pancakes. You want a few more eggs? It won't take long to fry up a couple."

Levi saw his opportunity and seized it.

"Malinda, if you're going to make more eggs, I could use another one."

Hannah's defeat was not accepted or acknowledged, the grumpiness in her voice holding it at bay.

"I don't know why you let Levi call you Malinda. He should know enough to call you Mam."

She swallowed a mouthful of scalding coffee, grimaced, shook her head, and said now her taste buds were cooked for the day.

"I'm sorry, Hannah," Mam trilled, whirling to the refrigerator, lifting a carton of eggs, and using her foot to close the door behind her. She had basically done a pirouette, Sarah observed, hiding a smile.

Well, that was alright. Let her long-suffering mother enjoy that flashy little dance to close the refrigerator door. Sarah had put her parents through enough as it was. Let her whirl all over the kitchen, her arms held high, her skirts billowing around her, her face lifted in praise to the Creator. She deserved to let her spirits soar.

At that moment, Sarah fully understood the depth of her love for her mother.

Hannah cleaned up her plate, swabbing viciously at the orange yolk with the well-buttered edge of her toast, and shook her head mournfully about Matthew's future.

"What is he supposed to do now, Sarah?"

"I'm sure there are many, many young girls who would be more than pleased to have him. Rose is dating him now, sort of. Maybe they'll get serious, and he'll return for her."

Eyeing the syrup on her dress, which had been joined with egg yolk, Hannah heaved herself from the chair and went to the sink. She yanked a dish rag from the drawer, wet it, and began to steadily clean up the remains of her breakfast.

"But you don't know how it's going with those two. Just like the last time. She's all giddy and happy to begin with, but then, sure enough, something turns her off, and she pouts. Matthew said they ate at the Olive Garden, and it cost them sixty dollars! I'm suspicious that they ordered an alcoholic drink. You know they serve them there. Amish people shouldn't even go in there.

"Well, I guess Matthew would be alright, he's not Amish, but still. Matthew says it's a good place to eat. I said I like McDonald's or Wendy's. It's good food and cheaper. Sixty dollars! Imagine! *Unfashtendich* (nonsense).

"Anyway, he said they were eating, and Rose didn't talk, just turned her head to the side and pouted. Now he's afraid to ask her out to dinner. Matthew says if you're English and classy, you say dinner for supper, and dinner is lunch. I guess breakfast is still breakfast, or what does it mean when they say sunrise service? Maybe that's breakfast."

Malinda coughed, sputtered. She could not meet Sarah's eyes, or they'd each lose their composure.

Innocently, Hannah lowered her eyebrows.

"What is a sunrise service if it isn't breakfast?"

Sarah told her it was an early morning Easter service. Mam's back was conveniently turned.

"Oh, is that so? Well, now that would be touching, *gel* (right)?"

Mam nodded as she turned, and Sarah said, yes, it would. Thankfully, Hannah dropped the subject.

"Well, then, I guess if you're going to marry Lee, you're going to marry Lee. I just have to give up. But *ach my oh*, it would certainly have been nice to see you two together. I think you would have been good with Matthew."

"We could have been, perhaps, Hannah."

When her chin wobbled and fat tears welled up in her eyes, Mam patted her friend's shoulder and asked if she wanted to make the scalloped potatoes for the supper at Sarah's wedding. That seemed to placate Hannah entirely, although she said sadly, "I should be sitting right up there with you, Malinda, side by side, as the parents. And there I'll be making scalloped potatoes with the rest of the church women."

She went on to say how long and hot the day stretched before her, with all the corn she had to do. The whole patch had ripened over the weekend, and here it was Thursday morning and not an ear pulled.

Sighing, she said she'd likely have to cream every ear. Dragging those big yellow ears of corn across the creamer gave her a crick in her neck and made her shoulder blades hurt.

Mam, in her newfound happiness, immediately offered her assistance, along with that of the girls. Levi could help shuck. He loved to sit beneath a tree and shuck sweet corn. All he needed was a brush, a paring knife, and two containers—one for the clean ears and one for the husks.

Hannah was so overwhelmed with gratitude that she told Mam if they helped her, she'd donate all the corn for the wedding. They were planning on having peas for the vegetable, but Mam told Hannah that would be just fine, they'd have corn for supper.

So Hannah let herself out the door, casting a worshipful glance at Mam. They smiled, and then Priscilla told Mam she wasn't going down to Elam's if Matthew was there. Mam raised her eyebrows in question, and Sarah stopped clearing the table, listening.

"Why ever not?" Mam asked.

"Mam, he wrote me a letter! He asked me for a date! I'm only seventeen. Is he crazy?"

Sarah stood stock still, chewing her thumbnail. He was desperate, this was very clear. Is that all his passionate pleas had been? A desperation?

Mam gasped. Suzie looked up and said dryly that Matthew was English. Did she want English?

Sarah washed dishes, tight-lipped now, angry thoughts swirling about her head. It was time she spent a weekend with Lee and got away from the upheaval that Matthew always created.

Saying nothing, she left the kitchen, walked across the lawn to the phone shanty, and dialed Anna's number. She left a message, asking Anna to call if she needed help with corn or tomatoes.

That was how Mam and Suzie and Levi found themselves at Elam's, knee deep in corn. Hannah was eternally grateful for their help, and Mam smiled and joked and laughed, that was how light her heart was. She lifted heavy bowls piled high with golden ears of corn, creamed them endlessly, and retained her exuberant spirits.

Hadn't she heard from her daughter's own mouth the stand she had firmly taken, and the right one, no doubt?

Yes, there was a *saya in die uf gevva heit* (blessing in sacrifice). This Malinda firmly believed, as her mother had before her. In matters of the heart, this was best, especially after Sarah's burning and the pain afterward.

Over at Anna's, Sarah and Priscilla picked two wheelbarrow loads and one garden cart full of corn. They shucked it, cooked it in the outdoor cooker, cooled it in huge plastic totes, and cut it off the cob for chicken corn soup. Anna buttered, salted, and ate so many ears of corn that Priscilla said it had to be ten. Or at least nine.

When Lee put the team of Belgians in the barn and came in for lunch, Sarah's heart became all fluttery, followed by a rush of genuine love. There was a sense of caring, a gratitude even, that proved to her, without a trace of uncertainty, that Lee was the real love of her life.

Chapter 18

Amish weddings are usually held after the fall communion services, sometimes the last week in October, but mostly in November and December. However, when a widow remarries, the service can be held at any time that is convenient, but preferably not in the hot summer months, because of the possibility of food spoilage.

Secrets are highly esteemed where second marriages are concerned, so in Lydia's typically quiet way, the announcement of the upcoming wedding for her and Melvin was a genuine surprise for many. Sarah figured it would be in the fall, but a September wedding was earlier than even she had thought.

Lydia's parents offered to have the wedding, saying they were not too old at 62. They only asked that not too many guests be invited.

Perhaps 200 would be a good number. Perhaps 220, but no more than 230.

Lydia blushed and beamed like a schoolgirl. The children seemed to be as pleased as their mother. The new dresses were brought out and showed proudly to Sarah that Sunday afternoon. Navy blue, plain fabric.

Sarah folded it between her fingers and told Lydia it was very pretty. She admired the black cape and apron that would be pinned neatly on top.

When Lee drove up to Lydia's barn with his black Dutch harness horse, the spokes in the wheels flashing in the September sun, Sarah ran down to meet him.

He climbed out of the buggy, his teeth gleaming white in his tanned face, and reached for her. Hearing the sound of horses' hooves on the gravel, he stepped back politely, his eyes never leaving her face.

It was Melvin, red-faced and exuberant, his spirits in high gear, his energy level off the charts, in his own words. No, Melvin was definitely not humble. He was talked about all over Lancaster County and in the sister settlements, and it suited him just fine. He reveled in the happy banter, the teasing, all the attention he garnered.

Well-meaning older men would reverently place their hands on his shoulders, telling him quietly what a *saya* (blessing) he would acquire, becoming a father to those dear fatherless children.

What a Godly thing to do, people said. So unselfish. So generous. He will make a good father. Lydia deserves this. Lord knows she suffered enough with Aaron.

Old Dan Dienner's wife, Leah, said Aaron wasn't all bad. People were just bringing a curse on themselves, talking that way about him after he was dead and buried beside his parents. She knew his mother well, and she was one of the most likable women around.

The Widow Mattie Stoltzfus said, so what, just because his mother was likable didn't make him that way, and Leah gasped and said she better watch it. Mattie didn't sleep very well for awhile, but in her heart, she knew she was right. Leah just tried to sugarcoat everything. That whole family did.

Talk swirled and circled, as these events tend to bring out people's opinions. There was praise from the generous of heart, and caution expressed and trials predicted from the more pessimistic, but all in all, people wished them well.

It didn't make any difference to Melvin what people said. He felt pretty sure he was Lydia's knight, come on a mighty steed to rescue her from her sad existence, and he set about making her happy.

True to his melodramatic fashion, an enormous

ornate grandfather clock showed up in Lydia's parents' plain kitchen on the day of the wedding. It was adorned with a huge lime green bow and the largest, most garish card Sarah had ever seen. It was completely out of character in an Amish home. Then two dozen red roses were delivered during the service, the likes of which Sarah had never seen.

Lydia was dressed as neat as a pin, completely flawless, her eyes shining with a glad light that touched Sarah's heart. She was so slender, so youthful in her appearance, especially considering she had an eighteen-year-old son. Melvin sat beside her, his reddish brown hair not quite right, a small section sticking out on back of his head, where he couldn't see. He, however, would never have imagined anything wrong with his own appearance. His white shirt collar was meticulously fitted with a black bow tie, his new *mutza*, vest, and trousers were immaculate, and his new shoes squeaky clean.

The position of his abundant eyebrows spoke of his anxiety, though, and only Sarah knew him well enough to pick up on this. After all, he did have to stand in front of the minister and the crowd and pronounce a *"ya"* at each of the proper times. With hundreds of pairs of eyes on him, it was enough to rattle even the heartiest ego.

The singing rolled in waves across the freshly

painted shop, ministers spoke, and everything went as planned, as tradition required.

When it was time to be married, Melvin did a good job, holding Lydia's hand tenderly, steering her to the proper position beside him. He answered at the expected times, in a low well modulated voice, although not necessarily a humble one. Lydia's voice was only a decibel above a whisper, but it sufficiently bound her to Melvin as his wife.

However, when it was time to leave the minister, Melvin turned the wrong way, and Lydia had to turn twice to accommodate his incorrect turn. She did it so gracefully that not everyone noticed.

Melvin knew though, and he blinked at least a dozen times, his eyebrows lifted another quarter of an inch. He sniffed and cleared his throat self-consciously, and then it was over.

Sarah could see the cloak of well-being return and settle across his shoulders, as his status as a married man sunk in.

She also knew if she ever wanted to rile him, she need only mention the fact that he'd made a misstep on his way down from the preacher. She had no intention of doing it, but you never knew when it might come in handy, she decided.

What a theatrical gift opening, Sarah thought. Leave it to Melvin to add drama to everything he did, but her admiration for him resumed as she watched the gentle manner he had with the hesitant Lydia. Melvin was smart enough to know she thought very little of her own ability to handle life, so in spite of his excessive smiles and tears and gesturing, he always thought of her.

Yes, Melvin would, indeed, be a genuine benefactor for his new bride. He would treat her well, as he would treat the children, especially little Aaron, who was his constant favorite.

So it was on that clear September evening that Lee and Sarah rode side by side in Lee's buggy after Melvin and Lydia's wedding. The black horse, Lino, moved along at a brisk pace, his shining mane and tail lifting and flowing as he trotted along.

The air was infused with late afternoon sun, a perfect ending to a golden day. The dust rose from a hayfield, where horses plodded, pulling a baler behind them. They dropped squares of newly baled hay, depositing them at neat intervals along the perimeter of the field.

The heavy cornstalks were turning brown, at least the ones left standing after the silage cutters had gone through, Sarah thought.

Suddenly, she slipped a hand behind Lee's arm.

"Lee! Imagine! I'll have to cook for silo fillers when we're married. I don't know how to make gravy now."

"You'll learn, hopefully. I love gravy. That gravy we had at the wedding today was absolutely unreal."

Sarah burst into laughter.

"You and your description of food! You really do love to eat."

"I do. I take it very seriously."

He grinned at her and placed his hand on hers.

"You better learn to make gravy, Sarah. I can be pretty mean when I'm hungry."

Sarah went to spend the evening with Anna and was surprised to find her scrubbing the front porch. She was using a broom and a hose with a nozzle attached to it, taking on her task with a renewed vigor. The three children were soaking wet, and Marianne's dress clung to her chubby form. Their hair was plastered against their skulls, and water dripped in rivulets down their faces as they ran and splashed across the wet floor of the porch.

Sarah helped Lee unhitch and waited while he checked on the cows. Then she watched as he fed his horse, closed the door of the cabinet where he kept the harnesses, and turned to accompany her to the house.

"My goodness, Anna. What ambition!" Sarah greeted her soon-to-be sister-in-law.

"I was hoping Lee would bring you!" Anna shouted, her face beaming from the confines of her *dichly*, which was tied behind her ears so securely it seemed to pull her eyebrows outward.

Sarah thought of Aunt Jemima on the box of pancake mix. Dear, dear Anna.

Anna shut off the water, coiled the hose on its

rack, and swished the broom across the remaining bit of floor. The three children were ushered into the bathroom for soapy baths and their pajamas, before returning to the kitchen.

Lee sprawled on the recliner, picked up *Lancaster Farming*, and was soon engrossed in an article. Anna and Sarah poured tea and cut cheese in neat slices. They put crackers, a plate of Rice Krispy Treats, and a container of chocolate ice cream on a tray to carry to the porch.

"I didn't bake. I hardly have anything in the house to eat. Sorry. Now tell me all about the wedding. Please do."

Leaning in, Anna began eating the cheese. She shook her head, clucked, sighed, and clapped her hand on her breast, as Sarah described the service and meal afterwards.

Finally, Anna sat back and rolled her eyes toward the sky. She clasped her hands across her ample stomach.

"But, you know, Sarah. I don't mean this in a bad way. Lydia's doing pretty good, marrying Melvin. But seriously, he just—you know—turns me off with his crazy ways. Nothing is calm and restful with him. To be honest, my eyebrows go straight up—and so does my blood pressure—the minute I see him. It's like, whoa!" Anna spread her arms, her feet thumping the floor.

Sarah jumped, then burst out laughing, Anna joining in with her.

"So now, you're feeling better, aren't you?"

"I'm getting there. Every day is a challenge, but every day I can rise to it better."

Sarah nodded, understanding. A silence enveloped them in its calm, providing a sense of rest, allowing them both space to contemplate the past and the future.

Finally, Anna spoke, her blue eyes twinkling with humor.

"Just do me a favor, Sarah. Don't let Melvin within a mile of my house for at least a month."

Despite the twinkle, Anna was so sincere, so genuine in her desire for avoidance that Sarah promised solemnly. She tried not to laugh, but it burst through despite her attempts. She and Anna both exploded into whoops and hollers that brought Lee to the door. Anna was wiping her eyes, her face in a grimace that was almost painful to watch, as they gasped for breath, and Sarah emitted a few more ungraceful guffaws.

Lee sat down and watched, laughing just to hear them, chuckling again as Sarah tried to stop.

"Sorry, Lee," Sarah said, placing a hand on his knee.

"It's okay, my love."

Anna's eyebrows shot up, her eyes widened.

"My love? Isn't that a bit much?"

Lee and Sarah shrugged their shoulders, and the three all smiled at each other. As the evening flowed along, they enjoyed the time together.

And each was inspired to help the others along the way as they realized the time was swiftly approaching when they would co-exist on this farm.

This home place, Sarah thought. That is truly what it is. My place to call home for the rest of my life with my handsome, kind, and loving Lee.

On the Beiler farm, Mam was trying to grow the celery for the wedding. She was a great traditionalist and remembered her own mother carefully tending to the long rows in her garden, fertilizing, watering, and finally bleaching it— covering everything but the tops with heavy layers of newspaper.

Mam fretted and stewed, worried and watered the stuff. Meanwhile, the heads of cabbage grew enormous, as that robust vegetable required very little care. The carrots were every bit as easy to grow as the cabbage. The tops were thick and heavy, the oblong orange roots below truly huge. They were amazing, for ordinary carrots.

Dat wanted to raise chickens for the wedding, but Mam said, no, they weren't going to put their *roasht leit* (people who make chicken filling) through that. Too many folks were unaccustomed to the fine art of beheading a chicken. Even if the men braved that gruesome act, the women would still need to scald and pluck them, not to mention remove that nauseating coil of, well, chicken guts. If Mam wasn't willing to do it herself, she was not going to make others do it on their behalf.

Dat said too many of these old traditions were being lost. Lots of young couples were no longer able to do their own butchering or smoking of meats. They no longer made cheese or churned butter. All of the old ways were being left behind, and Dat thought it was *shaut* (a shame).

"We still have so much, though," Mam said. "We want to be glad for what we do have. All in all, Sarah won't look much different than I did the day I became your bride, Davey."

Dat nodded.

"Yes, and I have to remember that we men use air-powered tools, milking machines, and generators to run electrical tools. You know, the list goes on and on. Times change, and so do we, very slowly. Change does come."

It was the end of a late summer day. There was still a bit more than two months before the wedding, and tension was building. They had to finish a thorough housecleaning and paint the shop, among many other things.

But for this evening, the time went by slowly. The air was mellow, their moods matching the quiet, peaceful time.

Levi was cracking peanuts, one by one. Suzie grabbed the shelled ones before his heavy fingers could retrieve them. Frustrated, he yelled at her, then drew his heavy arm back and fired a peanut against the side of her head. Suzie giggled and made a face at him.

A rooster crowed somewhere off in the distance. The caw of a crow answered the poorly-timed noise from the rooster.

The train zoomed through Gordonville, sending a rumbling across the fields as it always did. A dog barked. A siren sounded, far away.

"We won't be doing this too much longer, will we?" Mam asked.

"Listen!"

Dat held up a finger. Everyone snapped to attention, their ears fine-tuned to the sounds of wailing from the fire sirens. They faded off into the distance.

"You think we'll ever get over those sounds completely?" Sarah asked.

"Oh, I think so. This will all be a distant memory someday. Our children will talk about it to their children, until it's only a passing thought. The nights of terror, the fear, the rebuilding will all become lukewarm memories, then hardly worth mentioning, then forgotten. And that's as it should be. Why would you want to remember? What good could come of it? It'd certainly be of no help where forgiveness is concerned," Dat answered, his voice soft, relaxed.

Continuing, he told them that some things in life are best forgotten—the evil of fellowmen, the sins of others, the misdeeds of anyone around them, English or Amish, Mennonite or whatever. "But we will always remember the good, won't we?" he said.

His eyes were soft and liquid, bluish green and flecked with gold, like Sarah's. She could have watched the changing colors all evening, when Dat spent precious time with his family.

Levi threw another peanut at Suzie and said he would never be able to forget Suzie stealing his peanuts.

"I work hard to crack these, and she gets them all. It's just horrible."

Levi began to cry, and Suzie cast a guilty look in Dat's direction. She was sent to bed immediately with a stern reprimand.

Priscilla watched her younger sister go, her face soft with empathy. Discipline was a way of life in every Amish household. It was to be respected, especially when Dat doled it out.

Levi sniffed, then bent to his peanut cracking, his glasses wet with tears. Laboriously, he took them off, grasped his shirt tail firmly, and began wiping the heavy lenses methodically. Then he replaced them, sniffed, and went back to his chore.

A figure walked up to the house in the semi-darkness. He was unseen until he was almost at the porch.

Dat's head turned swiftly, clearly shaken.

"Omar!"

Relieved, Mam sat back in her chair. Sarah breathed out.

"Hey, Omar!"

"Hi, everyone. Priscilla, want to come for a walk?"

"Sure. I'm barefoot, not cleaned up at all."

"That's okay. Just come on."

Priscilla rose, rushed off the porch, and together they walked down the drive, their faces turned toward each other, talking.

"I never saw anyone who can talk endlessly the way those two can," Mam observed.

"I look forward to the time when we all stop snapping to attention every time someone shows up unexpectedly," Sarah said.

Dat laughed.

"Whether we admit it or not, we're still extremely jumpy. Even with the arsonist in jail, it'll be like this for a while."

"Has anyone heard what's going on?"

"It can take months. Even up to a year or two."

Mam nodded and wondered if any of the Amish would show up at the hearing.

"Probably," Dat answered.

"Who would?" Sarah asked.

"There are always the few disobedient among us," Dat said.

Mam drew her breath in sharply.

"There! Something is out in the rows of celery.

It's not a cat. I think it's a rabbit. No wonder my celery isn't doing well."

Grabbing the stiff straw broom, Mam hopped off the porch, moving fast and waving the broom.

Dat yelled the same time that Sarah screamed. "Mam! No!"

It was a skunk, and a very defensive one. He turned his backside, lifted his tail, and sprayed the garden, Mam's broom, the celery, and everything else within a ten-foot radius.

Levi roared with glee as Mam pivoted and made a stumbling dash for the porch. The evening came to an abrupt halt as they all scrambled to be the first one in the door, laughing and gasping, Levi shouting that he'd seen a skunk, a real one.

Mam took a shower and used her best talcum powder, but Dat said she smelled mildly of skunk all night. He shook with laughter at her indignation. Suzie said that's what they deserved, getting sprayed by a skunk, because they made her go to bed early.

Levi said he had spilled all the shelled peanuts. But the next morning, there was not a single one left on the front porch. He bet that skunk was up on the porch during the night, eating them.

Since the celery now smelled like skunk, Mam finally admitted defeat, much to Sarah's relief. They bought crates of celery the day before the wedding.

Chapter 19

Members of the school board had voiced their disappointment that Sarah would not teach again. Jonas King, however, had a genuine twinkle in his brown eyes, so Sarah figured he must have gotten wind of her upcoming marriage *aus grufa* (being published).

It was good to know her efforts had been appreciated by the school board. It was rewarding to understand the ways she had made a difference, for girls like Rosanna and for Joe, all the sullen eighth graders who had become her friends.

Suzie had gone back to school the last week in August, and Priscilla worked several days a week in the bakery at the farmer's market as Sarah had done. Mam and Sarah worked side by side through the busy fall days in anticipation of the approaching wedding season.

The organized, relaxed atmosphere in the quiet house allowed Dat a deep and peaceful nap after dinner. His glasses slid down his nose, and *Die Botshaft* (a weekly Amish newspaper) lay open across his stomach. With his head lolling to one side, he started softly snoring, enjoying a genuine, restorative power nap.

Mam yawned and yawned after dinner, but

she always said she had to keep going. They were "making wedding."

Sarah read a few lines of a book and dropped off to a deep, restful snooze. She woke with renewed energy and started in again.

Today, it was pears. Four bushels of the odd-shaped, green fruit were purchased from the fruit peddler at a whopping sum of fifty dollars a bushel. But Mam refused to do without her *beer* (pears). You could not buy the taste of home-canned pears, and that was all there was to it, she said.

Dat nodded vigorously as he wrote the check for the peddler. Yes, indeed. There was no better dessert than a heavy chunk of chocolate cake with rich caramel frosting and home-canned pear juice ladled over it, two succulent halves of pear beside it. Nothing better, not even vanilla cornstarch pudding.

It was the first real disagreement Sarah had with Mam. Pears and peaches were traditionally served at every wedding dinner. The golden yellow peach halves were mixed with the pale pears, and the juices combined. It was whole-some, delicious, and should be served, Mam insisted.

Sarah cringed at the thought of that common, everyday fruit being dumped into Melmac serving dishes and set on the wedding tables. Nowadays, many of her friends did not have fruit.

They only served pies, or Jell-O or tapioca dessert, and cookies and doughnuts at their weddings. If they didn't serve fruit, why should she?

Mam was firm, unmoving. She'd never heard of a wedding without home-canned fruit. Sarah told her it would be different if they didn't have to be served in those *koch-shissla* (serving dishes). Why, she, her own mother, would never serve fruit to company in plain old serving dishes like that.

Mam's lips tightened, her eyes narrowed. She said in rigid, clipped sentences that what had been good enough for her was good enough for her daughter. Sarah could either accept it or make it hard for everyone, and then they'd all be miserable just because of fruit.

Grimly, they sorted the pears, discord hanging between them like Plexiglas.

Pears were different than peaches. Peaches were spread on newspapers on the *kesslehaus* floor. Each day they were squeezed gently. The soft ones were chosen, put in large stainless steel bowls, and peeled. They never ripened all at once.

Aunt Lydia King had taught Mam, only a few years before, to leave pears in their bushel baskets and cover the tops and sides with heavy comforters or sleeping bags. Then they would check them each day, and eventually, they'd all ripen at once.

Today, they had all turned yellow, soft to the touch, every one of them, except a few tiny ones that had been picked off the tree way too soon.

They filled their bowls and washed the pears. Then they spread clean towels on their laps to absorb the juice that never failed to drip off their elbows. They took up their paring knives, cut the pears in half, expertly gouged out the centers, and began to peel. The heavy outer skin came away easily. Sarah popped the first peeled pear into her mouth, her senses infused with the perfect, autumnal taste of ripened fruit.

One by one, the pear halves made soft thudding sounds as they hit the bowls, and nothing was said. Sarah coughed. It was forced and unnecessary, but at least it was something. She ate another pear half and glanced sideways at Mam, whose stony features remained unchanged.

Levi shuffled out to the kitchen, helped himself to a pear from Sarah's bowl. He sat down heavily in the chair beside Mam, took a large bite of the fruit, chewed, swallowed, and looked at Mam.

"*Vell*, Malinda."

Mam raised her eyebrows.

"Why aren't you talking?" Levi inquired.

"Oh, we're relaxed, busy with the pears."

He looked into Sarah's face, his small brown eyes cunning, sharp.

"*Bisht base* (Are you angry)?"

Sarah shook her head.

"*Bisht an poosa* (Are you pouting)?"

"Stop it, Levi."

Levi grinned cheekily, turned to Mam, and said Sarah was both angry and pouting.

Eventually, Sarah told Mam it was alright to have peaches and pears if they put them in glass serving dishes. Mam thought that was completely unnecessary, but she did not want to be too set in her ways, so they reached a compromise. Pears and peaches would be served in glass "company" bowls.

As they worked, Levi was allowed to spear the pear halves with a fork and place them—every single one of them—in the wide-mouthed jars.

Mam scooped a half cup of sugar over the pear halves, then added water. She wiped the rim of each jar, placed a lid on top, added a ring, and tightened it. After she had filled fourteen jars, she set them in the heavy, water-filled canner, turned on the burner, and sat down to continue peeling pears.

The pears would cook for fifteen minutes before they were preserved, or cold-packed. Then each jar was wiped clean with soapy water. They would be taken down and set on the shelves in the basement.

They did 102 quarts that day. Levi speared every pear half, and Mam praised him with warm words of affection. He had done well.

Levi said he knew what Davey and Malinda

should do with their boy since he had worked so hard. They should take him to the Tastee Freez in Smoketown for a large swirled cone, the kind that had chocolate on one side and vanilla on the other.

Mam said she'd ask Dat, but Sarah watched her mother's shoulders droop with weariness and knew she needed a good long rest, not to have to get dressed up. Mam would never go away without a *halsduch* (cape).

So Dat took Levi and Suzie down to the Tastee Freez with Fred hitched to the buggy. Mam and Sarah stayed behind to clean the kitchen, wash the supper dishes, and sweep the porch.

Mam surveyed the rows of sparkling clean pears, the jars shining, ready to be taken down to the cellar in the morning. She sat, rocking slowly, eyeing the day's work. She knew it had been a day well spent.

Oh, it was a restful thing, going about her work, knowing the family would no longer have to live in fear now that the barn fires were a thing of the past. She thought of the troubled youth, Michael, and her lips began to move as she prayed for the teenager, who was so obviously misled. He had made bad choices, perhaps, but still.

He was always so terribly ill at ease, as jumpy and frightened as a newborn colt. Malinda prayed God would *fer-sark* (care) for his soul, show him the way, the truth, and the light. She wondered if

311

he read the Bible they gave him. She hoped so.

As for that other one, that older man—she forgot his name—he ought to know better, so he should. At his age, to be hanging onto that silly grudge against Aaron Esh, who was no longer even alive, was simply beyond her grasp.

It did serve him right to be sitting in jail, at least for a while. She guessed she should pray for his soul, but she wasn't sure she could just yet, at least not in the right way. Davey was much faster to forgive than she was. Sometimes, it felt pretty good to know that the arsonist was confined to jail. She'd heard the food was nothing to brag about in there.

Ah, yes, they'd all come through it, God be praised.

Well, the wedding was about seven weeks away, but she had enough time to manage things. If Levi stayed healthy, and nothing unforeseen came up, they should have everything in top shape by the end of November.

She lifted her hands, sniffed them, and thought of the skunk spraying her, or very nearly. My goodness, she thought. She could still smell that awful scent and almost feel that choking sensation that had accompanied it. And there went hours of labor, worry, and effort, the celery ruined by that odorous little creature.

Ach, so gates (it goes), she thought.

Upstairs, Sarah had showered, her shampooed

hair rolled into a towel. She lowered her right shoulder in front of the full-length mirror, the late evening sun slanting across it.

She bit her lip, and quick tears formed in her eyes, trembled there, and dropped on her cheek for only a second, before sliding off.

It just wasn't good. The skin looked too tightly stretched across her neck and shoulders. It was colored pink or white, depending where the lines zigzagged into each other. It was hideous. There was no getting away from it.

The side of her face was still discolored and uneven, but not like this. This ugliness was shocking.

The truth of her disfigurement hit her, caught her off guard. She couldn't marry Lee this way. She was too revolting. Her heart hammered in her chest, and her breathing became shallow as her eyes widened with fear.

She had to talk to Lee. She had to make him understand that he didn't want her. He would not be happy to live with an imperfect woman, one that was disfigured with a hideous scar all along her side.

Oh, he said he loved her, but he didn't know how bad it was. Perhaps she should show him, to make sure he knew. It would be like purchasing a team of horses. They checked their teeth, their hooves.

Surely somewhere, there had to be a miraculous

cure for scars such as these. She had used so many different homemade salves and lotions, burdock leaves, vitamin E capsules, oils, and all sorts of tinctures. Still, the scars remained, imprinted on her body, the mark of the arsonist.

Why me, she thought? Why do I have to carry the map of all the Lancaster County barn fires? Truly, it was like a map with all the rural roads and the ashes of barns that had stood for centuries. Like them, her skin was ruined, destroyed.

Suddenly, she couldn't understand how Dat could be such an advocate for forgiveness. When she saw her body at times like this, she was glad Harold Walters was in jail. Sometimes people had to reap what they sowed. That was all there was to it.

Anger churned through her, and self-pity descended, pushing her into the quicksand of despair.

When Priscilla came home from market, there was a light in Sarah's room, but by the time she got upstairs, Sarah's room had been darkened. It was a clear sign that her sister did not want to talk, so she went to her own room and figured she could wait to hear the local gossip till tomorrow evening.

On Saturday evening, they all loaded into a fifteen-passenger van and traveled to Dauphin County to spend the weekend with the married brothers and their families.

Abner had complained to Dat that he barely knew Lee. How was he expected to take charge of the wedding if he never met this guy?

Sarah laughed when Dat told him, and they made immediate plans to go with Sam's Danny's *freundshaft* (family). They packed their bags, and asked Omar Esh to do chores.

Lee was happy, joking with the men, courteous to Sarah, but only for the first hour of the drive. Sensing Sarah's detached manner, the tense position of her eyebrows, his stomach turned over with the same sickening flip-flop of former days, when Matthew had come around.

No, it couldn't be that. Not now. Not less than two months before their wedding. In spite of trying to reassure himself, he became increasingly skeptical until the evening stretched before him like an unattainable height, a slippery slope of doubt and fear.

They both laid their troubles aside when they arrived at Abner's home, a palatial one that spoke of well-managed finances. The yard was cut to perfection, the garden and flower beds immaculate.

Abner and his wife, Maryann, greeted them warmly, their curiosity shining through their polite smiles of welcome. Their two small children were already in their pajamas, peeping shyly from the folds of their mother's dress.

The evening flew by with board games and delicious food. It was late when they were shown to their rooms, and quiet settled over the house.

Almost as soon as Maryann went back downstairs, there was a soft sound on Sarah's door, a tapping.

"Yes?"

"Come. We'll go for a walk," Lee whispered.

She hadn't undressed, so she said, yes, she'd go. She followed him down the stairway and out the door, closing it softly behind them.

They walked down the drive and turned left onto the road. Lee's hand sought hers, and when he found it, he held it lightly in his own.

The night air was cool but not uncomfortably so. There was a woods, fields. Beyond them was the dark indigo color of the mountain. Overhead shone stars and a crescent moon, the same ones shining above Lancaster County.

Here, though, the houses were far apart, the farms dotting the countryside across much wider spaces. It was a younger settlement and smaller, but the ways and lifestyles were much the same.

Lee stopped. "Can we find someplace to talk?"

His voice was strained, the words short and almost clipped, lacking his usual warmth. Lee was terribly afraid, desperately sick at heart, but there was no use trying to avoid Sarah's pitiful attempt at covering up her feelings, so he plunged ahead.

"Here. We may as well sit on this little hill. There's a lot of soft grass."

He led her to a comfortable spot, then sank down beside her. She could feel the moisture forming on the grass, the dew that would be sparkling by morning. Her skirt felt damp already.

Headlights approached, the tires of the car making a dull whooshing sound as it passed by, the lights stabbing into the darkness as it continued on its way.

"What's wrong, Sarah?"

"Why? Nothing. Nothing's wrong."

"Don't lie."

"Lee! What do you mean? I seriously do not understand."

"You're not being your usual carefree self."

"Of course I am."

She couldn't speak to him now. Courage failed her.

"It's Matthew, right?"

"What?"

"Matthew. I know it's him. Our relationship has always ended like this before. You're just in too deep this time. It's okay, Sarah, if you can't go ahead with the wedding. I mean, it's not okay, but I won't make it hard for you. If you want to be set free, just say it. Don't marry me if your heart belongs to Matthew."

His voice was choked now, a near sob in his throat. In the darkness of the night, Sarah could plainly see the outline of his head, dropped low on his chest, a picture of abject misery.

She took her time, pondered her words.

"It's not Matthew."

His sharp intake of breath almost scared her.

"What else? What single thing on earth can make you feel so far away from me? Sarah, I do not want you to become my wife if you cannot love me. I've been selfish, inconsiderate, demanding. But I think I honestly love you so much that I want only your happiness. If I have to give you up for you to find true happiness, I will. It won't be easy, but I'll do it. For you."

Sarah had never been bold, certainly not with Lee, but now there was only one thing to do. Words were inadequate. Slowly, her hands gripped his arms, went around his shoulders. She lifted her face to his, found his lips, and conveyed her deepest feelings with the touch of her mouth to his.

The night became magical. The stars seemed to applaud and cast bright little sparkles all over them. The moon fairly skipped and whirled, before settling back into place with a happy sigh.

The Creator made this wonder, the love of a man for a woman. He created the ties that bind them until death parts the union ordained from the beginning.

She whispered, then, her deepest fears to him, and Lee listened in total disbelief.

Shocked, he shook his head, over and over.

"Sarah, you don't understand," he choked.

"When I say I love you, that means you, exactly the way you are."

She broke in, quickly, desperately.

"No. But you don't know how bad it is. I panic, Lee. I look at my shoulder, and it's so hideous. You can't know how bad it really is. It will disgust you."

"But Sarah. That has nothing to do with love. If a man truly loves a woman, he accepts her just the way she is. Her size, her looks, what she wears, scars, whatever—it's all insignificant."

"Lee, I simply can't believe that."

A moment passed, as Lee pondered her response.

"I guess I'll just have to tell you that after we're married. Maybe then you'll be convinced. Look at my sister Anna. She's not every man's ideal of the perfect woman, but to Ben, she was. He deeply loved every pound of her."

Sarah took a deep breath, inhaling all the happiness she could hold, greedily grasping it.

"You see, Sarah, I can't look at your scars now. But I imagine what they look like. And I've told you before. For me, they represent God's will for our lives. And if you really do love me, and . . ."

He broke off as a deep rumbling laugh emerged, and he said, "I really think you do, Sarah, and I almost can't contain my happiness."

"I do. Matthew is just simply no longer there for me. I can talk to him, and everything's changed.

He has begged me twice now to marry him. Can you imagine?"

Lee shook his head. She heard a deep breath as he jumped up from the hill. Suddenly, she was lifted to her feet in a crushing embrace. Then he held her tenderly, for so long, time was forgotten, until another pair of headlights appeared behind them. They sank back on the grass, giggling like schoolchildren as the car rumbled past, its headlights slicing through the night.

Sarah slept a deep and restful sleep, blinking awake to find brilliant sunlight shining through the sheer burgundy panels. The curtains made the whole room cozy. It was like wearing rose-colored glasses. Well, her world was not just viewed through those glasses. It was rose-colored without them.

She stretched, smiled to herself, and flung her arm across the pillow beside her, imagining being married to Lee, waking with her husband beside her, in his rightful place.

What had he said? Was that really how it was?

She thought of Anna's wide back, the ample legs, the rounded arms, her full stomach. Yes, she probably weighed more than 200 pounds, but to be with her, her weight was not what counted. Her pretty face, her neat hair, and her white, always ironed covering along with the energy, the quick smiles, and ready sense of humor—that's what made up the whole aura that was Anna. And her off-the-wall humor as well.

Sarah grinned and looked around at her brother Abner's wife's guest room with the neat bed and dresser, handmade, no doubt, but burgundy curtains? Pink artificial roses in cut glass vases?

A plastic cat stared at her from a pink doily, and two red roses protruded from a pink ceramic urn. My goodness.

She sat up and pulled the quilt up to examine it. She saw it was a Lone Star pattern done in brilliant red, white, and pink.

On the floor, lying on a decidedly magenta rug, were two pink crocheted accent pillows that had tumbled off the bed. Definitely rose-colored— her whole world, literally.

Maryann cooked them a huge breakfast with many different dishes to taste. And each one was delicious.

Abner made waffles, perfect ones, which Lee raved about. He wrote down the name of the heavy cast iron waffle maker, followed by instructions, step by step. He folded the paper and gave it to Sarah, saying that was one of the things that was a requirement for their marriage.

They sat around the breakfast table with second and third cups of coffee, talking comfortably, like old friends. In fact, it was as if they'd always known each other. Abner even tried to persuade Lee to buy a farm in Dauphin County.

"Look at what your place is worth!" he finished.

That was the moment when Sarah saw Lee's genuine humble attitude.

"Nah. Not more than this beautiful home."

He continued, saying Abner must have a special talent, the way this house was built. He diverted all attention away from himself, focusing on Abner instead. Sarah knew full well the farm Lee had purchased was worth three or four times the amount of this home, but Abner was very happy to accept Lee's praise.

Again, she reminded herself that she was not worthy of Lee.

Back home, Anna burst into tears the minute they walked into the house. She laid her head on the table and cried so heartbrokenly, they both rushed to comfort her. Sarah rubbed her back, Lee patted her shoulder. Then they made her a cup of tea and talked far into the night.

Her buddies, the married couples that she and Ben had run around with, had all visited. She knew they meant well, but the awful ache of missing Ben had only intensified as the day wore on.

She mopped up her tears and blew her nose, honking loud and long, then started shaking her head.

Omar had brought Priscilla to do the chores. Anna had watched them with so much longing. She could see the intensity of their attraction,

322

the easy way they could talk about any subject. They were simply so cute.

"Don't ever go to Dauphin County again," she concluded. "I can't handle it. You have to realize you have a dependent, fat, widowed sister who is going to be the biggest pain in your lives."

Sarah could only hug her soft, lonely body.

Chapter 20

And then, when everyone had finally relaxed, glad to be free from the fear of another barn burning, the fire sirens wailed from every direction. The undulating, deafening whistles rose and dropped off, only to have another, sharper one pierce the air.

Windows were closed that night, warding off the fall's chill. The call came towards dawn, when the bright October moon hung low in the sky. The same sickening, quaking feeling rudely roused slumbering households. Men stumbled around in the dark, shouting questions that made no sense.

Voss in die velt (What in the world)? Had they let him out of jail?

Half of them didn't even know his name.

Old Danny Dienner said to his wife, "*Grund da lieva* (grounds of love), Mam!"

She said it *was* grounds for love. Somebody

was going to have to come up with some forgiveness again, if that man was out of jail and back to his *umleidlich* ways.

"*Unleidlich* (mischievous)," Danny corrected her, but she was bent over, searching under the couch for her slippers. She was holding a flashlight that was barely usable, the batteries were so low, and she didn't hear what he said.

Sure enough, another barn was on fire.

Now what?

In stunned disbelief, families huddled on couches in the early morning hours, little ones wrapped in blankets, their eyes huge and dark in their faces. School-aged children cried like babies, imagining the devil himself breaking out of jail and lighting every barn in Lancaster County.

No one was safe. Locks on door were laughable. Someone was out there and would certainly come to get them. They quoted little German prayers, climbed up on their fathers' laps. Surely Dat would not let "the man" get them.

But where was the fire?

Men dressed hastily, held goose pimply vigils in phone shanties and unheated shops. The disobedient who owned cell phones talked plenty. Word spread rapidly, crackling through the air. The fire was close to the Vintage Sale Stables, at Aaron Zook's.

Ach, poor man. Poor family. But relief also

flowed like a healing wind, a veritable chinook of comfort.

Aaron had been out at 3:30, helping a cow with a difficult birth. He saw he really needed a veterinarian's assistance, so he left his naphtha gas lantern on the hay-strewn walkway and ran to the phone shanty. He had forgotten the LED flashlight, so he got it from the *kesslehaus*, and called Dr. Simms. He smelled the smoke the minute he opened the door and remembered the lantern.

Evidently, one of the barn cats had been chasing a mouse or another cat—who could tell? The lantern was knocked over, the mantles broke, and the little jets of blue flame continued to spurt out, igniting the hay. The gas leaked out, the flames roaring to life in seconds.

Aaron had tried bravely to beat out the flames with plastic feed sacks, but he saw he was only worsening a dire situation. He ran for the hose from the milk house, saw it was futile, and started loosening cows before he remembered to dial 911.

Poor Aaron, everyone said. He always had a struggle, scrambling to meet each monthly mortgage payment on his small farm. His crops were always a bit inferior, his thin mules working the fields until they all but collapsed. The animal rights people had turned him in once. He had borrowed money to pay his fine and then humbly paid it all back in weekly twenty-dollar installments. But he continued to feed the same poor quality hay and meager amounts of grain to his mules.

His wife, Nancy, was small and thin. She was a hard worker, who had faithfully borne her husband nine children, so far. Nancy never blamed Aaron for the overturned lantern. She never blamed him for anything. He was the head of the house. It was her duty to respect him, and respect him she did. He did the best he could. *Die guava sinn net gleich* (Talents are not alike), she said.

She kept her old farmhouse shining, scrubbed the cracked linoleum with Spic and Span, washed the old glass windows with cotton sheets and vinegar water. She washed countless loads of laundry in her old wringer washer, hung it all on her wheel line. She grew an enormous garden and canned well over a thousand quarts of vegetables and fruits each year.

She cried when the barn burned. She held her children to her thin breast and let the tears flow. When the neighbors came to stand with Aaron and watch the jets of water from the fire trucks hit the leaping, dancing flames, which were fanned by an unhandy October wind, her tears kept flowing.

When her mother and father came, they had to leave the horse in the neighbors' driveway, because so many fire trucks were parked all over the driveway. Nancy stopped crying, and no one ever saw her shed another tear, as far as the barn was concerned.

Perhaps relief that this fire wasn't arson brought the great outpouring of love. Whatever the reason, the response was overwhelming.

The family couldn't handle all the food. Some of it was given to the poor people at the homeless shelter in the city of Lancaster. A man came with a white minivan and loaded canned goods and pies and cakes and noodles and potatoes into cardboard boxes and drove off with them.

So many men showed up on the first day of the barn raising, they took turns working. The frame of the barn was up, ready for metal roofing, in approxi-mately six hours.

The Lancaster paper ran an article titled, "Practice Makes Perfect." It said that with all the recent barn fires, there was a new expertise and better management at barn raisings than before, which was probably true.

Sarah was serving coffee again. It seemed unreal to be at another barn raising, after everyone thought the whole nightmare was over. But here they were, the same black, stinking, smoking piles shoved into a field. There were piles of the same yellow lumber with that sharp odor of freshly sawed wood. The trucks came and went, the sound of iron tracks clashing and rumbling as dozers cleared the remaining debris, even as the new barn took shape.

Hungrily, Sarah bit into a filled doughnut. She grabbed a napkin when the filling squished out each side of her mouth. The 10X sugar rained on her black sweater, creating a mess that the napkin was completely worthless to remove.

Anna rushed over, her eyes wide. "Seriously! Did you taste these?" She held out a raisin-filled cookie, the sugary top held high by a generous mound of creamy raisin filling.

Rose Zook—this Aaron was her uncle—came up to the two of them. She squealed and hugged them, praised their sweaters, their coverings, and ooh, where did you get that doughnut?

Sarah enjoyed Rose's antics as usual, hoping she'd quiet down long enough for her to ask a few questions about her own life.

When Lee came for his coffee, Sarah smiled at him, reveling in the security of having Lee, being engaged. She caught Rose's eye and looked away.

They did get some time to be together, peeling potatoes, before others arrived.

Everything was great, Rose said. Single was the way to go. She had the chance to manage the restaurant at the farmer's market, so that was her latest thing. She was a regular career girl, she said, giggling at her own audacity.

"So!" she said pertly. "You're getting married, Sarah. Tell me the truth. Does it even seem real?"

They shared feelings, just like old times, laughing, talking fast, remembering times with

Lee and Matthew, the insanity of it all, Rose said.

She didn't know if she wanted Matthew. He was so English, so ungrounded, like a dandelion seed, just floating along with no direction.

"But Rose, think about it. The restaurant at the farmer's market! Perhaps Matthew just never found his calling."

"Yes, he did!" Rose snorted. "He's next to God."

"But he's doing better. Lots of young people, who come to the light and understand God's love, become a bit carried away. I don't think he's as airheaded, or whatever you call it. Why don't you see if Matthew could cook at the restaurant? I still think he would be okay once he found his niche."

"I can't stand his smarmy ways."

"If he'd cook at a busy restaurant, his smarminess might disappear. You'd have the old Matthew back pretty fast."

Rose tilted her head to laugh, and Sarah admired the porcelain doll prettiness of her friend all over again.

Yes, they'd make the perfect couple.

"Why don't you ask him?"

"Maybe I will."

Rose threw a large, peeled potato into the container of cold water, splashing Sarah's sleeve. They were joined by more women, who greeted them, but neither Rose nor Sarah had any idea who they were, so they gave up their paring knives and went back to check on the coffee.

At home that evening, they sat around the kitchen table, reviewing the day. Dat was in a pensive mood, remembering conversations with the members of the Amish church, men raised in the same culture, the same *ordnung*, and way of life.

He could only conclude that in the vast realm of God's earth, human nature didn't vary a whole lot. All goodness was a gift from the Father of Lights, exactly the way the Bible said.

Dat said Ammon's Amos's Eli thought all the barn fires were an act of God, whether they were caused by an arsonist or a lantern. Mam's eyebrows shot up, but she nodded, saying she could see his point.

They discussed Nancy's old house, the torn flooring and rattling old windows, and how nice it would be to help them remodel.

Mam shook her head. She said, No, Nancy is happy that way. She keeps that old house spotless, makes do. The children are clean and happy as larks. That home is blessed, she said. And if Aaron is a bit of an *aylent* (slow one), so what? That family is happy.

Dat nodded his agreement. Levi said he was happy, but he'd be a lot happier if he was allowed a *blooney brote* (bologna on bread).

Dat looked at the clock, then raised his eyebrows at Mam.

"What about a piece of fruit, Levi?" she asked. "Alright."

Obediently, he ate his apple, slice after slice, chewing methodically, his glasses bouncing up and down slightly, jarred by the movement of his cheeks, his bright eyes intense as he concentrated.

Levi loved his food, easily weighing 240 pounds now. But he was having difficulty breathing. He coughed relentlessly even in the summer. He would soon turn thirty-three years old, so the family knew they would not have Levi much longer, since his heart was weakened as much as some eighty-year-olds.

Dat's reasoning was to let Levi enjoy the foods that made him happy. Dat would have allowed the homemade bread and the slab of homemade bologna, but Mam maintained her vigilance with Levi's diet.

Their sleep that night was deep and restful, relief being the comfort in their dreams. No, another arsonist was not starting fires. It had been an accident this time. And so they slept.

About 10:30, Levi's bed creaked loudly. He stopped, held his breath, listened. Slowly, stealthily, he rolled over, swung his legs over the edge, found the wooden step stool, and lowered his great body to the floor, shoving his feet into his slippers.

Three steps and he was at his oak chest of drawers, pulling slowly at the drawer pulls. One hand crept inside, but he froze when a loud crackling escaped.

Eventually he managed to ease a bag of potato chips up through the opening, carrying them carefully between one heavy thumb and fore-finger. He laid them on his bed and kicked his slippers off. Pushing the potato chips aside, he crawled into bed.

Opening the bag, he thrust a hand inside, clutched about four potato chips, and stuffed them into his mouth, chewing rapidly. These chips were delicious. They were a very good kind of potato chip. Because he couldn't read, he remembered the colors on the bag—red, white, and blue.

Humming contentedly, he lay on his side, munching the greasy, salty chips, waves of happiness accompanying the steady, unrestricted supply. Potato chips were his favorite.

He slowed his chewing to savor them, then stopped. He heard something. It was a roaring sound, a dull, distant rumbling. He heard the leaves rustling in the maple tree, heard the wind pick up, bending the branches, and went back to eating potato chips. It was only the wind, and he was used to those sounds.

The bag was starting to feel weightless now, and he had to put his hand farther inside to find another handful.

Without warning, a brilliant, bluish-white light

ripped through the room, followed instantly by a loud clap of thunder. Levi's eyes flew open, and a great shout of fear tore from him. He forgot the chips, and the fact that he was not supposed to be eating them, as he squeezed his eyes shut and called for Mam.

"Fire! Fire!" Levi shouted.

Mam appeared almost instantly, her face white with shock.

"Levi! Hush! Hush! What fire? There's no fire."

The flashlight in her hand was trained directly on the potato chip bag. The beam moved to the crumbs and then the salt and grease on his heavy cheeks. All she said was, "You're probably thirsty, Levi." She said it in a dry, tight-lipped way that Levi recognized very well, and he knew poached eggs and dry toast would be his breakfast.

Dat called from the bedroom door, and Mam told him Levi was fine. She got him a drink of cold water and made him get out of bed while she cleaned it, but she didn't say a word.

"They should not allow flashlights," he said. "*Sie sinn aus die ordnung* (They are out of the *ordnung*)."

Mam's face stayed tight, her features buttoned into place by her anger at Levi's disobedience. But when she crawled back into bed, she began to laugh so hard the whole bed shook, and Dat rolled over and asked what in the world was wrong with her.

333

She gave up and let out a long guffaw. It was ungraceful, especially coming from the normally composed Mam. Between gasps, she told Dat what Levi had said, producing the same response in him.

As the lightning ripped across the sky and the thunder bellowed and crashed, Dat and Mam lay in bed and laughed long and hard at their erring son.

How they loved him! How many hours of pure delight had he brought into their lives? Indeed, the shock and sadness of having a baby born with Down syndrome had been great, but in the end, he had brought them much more happiness than they had ever dared to hope.

Dat reached for Mam's hand, squeezed it, and said, "Goodnight, Malinda."

They both fell asleep with smiles on their faces, as the thunder and the lightning roared above them. The rain beat against the house, filled the spouting, and sloshed out over the edge.

Levi burped quietly, said, "*Mude bin ich* (I'm tired)," and fell into a restless sleep, his stomach busily digesting all the carbohydrates, salt, and fat from the chips.

In the morning, the whole farm looked freshly washed. The grass shone with the wetness that clung to each blade, and the chrysanthemums burst into shades of red, yellow, and gold. The pumpkins in the garden were growing an inch every day, especially boosted along by the two inches of rain the thunderstorm had brought.

Sarah was in the milk house, banging milker parts against the stainless steel tubs, her curly hair creeping out beneath her *dichly* as she worked vigorously.

The sun cast a golden shaft of light through the steam. Her heart answered the sunbeam, a gladness she could not explain suffusing her entire being.

Thank you, God, for everything. Thank you for all You have given me. Because of You, I can feel joy again, feel Your love around me.

She spun on her heel and plunked the heavy milker on the rack to drip dry. She pulled the plug in the sink, grabbed the broom hanging on its rack on the wall, and swept the floor of the milk house thoroughly before heading to the house for breakfast.

She stopped to peer at the rain gauge mounted on the post by the bird feeder. Two inches. A little more. No wonder the rain had woken her.

Well, maybe they wouldn't be canning pumpkin after all. They'd sink to their ankles, carrying those cumbersome things out of the muddy garden. But knowing Mam's dosage of wedding preparation adrenaline, she'd probably find a way to get them off the vine.

Mam showed no sign of stress, however, standing by the stove flipping golden squares of

335

cornmeal mush. The sizzling increased each time she flipped a slice, but she stood back, away from the small spits of hot vegetable oil. The kitchen smelled heavenly, the air permeated with the crisp, golden flavor of the fried mush.

Levi sat in a kitchen chair close to the gas stove, making toast. He had learned to set a timer for three minutes, then open the bottom broiler drawer to check the slices. If the bread was not toasted to his specifications, he'd slam the drawer shut and set the timer for one more minute, before placing the toast carefully on a small plate.

This morning, however, he was scowling, his eyes hooded, his glasses sliding far down on his nose. The timer was nowhere to be seen.

Mam laid down the spatula, sighed, and let out a mighty, long, drawn-out yawn. She tapped her mouth with four fingers and said, "Shoo."

Levi sat glumly, staring at the broiler.

Mam wiped her eyes and sniffed the air.

"Levi, your toast."

Slowly, Levi pulled open the broiler drawer and glanced at Mam. He opened his mouth, then closed it again. He took up six slices of blackened toast, burning his fingers and shaking them against his knee, and silently stacked the slices on the small plate.

Getting to his feet, he shuffled to his place at the table, his face set in stone, completely silent.

Dat appeared at the *kesslehaus* door, looked at

Mam, and smiled a good morning at her, before taking his place at the head of the table. Priscilla and Suzie both slouched into their chairs, yawning, rubbing their eyes. They smiled sparingly at Dat's resounding, "Sleepyheads!"

Levi didn't give his usual response.

"Two inches of rain."

Dat's comment was met by a mere nod from Mam, as the silence clung to the room.

Sarah cracked eggs onto the two-burner griddle and turned the gas heat on low. She propped a closed fist on her hip as she leaned against the counter, watching the eggs sizzle and waiting till the whites lost their gelatinous look so they could be flipped successfully.

Mam scooped the sizzling slices of cornmeal mush onto a platter topped by two folded paper towels.

Levi swallowed.

Mam poured scalding hot milk into the Melmac serving dish containing saltine crackers. Then she set the fried mush platter on top to steam the stewed crackers.

Levi watched with grief-stricken eyes, then swallowed again. He bent his head low when they put "patties down." The family paused for a time of silent prayer, and Levi's mouth moved as he prayed fervently.

Dat lifted his head first, then Mam, followed by the girls. Levi was last. With a deep sigh of resignation, he folded his thick hands across his protruding stomach.

Mam helped herself to a fried egg and passed the platter to Dat, who had served himself four slices of fried mush.

When the platters reached Levi, he passed them on without putting anything on his plate. Sarah looked at him.

"Aren't you hungry?"

"Yes."

"Then why aren't you eating?"

"I'm not allowed."

"You're not?"

Priscilla stopped salting her fried egg and looked questioningly at her brother.

He shook his head sorrowfully.

"Why?"

"*Die Malinda iss base* (angry)."

Mam was totally caught off guard. A mouthful of hot mush came flying out as she choked and sputtered, her shoulders shaking as she laughed heartily.

The crow's feet at the corner of Dat's eyes deepened and spread outward as he watched his wife, but he did not laugh, seeing Levi's cheerless countenance. The girls smiled, waiting for Mam's response.

Wiping her eyes, then her mouth carefully, she dabbed at the tablecloth, shaking her head.

"Tell them, Levi. Tell them what you did."

"*Ich farich ich grick schlake* (I'm afraid I'll be spanked)."

Dat's eyes danced and twinkled, greenish pinwheels of merriment.

"What? What did you do?" Suzie asked.

"*Hop chips gessa* (Ate chips)."

Dat and Mam burst into peals of laughter, remembering the night before. Their laughter was as infectious as a yawn, and the girls joined in, not understanding completely what had occurred.

Still Levi did not smile. He admonished them all in firm tones about the boys who had mocked the prophet in the Bible. A bear came out of the woods and ate them, which set everyone into fresh gales of mirth.

"No, Levi, we are not making fun of you. It was just funny, the way you said Mam was angry," Dat said quietly.

Hope was rekindled, and Levi met his father's twinkling eyes.

"If Malinda isn't angry, can I have mush and eggs?"

"Yes, Levi, you may," Mam said, still smiling.

Sighing happily, Levi tucked into his breakfast. He polished off a wide wedge of fresh shoofly and told Dat that he imagined this family had *der saya* (a blessing).

Chapter 21

The rain did not deter the pumpkin canning. Sarah took off her shoes and socks and stepped into the garden in her bare feet. The cold, clammy earth sucked at them, hindering her steps.

Cold chills crept up her back, but she slogged on, bent over, and snapped off the first of the ripe pumpkins. They were dull golden neck pumpkins, shaped like oversized gourds in varying U shapes.

They were heavy, slippery, splattered with bits of wet earth. Their weight caused grunts of effort, as Sarah staggered from the pumpkin patch to the sturdy cart parked at the edge of the garden.

Mam stayed in the house to give Levi a haircut—after she had shampooed his hair. That was a job he usually did himself, but not always to Mam's specifications.

Back and forth Sarah went, her feet numb with the cold. Grimly, she bit down on her lower lip, determined to get every last one of these pumpkins out of the cold, muddy garden.

A pickup truck drove up the driveway and stopped near the house. The passenger door opened, and a man got out. He stood watching Sarah as she staggered along with the heavy pumpkins in the garden.

She dumped two of the awkward vegetables into the cart, then turned when she noticed someone approaching.

"Lee!"

A glad smile crossed her features, a light came into her eyes.

"What are you doing in your bare feet?" he asked.

"Can't you see?"

"In your bare feet?"

"It was that or have my shoes sink to the ankles."

"Sarah, our wedding isn't very far away. What if you got sick?"

"Oh, I'd get over it in a week, hopefully."

He looked deeply into her eyes, smiled, and asked if she could accompany him to the outlet stores in Rockvale Square sometime this week. She blushed, unexplainably embarrassed.

Yes, she could go, but her heart raced, thinking of the fine china, the tableware, the stemware—all the beautiful dishes he would be required to buy. Because of tradition or out of love, either way, he'd do it.

"Perhaps I'd better stay here now, help with these pumpkins."

"No, no. We'll get them done. You know you don't have time."

"Not really. We're starting on Anna's addition today."

Again, Sarah's heartbeat increased. Her mouth

went dry. She smiled a wobbly smile, her cheeks heating up again.

Lee looked down at his bride to be, the unruly curls springing from her white headscarf. She was wearing an old, torn sweatshirt, but her cheeks were rosy with health, the scars on the side of her face noticeable, but better. A mere discoloration, a constant reminder of God's hand leading them together.

He stepped forward.

"I love you so much, Sarah."

Her eyelashes swept her cheeks, as her eyes fell shyly.

"I love you, too," she whispered.

He reached out and tucked a stray curl behind her ear, straightened her headscarf, and said, "See you Wednesday night?"

She nodded and let her eyes find his, the message between them a complete story of love, anticipation, and joy.

The hard work of peeling pumpkins was definitely energized after seeing Lee. Sarah tackled the wearisome task with renewed vigor.

Pumpkin pies for the wedding dinner. She knew better than to try to argue against Mam's reasoning about pumpkin. All canned, store-bought pumpkin was inferior, even the best brand. The taste of home-canned neck pumpkin could not be replaced.

Sarah knew Mam's pies were a creamy

testimony to her theory, so she gripped the knife handle and sliced through the heavy, unyielding skin of the pumpkin, her mind churning with possibilities.

Why Rockvale Square? It was such a worldly, expensive place.

She was afraid Lee could not afford fine china. She had heard that Steven Stoltzfus gave his girlfriend Lenox china and paid close to a thousand dollars for service for sixteen. Oh, my goodness.

Well, Lee would never. He bought the farm and was building an addition. She'd be happy with serviceable stoneware or dishes from an Amish store. That price was bordering on sin. One thousand dollars.

"Mam," she blurted out.

Mam was at the sink, cutting the pumpkin into sizable chunks, filling a giant twenty-quart pot. She was preparing to set it on the stove to cook the pumpkin to a mashing consistency.

"What?"

"Lee wants me to go to Rockvale Square with him. That means expensive china. What should I do?"

Mam set the stainless steel pot on the stove with a clatter, turned, and asked Sarah what she meant.

Sarah thought expensive china would be a sin. Not really a sin, but sort of wrong.

Mam smiled a secretive, indulging smile, as if she meant to stay humble but couldn't quite carry it off.

"*My oh*, Sarah," she said. "Well. I guess if he wants to buy expensive china, that's his business. And, no, it's not wrong. How much do you think our ancestors paid for their china from England? It wasn't cheap. Not at all. I guess in the Amish heritage, dishes are cherished by the women. We don't have other things, like diamond rings or bracelets, whatever it is English men give their friends, their girlfriends. So, no, if he wants to give you fine china, that's his choice. Remember your great grandmother's? That pink and white?"

She pointed to the hutch cupboard, where the antique dishes resided with the more inexpensive set Dat had given her.

Sarah nodded.

Yes, she knew what Mam was saying. In each culture, there are cherished objects handed down from generation to generation, treasures of the past. Dishes were valued. They were taken carefully from cupboards made by Amish craftsmen to be used on special occasions and then washed and replaced with absolute care, these china dishes used by *de alte* (the old ones).

Sarah was relieved. She didn't need to worry about shopping with Lee. She and Mam then discussed the colors Sarah had chosen for her table, the corner table. The bride and groom would be seated on either side with the four attendants—two on each side—beside them.

Sarah had chosen white. All white. Her dress was blue, her cape and apron were white organdy, so that would be very different, unique, a touch of class. Sarah smiled at the thought.

She would need to wait, though, to plan the details until after she had the china.

Her hands were getting tired, her fingers stiff, refusing to slice through the thinnest skin, so she laid down her knife and washed her hands at the sink. She had to use a scrubbing brush as the pumpkin left a sticky, wax-like film on her hands. Cucumbers did the same thing, only that was lime green and this was yellowish.

She turned the burner on beneath the pot of coffee left out from breakfast and went to the pantry to look for a snack. Popcorn, oatmeal, noodles, flour, sugar, chocolate chips, baking cocoa, rice.

She lifted the aluminum foil that was covering a pie and found half of a peach pie covered with fuzzy, green mold. She set it on the counter. She'd allow Mam the pleasure of discovering that one for herself.

Sarah snapped open the lid of a Tupperware container and found a half dozen chocolate chip cookies. She squeezed one, and it broke into crumbs immediately. Hard as a rock. Taking the container, she set it on the counter beside the moldy peach pie.

Returning to the pantry, her gaze skimmed across the shelves. Peanut butter, honey, olive oil, grape jelly, graham crackers, saltines. Suddenly, she wanted a bowl of puppy slop—that mushy, milky dish from her childhood.

Taking the graham crackers, she broke five of them in half, placed them in a cereal bowl, and added milk. With a spoon, she broke the crackers into smaller pieces, soaking them well in the cold, creamy milk.

Mam smiled at her, watching her enjoy the dish.

"Nothing like puppy slop," Sarah grinned through a mouthful.

"I have a big notion to have some, too," Mam remarked.

"Who gave it that disgusting name?"

"If I remember correctly, it was Abner that started it. He was five or six years old."

Sarah nodded.

"You think that will turn into a tradition, too? Will my children also call it puppy slop?"

Mam nodded happily, her mouth closing over a large spoonful.

On Wednesday evening, Sarah dressed carefully, pinning her black belt apron with precision, settling it comfortably around her waist. The green of her dress matched her eyes perfectly, the black sweater around her shoulders carrying the black of her apron.

At Rockvale Square, Lee asked the driver to park close to the Lenox place. Sarah felt the color leaving her face. When he opened the door for her, she cast him a wild-eyed look, which he answered with a wink.

Two hours later, she was the stunned recipient of a large set of the most beautiful china dishes she had ever imagined.

It was white all over, except for a slightly off-white spray of wheat, or a fern, she wasn't sure, splayed along the right side. It was as if an artist had drawn it there, impulsively, as an after-thought.

She murmured about the price, which she wasn't sure about, and Lee would not reveal.

The knives, forks, and spoons to match it were so beautiful, she had to catch her breath. They chose a pitcher, clear crystal, and a dozen water glasses, a set of stemware, two white table-cloths, and cloth napkins.

Such a dizzying variety, but Sarah knew her mind, completely stealing Lee's admiration yet again for the quick decisions she made. She obviously knew what her tastes were and never wavered, once she saw what she wanted.

The evening flew by like a dream, albeit a real one that never faded away. At home, the dishes were taken from the box, admired, and fussed over. Then they were put away to be taken out the day before the wedding, when the *eck-leit* (corner people), the couples whose job it was to serve the bride and groom, would wash and prepare all the dishes needed for that special day.

Steadily, through the remainder of October and into November, the work continued. And on the weekends, Mam and Dat attended different communion services in neighboring districts.

The silos had been filled, and long, round snakes of white plastic covered the excess silage layered behind the barn. Fourth-cutting alfalfa was already in the haymow. The garden was cultivated, and a good cover crop sowed for the winter.

The cabbage remained undisturbed like squat, round little sentries, standing guard all alone after the celery was cultivated into the ground, including the newspapers that had been used to "bleach" it. Mam said she was glad to see the celery cultivated under, her failure now well hidden.

Melvin and Lydia came one Saturday to help paint the shop. Melvin had a fit that they were using rollers and not a sprayer.

If anything, marriage had only increased his chattiness. The expounding of his viewpoints reached new heights, the smiling Lydia swelling his already well-developed self-worth.

He eyed the good quality rollers, the metal pans, and gallons of white paint with a certain condescending weariness, resignation setting in as Lydia said rollers were fine. They didn't need to do the ceiling, she added, and this would be fun, working together with Lee and Sarah, the soon-to-be newlyweds.

She pronounced newlyweds as two separate words, putting grins of pure happiness on Sarah and Lee's faces. Melvin's face softened to a state of high emotion, his bushy eyebrows went straight up, and his nose became red as he began to speak in a most holy manner.

"You just have no idea what God has for you. I never thought I would be so happy on this earth. I mean, I was happy before, or I thought I was, but I wasn't. I lived for myself. Now I live for Lydia and the children."

On and on, Melvin spoke of his exalted position as stepfather, reveling in the assumption that he was counted as one of the best that ever held this position of such honor.

Lee opened the paint, stirred it with the wooden stirrer, dumped it into the metal pan, and began to spread it on the drywall. His grin was lop-sided, listening to Melvin.

Sarah couldn't hold it against her cousin. He was so obviously just being Melvin, genuine and sincere in his own belief in his abilities. She knew he wasn't blatantly blowing his own horn. He was just telling Lee and Sarah something he thought they needed to know. That was how harmless he was.

Lydia had acquired a bit of spirit as well. She

chattered like a busy magpie, her roller moving steadily across the vast shop walls as she talked.

She had to make new trousers for Melvin. He had already gained ten or eleven pounds, and he said it was her cooking.

She made the best fried chicken and meat loaf he had ever tasted. And her chocolate cake with peanut butter icing was unbelievable. Who would eat salad and apples if she cooked like that? Lydia beamed and dimpled, smiled and talked, until Sarah was completely in awe.

What a transformation! Remembering the sad, thin, cowering Lydia of old, Sarah felt the quick sting of tears in her eyes.

She could still see her the night the original barn had burned. That night she stood there, too thin, her face immovable, showing no emotion. Her feelings were hidden away, where they festered, damaging the thin hold on the emotional health she had left.

Her faith had been trampled as her first husband's harsh words had torn at her. She truly believed she had been what he chose to call her. Miserable, hate-filled man that he was. But he was gone, and he had had a chance to repent. The judgment of his soul was God's duty and none of theirs, the way they had been taught.

So there was a positive thing. Good had come out of evil. Sarah became Lydia's friend, introduced Melvin, and here they were.

It was an intricate design, this web of life. The good came with the evil. It just had to be sifted through, and the priceless lessons kept, while the rest was discarded.

"Where's your dat?" Melvin asked suddenly.

"He went to a farm auction."

"He just wanted to get out of painting these shop walls."

"I doubt it."

"No. I was teasing. He's a good uncle. Good guy."

Again, Melvin went off on an emotional bluster, exalting the many merits of Davey Beiler. He lectured on forgiveness then, reminding them all that in the end, Davey was right. Even if that Walters guy sat in jail for a hundred years, they still, in their hearts, needed to forgive.

Leaning against a door post, his elbow propping up his now slightly fuller frame, he informed them that they didn't have to go further than the Lord's Prayer to know about forgiving.

"You know, guys, it doesn't say how someone trespasses against you—if he walks across your property or burns your barn or shoots someone you know. We're still supposed to forgive."

"That's requiring the superhuman, right there," Lee broke in, stopping to adjust his roller handle.

"Oh, absolutely. But Lee, how can we be forgiven if we don't forgive? We can't."

Lee nodded, went back to work.

They discussed Michael Lanvin, who seemed to be doing alright. He was a work driver for Sam Fisher in Leola. Sam said he was punctual, always on time, no matter what. Michael now had an apartment in Leola, above the Laundromat. He had just gotten in with the wrong bunch before, and Ashley had known all along what was going on, poor girl.

Sarah nodded.

"It's over now. May that pitiful girl rest in peace. She was in an awfully hard place, between that violent Harold Walters and her boyfriend, Michael, who was under his influence as well."

"Did the trial ever come up?"

"Oh, I think so. Surely."

They became aware of another presence in their midst. One by one, they turned to see Matthew Stoltzfus standing in the doorway.

"Hey."

He said it quietly, with reserve.

"What's going on, Matthew?"

Effusive as ever, Melvin hurried over and shook his hand, pumping vigorously.

"It's been awhile. Sorry about your wife's passing."

Melvin rambled on, asking questions about Haiti, his church, his future plans.

Sarah cringed when Matthew's words became short, clipped, the questions answered halfheartedly or not at all.

"So," Matthew said finally. "Preparing the wedding chapel."

Lee had his back turned, rolling the paint furiously. He didn't stop or bother answering. Sarah became ill at ease, hurriedly acknowledging his words with a quick smile, a nod of her head.

That subject sputtered and died at take-off, so Matthew found an old folding chair and dropped onto it, stretching his legs and crossing his feet at the ankles, hooking his thumbs into the belt loops on his jeans.

"Go ahead, keep working. I don't want to hold you up."

"You're not," Melvin assured him.

They all continued with the job at hand, but with a note of discord, a certain tenseness making them do unsettling things. Sarah tripped over the metal pan, spilling paint on the newspaper, and some of it soaked into the concrete. Lee broke the broom handle that was screwed into the roller, and Lydia hurried off to find another one.

Matthew then informed them that Rose had asked him to be a cook at the restaurant where she worked. He was duly congratulated and went on his way, a smile of satisfaction on his lips, a new purpose to his step.

Lee watched him go and glanced at Sarah, but he said nothing.

Melvin began barking immediately, like an excited dachshund.

"Did you ever hear anything more perfect? He always liked to cook. He always wanted Rose. He'll be cooking with Rose!"

Slapping his knee at his own hilarity, Melvin went to fill his roller, chuckling to himself.

Straightening, he had to say what was on his mind and burst out, "I'm so glad that guy is out of the way. He used to irk me so bad. I could hardly stand how he treated you, Sarah."

Lee didn't answer. He just kept painting. Sarah watched the rise and fall of his wide shoulders, the blond hair above them, and she was filled with gratitude, and so much more.

Carefully, she laid down her roller, walked over to Lee, and slipped an arm around his narrow waist. On her tiptoes, she whispered in his ear, telling him of her love. Then she gently kissed his cheek, blushing to the roots of her hair.

Melvin blinked back genuine tears and could find no words to enhance the moment. Lee propped his roller along the wall and gave Sarah a look that could only be described as worshipful as he pulled her into a quick embrace.

They ordered pizza and sat in Dat's office to eat. They took a whole pepperoni pizza to the house for Levi and Suzie, and Levi was clearly beside himself at this wonderful opportunity. Mam wasn't even at home, so if he ate four or five slices, nobody would know, except Suzie, and she'd never tell.

Lydia finished her first slice of pizza and reached for another, shaking her head in wonder.

"You know, there was a time in my life when I didn't have enough money to buy five pounds of flour. Not even enough to make this pizza crust. And here I am, wolfing down pizza delivered to our—I mean, your—door."

"Oh, Lydia!" Melvin cried. "My dear wife! My darling girl!"

Gladly, Lydia accepted the unrestrained endearments, smiling at her exuberant husband. She ate three slices of the good, hot pizza and said it didn't seem right, being so blessed. That sent Melvin into an account of the day he met her, that very first time when she stood in her kitchen surrounded by all those women, her heart so burdened, her situation so dire. Through the dark valleys we walk through, he said, we become blessed.

Lee chimed in then, telling a bit about his own life, which hardly had any dark valleys, except for Sarah's tendency to leave him for Matthew. Lydia reassured him. She said he lived a life of unselfishness, always giving his time and energy to others. Trials were often withheld from people such as him, she told him.

He shook his head, humbled, but Sarah knew Lydia's statement was true.

A contentment, a unifying silence floated among them like golden fog. It comforted them with the knowledge that they had come through so much and had been blessed just as much.

"Look at us," Melvin chortled, "we'll still be friends fifty years from now, old and fat, sitting together drinking peppermint tea. Or, no—what is it old people drink?"

"Ovaltine?" Lydia asked quietly.

"That's it!" Melvin shouted. "Ovaltine!"

"We'll know every Nature's Sunshine product from A to Z," Lee said dryly.

Melvin slapped his knee and reached for his sixth slice of pizza.

Chapter 22

The day before the *risht dag* (day to prepare before the wedding), Levi came down with a terrible sore throat. His hacking cough tore through him, and his fever rose steadily, requiring all Mam's resources. She mixed a poultice of steamed onions and salt, plastered it on his chest, and tied a heavy white cloth around it. She almost drenched him with a dark, bitter brew of black tea laced with Southern Comfort whiskey. She put his feet in lukewarm water containing vinegar and red pepper, then massaged them with quick, sure strokes of her thumbs and fingers.

In between *fer-sarking* Levi, she barked orders. She sent Priscilla for the groceries she had planned to buy herself, wrote a list of jobs for Sarah, and did what had to be done for Levi, saying she didn't know how long they would have him. She would do what she could for him while he was here.

The weather was surprisingly mild, for the first week in December. The forecast in the daily paper predicted moderate temperatures with plenty of sunshine. It looked like at least the weather would cooperate for the big wedding day.

All through November, they had attended weddings. Lee was not always able to stay the whole time. He had his herd of cows to tend, the addition for Anna to build, and the fall work to finish up. He never complained and was always cheerfully on time to escort Sarah to yet another wedding. But by the time November came to a close, he appeared tired with a weary look around his eyes.

That was when Sarah decided to spend a weekend with her sisters Anna Mae and Ruthie, leaving Lee to a long, restful weekend of much needed sleep and plenty of Anna's calorie-laden snacks.

Now, on this day before the *risht dag*, the memories of the weekend with her sisters kept her smiling as she went about her duties.

They had been seated around Ruthie's kitchen table until four o'clock in the morning, drinking coffee and Pepsi. They made unhealthy buttered popcorn loaded with salt and sour cream and onion powder and Brewer's yeast. That strange but delicious mixture gave the popcorn such a unique flavor.

Anna Mae told Sarah in advance that they were preparing her for marriage with words of well-seasoned wisdom coming from them—women of substance, wives of experience. If she listened to them, she couldn't go wrong.

They weren't very far into the evening before her sisters decided Lee wasn't normal.

"You mean, he never says no?" Ruthie shrieked.

"I wouldn't know when."

"He never gets angry? Not even when he's stressed? Snappy?" Anna Mae asked in disbelief.

"I have never seen him that way."

Sarah's eyes narrowed, contemplating what to say next. Should she tell them?

"Okay, listen. Once Lee told me that if he knew I would be happier with Matthew, he'd let me go. My happiness is all that matters to him."

Ruthie placed both hands over her face and said she couldn't stand it. It was too sweet. Then she began sobbing hysterically, her shoulders heaving. She snorted, got up for a Kleenex, and said that was the single most unselfish thing she'd ever heard of. They decided then, for sure, that Lee wasn't normal.

Usually only sisters enjoy the bond they shared that night. They talked of their deepest fears, their greatest joys. They discussed life—all of it. They cried, they shrieked with hilarity, and then spoke in hushed tones of reverence, as the subjects changed.

Anna Mae gave Sarah a book to read about love and marriage with something about respect in the title. Sarah thanked her wholeheartedly and said even though she knew Lee was extraordinary, she was sure they would have their times. Everyone did. Simply everyone.

Ruthie added some extra salt to her popcorn and poured a handful into her open mouth. She nodded and chewed vigorously, before repeating the maneuver all over again. She wiped her mouth, chugged away at her Pepsi, and burped quietly. Then she opened her mouth and belched unrestrainedly, her eyes opening wide with surprise, her nose turning red as tears formed in her eyes.

"You are excused," Anna Mae said, sending a baleful glace at her.

Ignoring the stab at her lack of etiquette, Ruthie leaned forward and wiped her mouth with the sleeve of her housecoat. It was a ratty old blue thing she had had when she was a young girl at home.

"Hey, but you know what?"

Sarah was picking unpopped kernels of corn from the bottom of her bowl, crunching them between her teeth.

"Would you stop that?" Ruthie asked.

"Pure fiber."

"Salt and grease."

"Remember what Mam used to say? You'll get appendicitis. One of those kernels will get stuck in your appendix."

"That's an old wives' tale."

"Huh-uh. No, it's not."

"Hey, be quiet. I was going to say something," Ruthie paused. "Oh, I know. Love is never perfect. I wish it was, but it isn't. That wonderful, good looking, amazing guy we fall so in love with will eventually become the same person who sprawls on your new couch with feet that smell like road kill, snoring away, while you are feeding the baby with a whining toddler at your knee. Meanwhile you have a pile of unwashed dishes and a flabby stomach, and the best way you can think of to express your love is a quick thump on the head with a baseball bat."

Ruthie howled with glee at her own description.

"He'll be the same man that invites his parents for supper and forgets to tell you until Sunday morning, when you have a good book stashed away—one that you finally, finally planned on reading that day. And his mother is so *piffich* (meticulous), and you gave your Friday cleaning a lick and a promise. . . ."

"You mean you licked the floor and promised it you'd scrub it next week?" Anna Mae broke in, and they all burst into peals of laughter again.

"Then they arrive, and right away she says, '*My oh*, looks like I should send Rhoda to help in the garden.' You know exactly why she says it. You know the garden is not pristine, mostly because it was too hot, and you plain down didn't feel like weeding it."

Ruthie sighed. "And you know, Rhoda goes tearing through that garden, thrashing around with my hand cultivator. Not one vegetable is safe. She doesn't want to be there, so she plows through in double quick time so she can go home again."

"Sounds like marriage!" Anna Mae trilled, shaking her head from side to side.

"Lee wouldn't do either one of those things," Sarah said stoutly.

"Oh, but he will!" Ruthie sang out.

"He surely will!" Anna Mae chimed in.

Sarah laughed and looked at the clock.

"I have plenty of advice to last me for a long time. It's past one o'clock, and I'm going to bed now. I'm tired. There is still work at home to get ready for my wedding, you know."

Her sisters would hear nothing of it. They still planned on making soft pretzels.

Sarah groaned as Anna Mae leaped to her feet and began throwing yeast, salt, and water into a bowl. But the sisters talked and joked while they baked the pretzels and savored their salty goodness. There was not much sleep for any of them that night.

The weather was perfect, for December, on Sarah's *risht dag*. The air was nippy, but so clear you could see all the surrounding farms etched against the green of fall rye crops, the dark brown of bare trees in stark relief against the colorful backdrop.

Mam had been up since three o'clock, when she could bake her own pumpkin pies with no interference or well-meaning advice from sisters or mothers-in-law. Mam knew what she was about when it came to pumpkin pies.

For one thing, the egg whites had to be beaten until stiff peaks formed and stood up to a point, all by themselves. They couldn't be folded over in the least bit, the way they had when Davey's mother did them for Ruthie's wedding. She could still feel the dismay that came over her, sitting at the special table with the close relatives, when she cut into the pumpkin pie that had not met her standards. A thin telltale line of *bree* (juice) had formed around the crust, spoiling it and making it soggy.

She remembered the quick stab of irritation, though she had quenched it just as quickly, the smile on her face folding for a mere second before being put back into place.

She had seen it. Those peaks had not been stiff. They had folded over easily. Plus Davey's

362

mother had taken the pies out of the oven a few minutes too soon. Yes, she had. Malinda had seen the centers jiggle. Centers of baked pumpkin pies do not jiggle. She had told her mother-in-law that, but she was snapped off with quick tones of reassurance. The tops were golden brown, and she didn't want dark tops on pumpkin pies for a wedding.

Well, Malinda knew what she wanted, but Davey's mother wouldn't listen, so it was up and out of bed at three o'clock for these wedding pies.

She giggled a bit, a quiet burst of mirth. She felt very much like the little pig that got up especially early and beat it to the apple orchard before the cunning fox appeared. No one was going to bake these pies but her.

And another thing, the oven had been about twenty-five degrees too hot when Davey's mother made them for Ruthie's wedding. That was why the tops would have been too brown. But you couldn't tell Davey's mother one thing, so here she was. Well, no use spoiling this *risht dag* with thoughts like that. She'd just make her own pumpkin pies. That was all.

So at five o'clock, when the first couple, Sam Kings, arrived, Malinda had just put the first of the pumpkin pies into the oven. She wiped her hands on her apron and turned to greet Mary, the energetic, very large woman who entered her kitchen.

"Malinda."

"Mary. Good morning."

Mary's kindly brown eyes sparkled from her smooth, tanned face like wet acorns. Her cheeks were puffed up and smiling.

"*Ach* Malinda, I'm just going to come over there and hug you."

This she did, wrapping Mam into a pillowed embrace. Then she stepped back and said with tears sparkling from her dark eyes, "Such a blessed day. Oh, I felt so much joy as we drove in the lane. I told Sam, these people have been through so much. It gives me goose bumps to think of the blessings pouring out on you now. God has truly brought you through."

"Oh my, yes!" Mam answered, her own tears reflected in Mary's.

"This is a special day. I can feel it in the air. The new barn standing there as if nothing bad has ever happened and was never going to again."

Mam nodded, smiled.

"Well, I came to make *roasht* (chicken filling). I guess everything is ready for us out in the shop?"

"Oh, yes. If you need anything, just give us a holler."

Mary nodded, eyed the pumpkin pies, and shook her head as she voiced her admiration. No one made better pumpkin pies than Malinda.

Smiling her acceptance of Mary's praise, Mam said, "Well, now."

Sarah awoke a bit after five o'clock, long before her alarm went off. Then she lay in bed for only a minute, embracing the day's wonders. This day, the *risht dag*, was every bride's anticipated day of joyous preparation for the actual wedding day.

She dressed carefully in a bittersweet-colored dress, a black bib apron, a clean, fairly new covering. Her eyes shone back at her from the bathroom mirror as she applied the concealing lotion on her scars. She turned her head to assess them carefully, willing herself not to panic.

He'd said it was okay. She had to accept that. She ran down the stairs, finding Mam bristling with tension, leveling the top of a pie crust before crimping the edges. Her huge bowls of pumpkin pie filling stood ready, and the smell coming from the oven announced that pies were already baking.

Mam stopped, smiled at Sarah, and said, "Good morning, Sarah," but her face was flushed, her eyes puffy from lack of sleep. Her hair wasn't combed quite right, her large white covering was a bit off center, and she had one shoe lace dragging from her sturdy black shoes.

"Good morning, Mam. What time did you get up?"

"Three."

"What's wrong with you?"

"Davey's mother, Mommy Beiler, is what's

wrong with me. Remember Ruthie's wedding? The pumpkin pies?"

Sarah poured a mug of good, hot coffee from the pot, splashed a dollop of creamer into it, and sipped appreciatively as Mam recounted step by step what she considered the failed pies. Sarah hadn't remembered that there was anything wrong with them, but there was no use saying this to Mam now.

Sarah wouldn't give her mother a hug this morning either. It would be the same as hugging a porcupine, with her quills of irritation and tension sticking out all over. A lot of weight lay on Mam's shoulders this morning.

"Sarah, when you've finished your coffee, you should go check to see if the celery was placed in the washhouse. Just make sure it's there. There's not very much laundry, but wash what's in the hampers. And Sarah, you better hurry. It's later than I like it to be. Oh, and don't forget, the rinse tubs Dat brought in? Be sure and scrub them well, with a splash of Clorox before Lee comes to wash the celery. I'd sure feel bad if the taste of Downy fabric softener was in the celery."

Sarah nodded, set down the mug of coffee, and ran back up the stairs for the hamper of dirty clothes. She was bent over the rinse water at six o'clock, when she felt two strong hands on her shoulders.

Lee. Her bridegroom.

She turned and went straight into his arms, placing her own snugly around his waist. The closeness of him was a homecoming, a place she felt loved, secure, safe.

"Good morning, my lovely girl," he murmured against her hair.

"Good morning, Lee," she answered, her arms tightening momentarily.

They stood together by the washing machine, sharing this moment of closeness before the rush of the day.

Neither of them heard Mary King open the door and peer inside, looking for a plastic bucket. Her brilliant brown eyes lit up at the sight of them in an embrace of true love. Her eyes filled with tears, her shoulders shook with emotion, and she snorted a few watery sobs outside the door as she felt another set of chills across her heavy arms.

She bit down on her lips and got control of herself, reaching under her black apron for a handkerchief. She honked loudly into it, sniffed, replaced it, and went back out to the shop to make *roasht* without the plastic bucket. She'd tell them she couldn't find it. They didn't have to know what she'd seen. It was too precious.

The job of washing celery was to be done by the bride and groom, along with the four people who would be their attendants, their *nava sitza* (beside sitters).

Priscilla would be seated with Omar, Lydia's

son, who was closer to Lee than anyone else. He was like a brother and was chosen to be in the bridal party because of that. Priscilla radiated high excitement, being chosen to *nava sitz* with Omar. It was a long-awaited event, a wonderful duty in her life, being Sarah's sister. She was chosen by tradition but felt extra fortunate to be allowed to sit beside Omar.

A cousin of Lee's, Marvin Stoltzfus, would be seated with Rose Zook, Sarah's special friend. To her knowledge, they had never met, but, hopefully, it would work with them being seated together at the bridal table for one day.

Lee and Sarah broke the celery into individual stalks, washing them well with cold water, and stacking them into large plastic dishpans. The full pans were whisked away by happy aunts and sisters. Ruthie and Anna Mae descended on them, furiously animated into whirling dervishes of excitement, teasing, and laughter. They splashed Sarah with cold water, batting their eyelashes at Lee and acting like twelve-year-olds who had a crush on him.

The *risht dag* was something, wasn't it?

The kitchen was alive with happy chatter, punctuated with peals of laughter. Mam's sister Emma was cooking "cornstarch," a creamy vanilla pudding cherished by the Amish.

Mam acknowledged Emma's skills at making cornstarch. She just had a way of producing the creamiest pudding, not too thick and not too thin.

The celery chopping began as the two grandmothers seated themselves at one end of the extended kitchen table, wooden cutting boards in front of them, paring knives flashing as they sliced and chopped their way through the mountain of celery. They talked quietly, their shoulders periodically shaking softly with laughter.

They needed three sixteen-quart kettles full.

"*Unfashtendich, vee feel leit henta* (Nonsense, how many people are invited)?" Emma asked, adding that there would be way too much celery.

Mam informed her tersely that a few more than four hundred were invited, but they wouldn't all show up.

Emma turned her back and stirred her cornstarch pudding. She thought that Malinda was as crazy as ever when she planned a wedding, but she'd better keep her mouth shut. Well, three sixteen-quart kettles of *tzellrich* (celery) was too much. She didn't care if four hundred people showed up or not. She'd be canning celery till January.

Two of Malinda's brothers came in to cut celery, since the grandmothers weren't doing the job fast enough. The *roasht leit* needed celery out in the shop. They promptly sat down and cut in double quick time, and Aunt Barbara joined them. The brothers began a heated discussion about politics, voicing their conservative Republican views. They predicted doom and gloom, citing the ineptitude of the president, and the two grandmothers nodded in agreement.

Barbara, however, became stone silent, her lips compressed, listening to her brothers. They thought she'd brought outright sin into her life, arguing with them before and leaning much too far towards the Democratic view of things. She only upset other members of the family when she voiced the left wing's opinion. Her own husband had shunned her for a few days for being the rebel she was. She was politically incorrect, everyone thought.

So she'd learned to be quiet, being a woman and Amish and therefore subject to her husband and men in general. It was all, in her opinion, a lot like in Iraq, or wherever it was that they wore those burqas, the long, loose coverings with just little screens to see out. The only difference was Henner never beat her, the way those men did— some of them, anyway.

When Grandma Beiler became tired of the political blather, she quoted Scripture, saying all rulers were ordained by God, even if we don't understand it. Barbara began to smile again, even if it was only halfheartedly.

Anna Mae and Ruthie, along with two of their brothers' wives, were *eck leit* (corner people), meaning they would serve the bride's table. It was a high honor, one with prestige on a day when they were trying to achieve perfection.

One corner of the shop was partitioned off and filled with tables and chairs. It was decorated with Sarah's colors—mostly white with little accents of blue—and the fabulous china, silverware, and stemware were brought out. Everything was fancy and elegant, for this was a wedding, even though there were no candles or flowers on the bridal table as neither were allowed in the *ordnung.*

Sarah was not allowed to see anything the *eck leit* prepared. It was all a surprise for her after the ceremony.

Carpet was unrolled across the cement floor of the shop and duct taped at the edges, ensuring a smooth floor for the many guests and servers. Propane heaters purred from corners, doing their best to heat the chilly shop, as doors continually opened and closed. The bench wagons were emptied of their contents, as the men set up tables along every wall and a long one through the middle. They marked them with pieces of freezer tape and placed corners of duct tape on the carpet, ensuring they would be arranged in the same way after the ceremony on the following day.

There was lots of banter and well-wishing as the whole shop transformed into a place lit with warmth and high anticipation. This was the *risht dag*, as exciting as the wedding day itself.

The tables remained until after lunch was eaten. It was a sort of trial run for the wedding day. The lunch was provided by two helpful ladies from Davey's church district. At precisely 11:30, they delivered lasagna, creamed peas, and a lettuce salad with cake and fruit salad for dessert.

Lee and Sarah sat at the head of the long table, as tradition required, flanked on either side by their parents.

After lunch was eaten, the tables were taken down and the benches set for the actual service. Hymnbooks were distributed, and a last polish given to the windows by anxious women. The yard had been raked to perfection, the driveway cleaned with the leaf blower, and the cow barn was immaculate.

Upstairs in the house, Sarah and Priscilla dusted and swept. They put the new quilt on Sarah's bed, the one Mam had bound only a few weeks before. It was a solid off white and quilted with thousands of tiny stitches with two pillow shams to match. It was absolutely breathtaking, the pattern so fine and intricate.

Mam told Sarah if she thought that was a lot of work, she should see how they used to embroider and crochet the edges of the pillowcases to put in their hope chests. Then, when the couples visited every wedding guest as newlyweds, the women would make pillow tops out of yarn, pulling it through latticed plastic to create pillows with colorful designs. These pillows often went on the seat of a rocking chair in their formal living rooms, *die gute schtup.*

Mam shook her head, keenly feeling the sadness of lost tradition and telling Sarah the Amish homes appeared more and more *vee die Englishy leit* (like English people). No one had a *gute schtup* anymore, a closed room that would only be opened for important company on Sunday.

But Sarah did cherish her quilts. All four of them. She just did not want to embroider pillowcases. Or make those yarn cushions. They were stodgy and old fashioned, but maybe someday—who knew?—they would be more important to her again.

She was happy to have all her packaged sheet sets from Walmart or Kohl's or JCPenney, wherever Mam found them on sale. She even had a stack of Ralph Lauren towels that Mam bought on clearance at Park City. A kindly neighbor lady had alerted her to the sale.

Life and times move on, tastes change, and styles come and go for the Amish or English or whatever culture. Traditions are precious, indeed, but some things just didn't make a whole lot of sense in this day and age.

Chapter 23

True to the forecast in the *Intelligencer Journal*, the next day dawned perfectly with a sunrise of gold, yellow, lavender, and deep blue heralding the arrival of Sarah's wedding day. The Davey Beiler farm was bathed in a glow of blessed light.

Even Levi's throat had improved quickly, aided by Mam's adrenaline-fueled ministrations. She had heaped his chest with steamed onions and spread copious amounts of Unker's salve on a clean white cloth, pressing it to his throat and kneading the salve into the bottoms of his swollen feet. She gave him cup after cup of tea laced with whiskey, as well as vitamin C, echinacea, and goldenseal tablets. The poor man was over-whelmed with home remedies, complaining loud and long to anyone who would listen.

On the morning of the wedding, this had all paid off, and Levi sat dressed in his new suit, his shirt collar big enough, finally, that it felt comfortable. His hair was washed and combed, his teeth brushed, and he smiled eagerly as he greeted guests from where he was seated in a comfortable chair just inside the door. He had breakfasted well on rolled oats and the breakfast casserole Aunt Emma had brought.

Sarah's hair behaved better than usual, as if it somehow knew that this was not the time to be out of control. Priscilla said she'd never seen anyone spray so much hairspray. She claimed Sarah would get lung cancer from the fumes, but Sarah only smiled tightly and told her to watch what she said.

The blue dresses were worn by Sarah, Priscilla, and Rose. They were covered with immaculate white capes and aprons, pinned to perfection. Their white coverings were placed carefully on the much-sprayed heads.

Rose was as blonde and beautiful as ever, giggly and nervous, elaborate in her praise of the good-looking Marvin. He acted like a typical guy where Rose was concerned, completely enamored, appearing extremely pleased to be *nava sitzing* with her on his cousin's wedding day.

Omar was groomed to perfection as well, his dark hair cut nicely in the *ordnung*, as was required on a wedding day. He had eyes only for the radiant Priscilla. His heart was worn on his sleeve all day, the hope of having her for his bride some day carried within and shining from his eyes.

Lee appeared relaxed, but Sarah noticed a certain tightening of his jaw, a twitch in his cheek, as he shrugged on his new *mutza* and ran a comb through his thick, blond hair one final time. Sarah adjusted his black bowtie and stepped back to admire him, her eyes conveying all the love she felt on this perfect, beautiful morning of her wedding.

Anna wore blue as well, choosing to dress for

Lee and Sarah, instead of the usual black worn long after a close relative or spouse passes away. She looked radiant, her pretty face wreathed in smiles of congratulations, but Sarah knew there was a shadow behind the happiness, a cloud of grief and loneliness that was ever present.

"I can't hug either of you," she remarked as a greeting, indicating the easily wrinkled organdy fabric used for Sarah's bridal cape and apron.

Mam appeared to have settled down after the *risht dag*, but she didn't waste very many smiles on anyone. She spoke in short sentences, giving orders she expected to be carried out immediately. Sarah knew she had swallowed every herbal concoction meant to calm the nerves—vitamins B12 and 6 and something called Nature's Calm, which was likely supposed to provide exactly what its name implied. She squirted a vile-smelling tincture called Ladies' Formula, a blend of herbs from Dr. Schultz's, into a glass with a bit of water and swallowed it. She rinsed the glass, banged it back into the cupboard, and went briskly on her way. She always ate a few pretzels or crackers soon after, so Sarah knew it must have tasted absolutely horrendous.

When guests began arriving at 7:15, there was no doubt about it. Mam's management skills had paid off. She had missed nothing. The two large meals planned for 400 people were both taken care of to the last fork and pie.

Out in the shop in the room sectioned off for *die shoff leit* (work people), potatoes were being peeled by helpful church ladies. The *roasht leit* were finishing the preparation of the forty fat roasting chickens with the cubed bread, celery, eggs, and seasonings. Cabbage was being grated for huge dishes of cole slaw. Dat had made sure — his own management skills also apparent— that there were five gas stoves with working ovens set up at different places throughout the work area. One was for potatoes, one for coffee, another for gravy, celery, or whatever.

Aunt Emma and her sister Barbara were the ones with "the paper," the important piece of tablet paper stating each person's job. As the helpers arrived, Emma and Barbara told each one who would make gravy, who would cook the celery. That lowly piece of tablet paper was what kept the whole work area going, with every last job assigned to someone by Mam's sisters.

Lee and Sarah sat on a bench, side by side, flanked by their attendants, greeting guests as they arrived. They smiled, shook hands, and acknowledged the beauty of the day.

Through the shop windows, Sarah could see the brilliance of the December sun, the yellow glow it cast across the prepared shop. The *fore gayer* (managers) scurried about, ensuring last minute details were taken care of.

Then they began seating people in earnest—

ministers, parents, grandparents, other family members, workers or co-workers, and on down the line, the way people had been seated for many generations at Amish weddings. The men were on one side of the room, and the women on the other. The last ones to be seated were the single youth, all dressed in their very best, for this was a wedding day.

The announcement of the opening song was swallowed by the vast number of people, but everyone knew the hymn sung first at a wedding, so after the first line was sung, a crescendo followed with the second and third lines.

Sarah's heartbeat accelerated when the first minister stood up, followed by ten others. They watched them file out, then Lee stood, reached for her hand, and led her after them into a small area set aside as a conference room.

After they were admonished, blessed, and given spiritual advice, they were free to rejoin their attendants. They filed slowly into the middle of the large shop, where six additional folding chairs now stood, three facing three, waiting for them to be seated in the row of ministers as the singing went on.

Sarah took a deep breath, concentrated on relaxing, and kept her eyes downcast as a demure bride should. There were no smiles, only slightly bent heads, signs of true humility and obedience. Around them, the singing rose and fell, a comfort Sarah had been used to all her life. It was now especially beautiful, this well recognized wedding hymn.

Someone coughed. A throat was cleared. A baby set up an earnest howling. A frustrated mother got up and edged her way carefully past the bent knees of others, as her tiny infant continued to wail. Color appeared in the mother's cheeks, embarrassment setting in from having to get up and move among all these people. She wondered if her baby truly had colic, as little sleep as she got every night.

When the ministers returned, the singing stopped. David Beiler stood, rubbed his hands together, and cleared his throat. He lifted his eyes to the large shop filled with his daughter's wedding guests—his guests and Malinda's.

A great swell of emotion took away his ability to speak. He stood quietly, lifted his eyes to the shop ceiling.

When Sarah realized Dat was unable to speak, she felt the sting of emotion in her eyes and nose. She knew her tears would spill over, so she reached as delicately as possible for the folded white handkerchief in her pocket and lifted it discreetly to her face.

Finally, Dat spoke in the deep baritone she was accustomed to hearing, with the roughness of emotion changing it only slightly.

He spoke from the heart on his daughter's

wedding day. He recalled the barn fires and Sarah's deliverance from death by God's hand. He spoke of the men who had done this and the insignificance of the jail term. The only necessary thing was the genuine forgiveness in each individual heart.

He spoke of past trials and the mighty hand of deliverance that allowed Lee and Sarah to be together and to live in a land that was blessed with religious freedom, allowing them to have their horses and buggies, their Amish lifestyle. Sarah bent her head and held her handkerchief to her nose. She sniffled as tears plopped on the white organdy of her apron. She felt Lee shift in his chair and heard him pull out his own handkerchief, blowing his nose quietly, not wanting to draw attention.

Lee's bishop, Amos Esh, was the one who would "give them together." After the short prayer and the reading of the Scripture, he stood, a small man with a mighty voice, and rattled off every story in sequence. He told all the required stories for wedding sermons—Naomi and Ruth, Samson, and many others. They were all Old Testament tales that were filled with good advice and precious lessons of love and marriage.

How many young brides had the love for their mothers-in-law that Ruth did, wanting to dwell with her and worship the same God she did? Sarah thought of Mam's pumpkin pies and doubted if she ever felt like Ruth. She had to stifle a smile that threatened to surface.

Indeed, how many women were guilty of cajoling and seducing their husbands by their own foolish whims, thereby robbing their husbands of their power, the way Delilah did to Samson? Women could be devious creatures, propelled by their own wills, depleting strong men of their strength.

Sarah shivered and covered her forearms with the palms of her hands. She loved the Old Testament stories; she always had. She had usually been the preacher when they played church. She loved to get up and wave her arms and tell Priscilla and Suzie and Mervin about Moses in the basket and Pharaoh drowning in the Red Sea and manna falling from heaven. She had even stolen a few slices of white bread from the drawer in the kitchen, broken it into pieces, and said they were the children of Israel eating their manna.

Her heartbeat thudded against her ribs when Amos Esh launched into the story about Tobias, a revered story from the Apocrypha and the one used at every Amish wedding to unite two people as husband and wife.

The bishop wasted no time, and when Sarah thought she just might faint from her rapid heartbeat, she heard him say their names, Levi Glick and Sarah Beiler. Then Lee stood, reached for her hand, and walked with her to stand in front of the bishop, who was dwarfed by Lee's height.

Obviously undaunted, his mighty voice continued, asking them the required holy questions. They each pledged their commitment in the age-old union of marriage with a soft *ya* (yes).

They received the bishop's blessing and turned to go back to their seats. Lee maneuvered the correct turn flawlessly, though Sarah would not have noticed if he did it all wrong.

She kept her eyes properly downcast through the remainder of the sermon, but when the rousing swells of the last hymn rose to the confines of the ceiling, she dared one furtive glance at Lee. Her eyes connected with the blueness of his, and she wondered if she had ever known that love was a color.

The remainder of that day was as close to perfection as possible. The corner table was every girl's dream. The china dishes Lee had given her were so gorgeous that Sarah was hesitant to put food on the plates, let alone eat from them.

The cakes and dishes set all over the table, given as gifts in the traditional way, were enough to inspire awe. The array of gifts and food was endless, and Lee stayed by her side as they opened and recorded each one.

In the afternoon, Priscilla led the old German hymn "Wohlauf" about the church being Christ's bride. Her voice was rich and steady as the remainder of the people seated around them chimed in. Omar sat beside Priscilla, his heart in his eyes, his gaze never leaving her downturned face as her eyes followed the German words of the hymn.

On the other side of the newlyweds, Rose kept up a string of witty conversation topics, and Marvin was obviously enamored, but no one could tell if anything would come of it. Rose later gushed about Marvin continuously, but who knew? She had also just asked Matthew to be the short order cook at the restaurant where she worked, giving Matthew hope that she would take him back. But would he come back to the Amish for her sake? That was obviously a huge question, carrying a doubtful answer.

And there was Sarah, Mrs. Lee Glick, with her manly husband of approximately four hours by her side. All the doubts and fears, all that senseless heartache, erased, gone. Or had it been senseless? Did everything, including mistakes all add up to a richer, more enduring maturity in the end?

Suddenly, she noticed Matthew, tall, handsome, his dark good looks accentuated by his smartly cut gray suit. He was watching Rose, a confused look in his brown eyes, a sort of embarrassed bewilderment, as if he wasn't sure what he was seeing.

He had come to her wedding, and Sarah was

glad of it, but seeing him this way tugged at her heart in spite of the pain he had caused in her life. He still loved Rose. He always had, always would.

His love for her had likely been the driving force that caused him to leave the Amish and the sole reason he had ever lowered himself to date Sarah. Everything in his life had revolved around his desire for the lovely Rose, who, it seemed, was happily embarking on another flirtatious fling.

What would happen to Matthew?

Suddenly, Sarah realized that it wasn't up to Rose to fix Matthew. No one could blame another person for their situation in life. It was up to Matthew to find the resources to learn to give up his own will. Sarah realized Rose was Matthew's will but not necessarily God's.

Poor Hannah, having thoroughly spoiled her son, now lived on antacids and anxiety medication. She lay awake at night, praying and worrying about his life.

Sarah looked at Matthew with his puzzled stare. She smiled at him and looked away, but not before he had returned her smile. It was a small, unsure widening of his lips, with a hesitant, almost humble expression in his eyes.

So the world kept spinning, Sarah thought, and only life's trials would help to mature the charming Matthew. It was simply the way of it.

At nine o'clock that evening, the string of well-wishers filed past Lee and Sarah at the corner table. They shook hands and wished them well, giving their congratulations and good-byes. There were promises to visit as the bride and groom gave away the trinkets with their names and date of the wedding day. Sarah's head spun with weariness.

Rose and Priscilla had gone off with their guys. Anna Mae and Ruthie sank onto their chairs, their shoes kicked off, and said if they had to walk one single step more, they'd collapse, and someone would have to bring in a skid loader to move them.

Lee said he would; he was pretty good with a skid loader, which sent them into shrieks of glee. Sarah thought they still acted like kids when Lee was around.

Levi came to wish them a goodnight at their table. It was past his bedtime, and he was sleepy. They gave him a large Ziploc bag filled with all sorts of candy, which he hastily stuffed into his vest pocket, his eyes darting back and forth, making sure nobody saw him hide it away.

He said he was glad he had a new brother-in-law and wished them *Herr saya* (God's blessing).

He lumbered off, one hand on his vest pocket and a smile on his face, heading to tuck the candy in a bureau drawer and settle himself for a long night of rest. The next day promised to be a good one with all the wedding leftovers to eat.

At last, Lee and Sarah could leave the corner table. They found Mam and her sisters clattering dishes in the work room. Dat was reclining on a folding chair, a steaming cup of coffee in his hand, his hat pushed to the back of his head, smiling contently as he listened to the ramblings of his wife and her sisters. Emma shrieked some nonsense about the amount of *roasht* they had packed into gallon Ziploc bags and carted off to the freezer.

"Malinda, you do it every time. Way too much food."

Mam set her mouth determinedly, shook her head, and said she would be happy to have all that *roasht* and *tzellrich* for quick meals all winter long.

Emma grumbled about the work she put on everyone, making all that extra food, but Mam threw an apple at her, missing her completely. Barbara giggled like a schoolgirl, and Dat leaned over to pick up the apple. He lobbed it at Emma, and she whirled and said, "*Unfashtendich*, Davey, *doo bisht kindish* (nonsense, you are childish)."

Such goings on were completely common. The tension lifted, the pressure released. Everything had gone well, and now it was time for fun.

Mam delicately put a finger through a corner of a half-ruined wedding cake. She thought no one had seen her until Dat called loudly, "Malinda, I'm surprised at you!"

She jumped, caught red-handed, then looked up and laughed with the abandonment of a teenager.

The wedding was over.

Lee and Sarah stood together, taking in this whole scene of carefree release. Lee slipped an arm around Sarah's waist and pulled her close against him, under Dat's warm gaze.

"Well, Mrs. Glick, how does it feel to be an old married woman?" he asked, smiling at Sarah.

He had barely finished the sentence, allowing Sarah no time to reply, when the door burst open, and six rowdy young men charged through it. They whooped and yelled, grabbing Lee by his arms and legs, in spite of his fervent yells and his flailing and kicking. They carried him out the door, as Sarah clapped a hand to her mouth to keep from crying out.

Dat laughed out loud.

"He may as well give himself up!"

"Over the fence," Barbara chortled.

"That's so ignorant," Emma snorted.

"I hope they don't hurt Lee," Sarah said.

"He'll be alright. The more he resists, the harder it will be for him. If he quiets down, he'll get dumped over safely," Dat said.

And sure enough, as Sarah later found out, the youth had also placed a broom across the doorway to the upstairs. Sarah tripped on it, catching Lee's arm to stay upright, as they headed to her bedroom.

Well, they'd gotten her good and proper, too, so now she and Lee were traditionally fit to be husband and wife. They'd thrown Lee over the fence (Sarah detected the smell of manure on his shoes when they left them in the *kesslehaus*), and now she had "stepped across the broom," enabling her to be a true wife. Old wives' tales, traditions, myths—whatever one called them— they were all done in the spirit of fun. They were endearing pranks that tied them all together as one culture, the way English people threw bouquets and removed garters.

Sarah's bedroom was strewn with red rose petals and a sea of white balloons, decorative and romantic. It had all been done by her sisters and best friends, bringing a lump of appreciation to her throat. The room was lit by soft candle-light, making it ethereal, almost heavenly in appearance.

They would spend their first night together here in Sarah's room on the home farm, following tradition. And they would live with Sarah's family until they had visited most of their wedding guests. Then they would move to their farm, making a life of their own. That would be soon, Sarah knew, with the chores to do and the whole farm to look after.

Now she looked around the room, taking it all in. But what was that in the corner?

Softly, the magnificent grandfather clock

bonged eleven times. The sound was rich, muted, and elegant, the golden glow of the oak finish luminescent in the candlelight.

Shyly, her eyes wide, she turned to her husband, questioning him with her gaze, speechless.

"Your clock," he said.

She could only shake her head in disbelief, as she went across the room to touch the smooth oak wood and listen to the great pendulum swinging slowly back and forth.

"You never did give me a clock," she said softly.

His answer was his strong arms around her, as the white balloons bobbed and floated, and the candle flames sputtered. Sarah did not know this much happiness was possible.

It was so much like Lee to keep this clock hidden from the guests at the wedding. He had chosen, instead, to have it delivered late in the day as a secret, a surprise for her alone. It somehow made it seem almost sacred, this wonderful gift.

"Sarah, you'll be a farmer's wife, and who knows if we'll be poor someday, but at least we'll have a beautiful clock, won't we?" Lee said, as they watched the pendulum's movement together.

Sarah nodded.

Yes, time moved on, the great clock ticking it off with every movement of its second hand. Life would be measured in seconds, minutes, and hours, with days turning into weeks. The weeks would turn to months, and the months to years. Through time, they would live together, evolve together. Their love would grow into a sturdy tree, swayed by winds of adversity, storms, and trials, but the foundation of their deep roots would hold.

Hadn't they experienced firsthand the fires of life? One after another, the arsonist had set fire to men's hard labor, their very livelihoods, and one by one, they had overcome, growing stronger in faith, understanding forgiveness as never before.

Lee placed the palm of his hand on Sarah's scarred face, then bent his head to the dearest sign of God's will for their lives, to be together always.

Epilogue

The sturdy grandfather clock stood in its corner of their home for many years, faithfully recording the time. It was wound by Lee at the end of every week on Saturday evening.

Sarah polished the oak wood, wiped the glass clean. When housecleaning time arrived every spring and every fall, she would take down the great gold weights and the intricately engraved pendulum. She polished them with great care, lovingly rubbing them with a soft cotton cloth.

The clock bonged out the hour when their first child was born one stormy winter night, when the local midwife had to use her four-wheel drive and every skill she possessed to maneuver through the cold and the wind and the drifts. It chimed joyously when Lee carried his newborn son across their living room to show Malinda. They named him David Lee, for Sarah's father and for Lee.

When Levi died and was buried in the cemetery at Gordonville, both Sarah and Lee neglected the usual winding of the clock. It stopped, the motionless pendulum paying tribute to Levi, the great and beloved man who had brought joy and simplicity to the whole family. He was 38 and had lived a happy and blessed life, his memory living on in their hearts.

The ticking of the great clock witnessed the sight of Lee with his head bent, his elbows on his knees, his shoulders heaving with the weight of having been ordained into the ministry the day before. Far into the night, he wrestled with fear and doubt and his own insignificance, for he was a humble young man and could not imagine why the lot had fallen on him. Sarah was his loving helpmeet, his staunch, unfailing supporter, having been raised in a home where they always expected their father to expound God's word.

The sun shone again for Lee. It glinted off the gold pendulum as it swung steadily back and forth one bright summer morning when he realized his joy had returned as he learned to again give himself up to God's will.

As the contours of the land were filled with crops, the cycle of life moved on. Corn and alfalfa were planted, grew, and were harvested. There were seasons of plenty, of rain and of sunshine, of storms, and always the beauty of sunrises and sunsets.

Changes came, as they are bound to do. More children were born to Lee and Sarah, filling the table in the kitchen.

The glass on the grandfather clock was smudged by sticky little fingers, the sides beat upon by sturdy little fists, and yet it continued chiming out the hour, day after day.

The clock could not speak; it only ticked away the minutes. Every evening after the *gebet* (prayer) was said, Lee bent to the rhythm of the ticking clock. He kissed his wife goodnight and touched her still scarred face. Time had not completely removed those reminders of the hard times they had been through and God's continuing presence with them.

The Glossary

aus grufa—A Pennsylvania Dutch dialect phrase meaning "being published."

aylent—A Pennsylvania Dutch dialect word meaning "slow one."

babeyly—A Pennsylvania Dutch dialect word meaning "paper," particularly a paper with a list of duties to be done the day before a wedding.

bann—A Pennsylvania Dutch dialect word meaning "ban" or "shunning."

base—A Pennsylvania Dutch dialect word meaning "angry."

beer—A Pennsylvania Dutch dialect word meaning "pears."

begrabnis—A Pennsylvania Dutch dialect word meaning "burial."

bekimma—A Pennsylvania Dutch dialect word meaning "bother."

bisht alright—A Pennsylvania Dutch dialect phrase meaning "are you alright?"

blooney—A Pennsylvania Dutch dialect word meaning "bologna."

bree—A Pennsylvania Dutch dialect word meaning "juice."

buze fertich—A Pennsylvania Dutch dialect phrase meaning "repentant."

dale—A Pennsylvania Dutch dialect word meaning "share" or "portion."

Dat—A Pennsylvania Dutch dialect word used to address or refer to one's father.

de alte—A Pennsylvania Dutch dialect phrase meaning "the old ones" or "ancestors."

denke—A Pennsylvania Dutch dialect word meaning "thank you."

dichly—A Pennsylvania Dutch dialect word meaning "headscarf."

Die Botshaft—A weekly periodical in which volunteer "scribes" report on the events of their communities. Its name is a Pennsylvania Dutch term meaning "The Message."

do net—A Pennsylvania Dutch dialect phrase meaning "don't."

Doddy—A Pennsylvania Dutch dialect word used to address or refer to one's grandfather.

eck leit—A Pennsylvania Dutch dialect phrase meaning "corner people." They are the ones who serve the bride and groom's table at a wedding.

fer-fearish—A Pennsylvania Dutch dialect word meaning "deceiving."

fit—A Pennsylvania Dutch dialect word meaning "capable."

fore-gayer—A Pennsylvania Dutch dialect word meaning "managers," usually for a wedding or funeral.

freundshaft—A Pennsylvania Dutch dialect word meaning "family."

gebet—A Pennsylvania Dutch dialect word meaning "prayer."

gel—A Pennsylvania Dutch dialect word meaning "right."

gix—A Pennsylvania Dutch dialect word meaning "needle."

goot zeit mach—A Pennsylvania Dutch dialect phrase meaning "making good time."

gute schtup—A Pennsylvania Dutch dialect phrase meaning "formal living room."

halsduch—A Pennsylvania Dutch dialect word meaning "cape." It is part of the traditional attire worn by Amish women, covering the upper part of the body.

helf mich—A Pennsylvania Dutch dialect phrase meaning "help me."

Herr saya—A Pennsylvania Dutch dialect phrase meaning "God's blessing."

hesslich goot—A Pennsylvania Dutch dialect phrase meaning "awfully good."

kalte sup—A Pennsylvania Dutch dialect phrase meaning "cold soup."

koch-shissla—A Pennsylvania Dutch dialect word meaning "serving dishes."

komm—A Pennsylvania Dutch dialect word meaning "come."

laud—A Pennsylvania Dutch dialect word meaning "casket."

Mam—A Pennsylvania Dutch dialect word used to address or refer to one's mother.

mein Got—A Pennsylvania Dutch dialect phrase meaning "my God."

mutza—A Pennsylvania Dutch dialect word meaning "Sunday coat."

nava sitza—A Pennsylvania Dutch dialect phrase meaning "beside sitters," the members of a wedding party who sit beside the bride and groom.

ordnung—The Amish community's agreed-upon rules for living based on their understanding of the Bible, particularly the New Testament. The *ordnung* varies from community to community, often reflecting leaders' preferences, local customs, and traditional practices.

piffich—A Pennsylvania Dutch dialect word meaning "meticulous."

risht dag—A Pennsylvania Dutch dialect phrase meaning "day to prepare before a wedding."

roasht—A Pennsylvania Dutch dialect word meaning "chicken filling."

roasht leit—A Pennsylvania Dutch dialect phrase meaning "people who make chicken filling."

s'ana ent—A Pennsylvania Dutch dialect phrase meaning "other end."

sark—A Pennsylvania Dutch dialect word meaning "care."

saya—A Pennsylvania Dutch dialect word meaning "blessing."

schlakes—A Pennsylvania Dutch dialect word meaning "punishes."

schloppich aufangs—A Pennsylvania Dutch dialect phrase meaning "sloppy now."

schtrofe—A Pennsylvania Dutch dialect word meaning "punishment."

shaut—A Pennsylvania Dutch dialect word meaning "a shame."

shoff leit—A Pennsylvania Dutch dialect phrase meaning "work people."

smear—A Pennsylvania Dutch dialect word meaning "cheese spread."

snitz—A Pennsylvania Dutch dialect word meaning "dried apple."

tzellrich—A Pennsylvania Dutch dialect word meaning "celery."

unfashtendich—A Pennsylvania Dutch dialect word meaning "nonsense."

unleidlich—A Pennsylvania Dutch dialect word meaning "mischievous."

unna such—A Pennsylvania Dutch dialect phrase meaning "search."

vesh bengli—A Pennsylvania Dutch dialect phrase meaning "washbowl."

vissa tae—A Pennsylvania Dutch dialect phrase meaning "meadow tea."

voss—A Pennsylvania Dutch dialect word meaning "what."

Wohlauf—A traditional German hymn sung after the meal at Amish weddings. It is about the church being Christ's bride.

ya—A Pennsylvania Dutch dialect word meaning "yes."

zeit-lang—A Pennsylvania Dutch dialect word meaning "missing/longing."

About the Author

Linda Byler was raised in an Amish family and is an active member of the Amish church today. Growing up, Linda loved to read and write. In fact, she still does. Linda is well-known within the Amish community as a columnist for a weekly Amish newspaper.

Linda is the author of the *Lizzie Searches for Love* series and the *Sadie's Montana* series, as well as the *Lancaster Burning* series, which includes the novels *Fire in the Night* and *Davey's Daughter*. She is also the author of *The Little Amish Matchmaker* and *The Christmas Visitor*, as well as *Lizzie's Amish Cookbook: Favorite recipes from three generations of Amish cooks*!

Center Point Large Print
600 Brooks Road / PO Box 1
Thorndike, ME 04986-0001 USA

(207) 568-3717

US & Canada:
1 800 929-9108
www.centerpointlargeprint.com